Covert Reich

By

A.K. Alexander

San Diego, Ca

A.K. Alexander Thrillers

Daddy's Home

Mommy, May I?

The Cartel

Saddled with Trouble

Death Reins In

Tacked to Death

Michele Scott Mysteries

Murder Uncorked

Murder by the Glass

Silenced by Syrah

A Vintage Murder

Corked by Cabernet

A Toast to Murder

Dedication

This book is dedicated to the two Alex's in my life. The first Alex is my son. His entry into this world is the reason why I ever decided to write the book. He truly set me on my path. Thank You, Kid.

The other Alex helped set me straight when I doubted myself as a writer. He encouraged me and helped me see a light I was not seeing. He is a true and good friend. Thank You, my friend, Alex Johnston.

CHAPTER ONE

Press it. Just fucking press it!

Sweat beaded Ryan Horner's forehead as he stared at the computer screen. His next move could…no…*would* impact hundreds of thousands of lives. And his family. And him.

He lifted his right hand off the mouse and took a deep breath. Images of his beautiful wife, Jeanine, their twin girls, Chloe and Taylor, and his gated home in Blankenese, Germany darted through his head. He thought about his mom and dad back in the States, finally living the life of luxury they so deserved—a life he'd been able to provide them. But at what cost?

The sweat trickled down past his temples. Ryan put his finger back on the mouse, closed his eyes, and clicked "send." He felt instantly sick to his stomach and dropped his head into his hands. *God, oh God, oh God.*

He took a moment to compose himself. Then, after another deep breath and a quick glance to ensure he wasn't being watched, Ryan stood, gathered his things, and walked as casually as he could out of the internet café towards his car. He'd driven for over two hours to find a place where he could safely and anonymously send the email. He opened the door to his sleek Audi, stepped in, and started the engine. Once on the Autobahn, he allowed himself to relax slightly and his thoughts drifted back to that fateful day three years ago in San Diego. The date was etched into his memory—October 22, 2008.

* * *

"Dr. Horner?" Ryan had just reached his SUV after a long lunch at his favorite café. He was tired and not in the mood for conversation. He turned to see who'd spoken. Tall guy, lean, in his early thirties with light brown hair and icy blue eyes. Ryan didn't recognize him at all. That should have been his first clue.

"Dr. Ryan Horner?" the man asked again. He spoke with an accent. Ryan thought it might be German.

"Yes. I'm sorry, do I know you?"

The man came closer, stuck out his hand. He wore what appeared to be an expensive grey suit and silk tie. "My name is Frederick Färber, and I'd like to speak with you about the Petersens."

"The Petersens?" Ryan was instantly uneasy. He shifted his weight from one foot to the other, fiddling with his car keys. "Who are you? I told the police what I knew and honestly, it wasn't much."

"I understand. But I need to speak with you about them. Please come with me."

"No." Ryan shook his head and opened the car door. "I have nothing further to say about the case and I need to get back to work."

"You don't work for Centurion Pharmaceuticals any longer. And as I said, you need to come with me." The man's voice was slightly deeper now, with the faint hint of a threat running through it.

Ryan turned, "Excuse me?" Suddenly he was grabbed roughly from behind. Someone had been waiting inside his car all along. He felt a sharp jab to his right shoulder—a needle—and then was shoved into the back seat. The rest was a blur until he woke up. He wished he'd never woken up.

***

Now all Ryan could think was he'd made a huge mistake sending the email. They paid him well. Gave him shit…good shit. This car for one thing. The house…a good salary.

His eyes stared bleakly at the road in front of him. What if he drove into the guardrail? Let the car bounce off, spin him— round and round—until he eventually died on impact. What if? But *they* would know…

They would know he'd done it intentionally. And his family would suffer as a result.

He prayed to God *they* didn't ever discover he'd sent the email to the journalist in Los Angeles. He prayed to a God he wasn't sure he believed in the journalist would read between the lines. Spur an investigation. Research what had happened three years ago and, most importantly, start paying closer attention to her neighbor.

And then what? Then what!? He slammed the palms of his hands against the steering wheel. Tears streamed down his face as he recalled the video *they* had showed him. The blood. The torture.

The tears blurred his vision and he wiped them away, wishing he could clear the memories just as easily. Wishing he could vanish. Or die.

But *they* had him by the balls.

He was trapped in hell, because of what *they* had shown him and what *they* would do to his family if he took *the cowardly* way out—or worse—told anyone about *their* plans.

The agony on the faces of the Petersens in that video— from Bren who was only six-years old and had made silly faces with Ryan's then two-year old twins, to their father, Andrew, who, from the brief time Ryan spent with him, seemed like a good guy. It didn't matter because good or bad, no one deserved what had been done to Andrew and his family. *They* had bound them. Raped Selena in front of her husband and children. God, Selena. She had been so sweet when they had moved from New Jersey to San Diego. She had brought his wife Jeanine into her fold of friends. They'd gone to yoga together and went for morning coffees.

Jeanine had known Selena better than Ryan knew Andrew. The guys were simply colleagues, but the women bonded at a work picnic. Jeanine had been devastated when they were murdered.

Selena's silent tears were what always popped into Ryan's mind. She'd been brave and clearly didn't want the children to hear her pain, although it wasn't easy to hide. Ryan had seen the horror in their faces. And their father had been purple with pain and rage. All because he had said, "No." All because he had not believed in what *they* represented and they're threats. He'd thought it was a joke.

After murdering Selena, the men slit the throats of all four children in front of their father. Ryan could see in Andrew's eyes how badly he'd wanted to die then—any way they could put him out of his misery, he would have gladly accepted. But they tortured him first. And now, Ryan understood why. It had all been for *his* benefit. The group who referred to themselves as The Brotherhood needed to be certain there was no way in hell Ryan would refuse them. They had forced him to watch the video. Gun to his head. Wrists and feet bound. A gag in his mouth. No, he could not refuse their offer. But then it wasn't really an offer, was it? Because offers can always be turned down.

The men put a bullet in every non-fatal place possible in Andrew's body, until finally, they shot him through his stomach and allowed him to bleed to death. All because Andrew was a chemist, like himself—and because Andrew Petersen had said, "No."

Ryan reprimanded himself again for sending the e-mail. But if there was still a God—the One he had believed in growing up—if that God existed, sending the email, no matter the consequences to him and to his family, had been the right thing to do. Because as horrific as The Brotherhood had been to the Petersens, their plans for humanity were even worse.

CHAPTER TWO

A shrill whistle rang out from the fetal heart monitor as the baby's heart rate plummeted. The emergency room staff flew into an organized chaos with rubber gloves sliding over hands, instruments exchanging sterility for human flesh, and various orders voiced loudly above the other noise.

"Let's go! Let's go! She's crashing. Baby is crashing!" Dr. Kelly Morales yelled. "Watch out for Mom."

"She scratched me!" a nurse cried out, while placing an oxygen mask over the teenager's face. The sixteen-year-old thrashed wildly, her arms outstretched. Each fingernail was over an inch long, curving at the end, and decorated with a skull and crossbones motif. The girl moaned in pain. Or maybe panic or protest. Likely a combination of the three. She was involuntarily doing everything she could to keep the medical staff from doing their jobs. At least she had some fight left in her. The only positive sign so far.

"Someone get her arms!" another nurse yelled.

Kelly saw a window and took it. She pinned the girl's arms down and bent directly over her face, looking into a pair of panicked brown eyes. *Jesus, what was going on with this kid!?* Kelly didn't really want to know. She witnessed enough tragedy every day inside the Neo-Natal Intensive Care Unit. But at least in her protected NICU bubble she could make a difference. She'd been the available doctor when Lupe Salazar arrived at the hospital, and so here she was. A sixteen-year-old in severe distress was not Kelly's specialty. Babies were easier.

Kelly bent over the girl, her face within inches of the teen's. The girl's eyes widened, clearly surprised at the lithe doctor's strength. Dr. Morales lowered her voice to a calm whisper. "Listen to me, Lupe. I want to help you. I need to know if you've taken anything. Any alcohol or drugs?"

Lupe focused. She shook her head. "I don't do drugs!"

"I won't be angry. I just need to know."

"No," the teen managed to say. "I promise. Nothing. Let me go!"

"I can't. You need to stay calm and listen. Have you been getting regular prenatal care?"

Lupe nodded, crying loudly now.

"Have you had any problems with this pregnancy? Anything your doctors mentioned? High-blood pressure? Any bleeding?"

"Nothing," Lupe sobbed. "Everything's been fine. It hurts so much. Make it stop. Just make it stop!"

"What about family? Where are they?"

"I don't have any," she spat.

"Where do you live, honey? Can you tell me that?"

"The shelter on East Fifth. Please make it stop hurting!" Tears streamed down her face.

Kelly hated this part of the job. Despite her skill and ability to keep her emotions in check, watching this girl suffer was not easy. Particularly because Kelly was no closer to figuring out what in the world was going on. So far, Lupe was a medical mystery. And where the hell was Dr. Brightman? He was the head of O.B. and she needed him now.

"I'm sorry it hurts. I'm trying to get a monitor attached to your baby's head so we can study the heart rate. Okay? Stay with me, Lupe."

Kelly lifted her head. A nurse wiped it with a towel. The girl started to struggle again, pushing forcefully against Kelly's tight grip. "Ten ccs of epi, stat!" Kelly fought back an exhausted sigh. This was too much. Whatever had landed Lupe on the ER table was serious. She was losing her grip on the girl when suddenly her eyes rolled back into their sockets.

"Pressure is dropping!" the intern reading vitals called out.

Kelly glanced up at the crew around her…a look that lasted a mere second.

The girl on the gurney started to shake and writhe.

"Seizure."

The air around them was dense and still, the way it gets when the threat of death enters the room. Kelly understood the stakes and implications in a second. She had been in this situation too many times to count. Her vision narrowed, sounds faded, and everything extraneous drained from her mind. The analysis and course of action took only seconds. Because seconds are all you get when a life is on the line.

It was time to make a tough call. Kelly braced herself.

But before she could say or do anything, Lupe's body went still. A monotone buzzing echoed through the room.

The girl was flat-lining.

"Goddamn it!" Kelly yelled.

Dr. Pierce Brightman pulled back the curtain. He was tall, slender, and handsome in a surfer sort of way. He didn't really look like a doctor (but he could have easily played one on TV). Kelly had never been so happy to see anyone.

"What the hell is going on?" His normally relaxed face was drawn up in a tense frown.

"I don't know! Normal pregnancy, from what I can tell. Pressure is dropping. Baby is crashing. Now we've got flat-line." Kelly glanced at the monitor. Dr. Brightman saw the screen. Heard the tone. Everyone did. "We don't have many options here, Pierce. We're losing both of them. The baby is thirty-two weeks, and I can probably save it."

Code Blue in ER number three! The intercom crackled to life as more nurses and techs scurried into the room.

"Epinephrine," Brightman ordered. He administered the drug, trying to raise Lupe's blood pressure. There was no response. "More epi! Give me more epi!"

The team hooked up the defibrillators and applied CPR.

"Clear!" The harsh popping sound echoed in Kelly's ears. The baby was dying inside the young woman. The infant couldn't take much more. Lupe didn't have a prayer unless a miracle occurred. Kelly knew it in her gut.

And tonight her gut told her before the night was through, the poor sixteen-year-old lying on the gurney—a child herself still —would be lying in the morgue.

CHAPTER THREE

"Clear!" Brightman ordered again. Lupe gave no response.

Kelly continued to watch the fetal monitor. "Pierce, we have to get this baby out now. There are no more options left. She's gone. We're wasting time."

"Clear!" Brightman ignored her, acting as if he hadn't heard a word she'd said.

The baby's heart rate continued dropping. "Damn it, Pierce, call it or they'll both be dead!" The helpless feeling she had seconds before was replaced with anger. Adrenaline coursed through her and lit every nerve on edge. *Screw this guy!*

"I'll call it when I'm goddamn ready!" Brightman shouted.

She was hit by a surreal out-of-body moment where she felt oddly detached from the scene unfolding in front of her—white walls, blue curtains, silver instruments, dead mother, dying infant, a frantic medical staff trying to fix the situation. Dr. Brightman was good. Kelly knew this. But she could see he was fighting a losing battle, and she hadn't lost hers yet. She could save the baby if he would let her.

"Get the hell out of my way, Brightman, and call this patient's time of death, or I will be the first in line to file a law suit against you."

Brightman looked at her, took survey of the room, and then stared down at the girl on the gurney. Three seconds later he glanced at the clock and wiped his forehead with the back of his arm. "Time of death, sixteen hundred hours. The baby is all yours, Dr. Morales. And good luck." He swore under his breath and slipped away behind one of the curtains, off to file his report.

The charge nurse from labor and delivery and the two nurses from the neo-natal intensive care unit waited for Kelly's next call. With their help, she went to work with quick and determined efficiency. "Sponge," she said and wiped down the mother's stomach with a mixture of alcohol and iodine. "Scalpel." With proficient hands, she opened up Lupe's abdomen, retrieving the baby within minutes. A girl. The doctor suctioned the infant's mouth and nose clear.

The tiny infant resembled an extraterrestrial being, with her transparent skin and spindly limbs. A nurse placed the baby on a radiant warmer. Three others gathered around, gently drying her with warm towels. "Let's get a heel stick stat and into the incubator immediately," Kelly said. "This one is going to need to oxygen, among other things, I'm sure. Get her weight and length. What do we have?" She noted the baby's weight on the scale as a nurse took the blood sample and hurried off. "3.2 pounds and 16.53 inches. She's a little one."

Kelly took the baby's APGAR score to check how well she was doing after her traumatic birth. The score rated the infant's breathing, heart rate, muscle tone, reflexes, and skin color. At only four, it was not good. She'd take it again in a few minutes to see if things improved.

Kelly and Eric Sorensen, the NICU nurse in charge, transferred the baby to the intensive care nursery. As they rolled the warmer down the hospital hallway, a lab technician came running after them. "I have the mom's initial blood work back. Here you go."

Kelly took the reports. "Thank you."

Once inside the unit, the baby was placed inside an incubator, likely her home for the next several days, if not longer. Eric began hooking up the monitors and leads onto the infant. There was a lot to be done: blood gas, chest x-ray, continuous cardio-respiratory monitoring, feeding tube…and a lot to watch for: apnea, anemia, jaundice, respiratory distress, underdeveloped lungs, infection. The list was endless. But Kelly could tackle all of that. She took a step back and opened the mom's file, figuring she would find Lupe had some kind of drug in her system. What else could explain the scene back in the ER? The more Kelly knew, the better she could help the baby.

"I don't believe it," she muttered, shaking her head.

"What?" Eric asked, glancing over at her

"Inconclusive for any kind of narcotics or alcohol. Nothing apparent in the mother's system to indicate she was using." She shrugged. "According to these preliminary reports, we have no clear signs the mom has any drug, legal or illegal, in her system. I was so sure. I mean, I have no idea what happened on that table in there. Obviously we have to wait for an autopsy report, but I don't know what to think. These test results say we are probably dealing with a perfectly healthy sixteen-year-old girl who, for no explicable reason, completely crashed on us."

"I don't know what to say, but I need some help here, Doc. I'm having a hard time getting this IV started on her," Eric said.

Kelly focused back on the baby, scanning her body. The poor thing let out a fragile cry, similar to a puppy's whimper, as Kelly found a vein on the top of her head and inserted the tiny catheter. *God, please help me save her.*

The baby girl was hooked up to numerous monitoring sensors in order to regulate heat, oxygen, and carbon monoxide levels as well as her heart and breathing rates. "Okay, I'll get the tube in, and then let's get this little one a dose of surfactant," Kelly told Eric. The baby's underdeveloped lungs hadn't had enough time to produce their own surfactant, but thank God Kelly could give it to her. Machines and drugs could do pretty damn well, sometimes almost as well as a mother's own uterus.

Kelly expertly threaded a tube through the baby's nose, down the back of her throat, and into her trachea. Eric then connected the tube to the respirator and started the machine, regulating the flow of air, oxygen, and air pressure in and out of the lungs. "Thank you," Kelly said to Eric, who smiled back at her.

He had a great smile—perfect white teeth and dimples to boot. His grey-blue eyes matched the surgical gowns he wore. His black hair and superb physique caused many women to take second and third looks because the guy could easily have been a Calvin Klein underwear model. It was a shame he was gay. At least for all of those swooning women, anyway.

Eric was fairly private about his sexual preference. The only reason Kelly even knew was because of an embarrassing incident that had occurred at last year's holiday party. Kelly had gotten drunk and made a complete fool out of herself, telling Eric how hot he was, and more. Frankly, this was pretty out of character for her, but who can resist the pull of a frozen margarita (or four)? And then he'd told her he was gay, and she was mortified. When Monday rolled around, she could hardly look him in the eye.

At lunch time he'd sweetly taken her by the hand and said, "C'mon, Doc, let's get something to eat."

Over turkey sandwiches and Diet Cokes, she tried to apologize.

"For what? Are you serious?! First of all, I'm flattered." He leaned in closer, flashing his adorable smile. "Second, if I wasn't gay, I'd do you in a heartbeat. I actually gave it some serious thought the other night. You looked good enough to eat in that red dress. Maybe you could have converted me." He'd winked at her, and they both burst out laughing, causing heads to turn in the cafeteria. From that day forward, their friendship was permanently cemented.

There was no one Kelly would rather have at her side.

"She is a very sick little girl, isn't she, Doc?" Eric asked, placing soft cotton bandages over the infant's eyes, shielding her from the Bilirubin lights.

Kelly nodded. "I'm going to do my damndest to see she makes it. Right now, I'm just concerned with stabilizing her." She frowned. "I don't know what to think with the reports. From everything I saw in that ER room and seeing how sick this baby is, I would have assumed there were narcotics involved. I would expect to see some withdrawal signs in this one's early weeks, but…well, now I don't know."

"Huh."

"What?" Kelly asked.

"You heard about the other cases from last week, right?" Eric asked. "They happened while you were off."

Kelly nodded slowly. "Yeah…I heard a couple of maternity patients passed away, but I never did get the full scoop. What happened?"

"Our team was called in to stand by for the infants but neither baby survived. They were both stillborn. They had heartbeats until a few minutes before delivery, but once the mothers died, well, things went rapidly downhill from there," Eric replied.

"Who were the attending OBs and who was on for NICU those days?"

"Dr. Pearson was on both of the cases for NICU. Brightman was the attending OB," Eric shrugged as he adjusted an IV. "It seems a little weird. Kind of coincidental, don't you think?"

"I hear you. I think I'll track Pearson down and see if he can enlighten me a bit. Something tells me Brightman may not want to talk to me after our little showdown in ER."

"You may have to wait to speak with Dr. Pearson. I heard he left on vacation the day after the second baby died. Rumor is he was pretty distraught. He may have even been forced by the chief to take some time off. Someone said he's in southern Europe…Greek Islands, maybe?"

"Must be nice," Kelly muttered and then sighed loudly. "I suppose I could go and see what I can get out of Brightman. But I really don't know if I want to deal with him today. Maybe I'll visit

Hamilton instead." Jake Hamilton, the chief pathologist, was the only other man in the hospital corridors besides Eric to catch her attention. "Maybe he has some ideas. He can at least tell me what he found in the autopsies."

"Makes sense. But before you go, why don't you take a load off and rest ? You look beat. What time is your shift over?"

"God, I don't know." Kelly ran her hands through her hair. "I don't think I care anymore. I feel like I live here. Any time off I typically spend sleeping."

"You need a life," Eric said.

"I probably do." She wiped the perspiration from her forehead.

"Go grab something to drink, take a few. I've got things here." He glanced down at the baby in the incubator. "I think she's as stable as we're going to get her for now. I'll page you if I need you."

Kelly scrunched up her nose and shook her head. "Hmmm, I don't know. I don't want to leave her yet."

"You can't keep twenty-four hour vigil, Doc. Get a cup of coffee, think, and breathe for a minute. Regroup and come back. You can't go very far, so if something goes wrong, I'll have your ass back here in minutes. I insist." Eric crossed his arms and gave her one of his no-nonsense looks. He'd make an awesome parent. He had the expression down pat.

"Fine. But page me if anything happens. I don't care how minor. I mean, even if her lead comes off, page me. Promise?"

"Cross my heart."

Eric was right to send her away. A lot of what they called "the waiting game" was starting now. There would likely be many stressful, difficult moments before they could envision a healthy future for Baby Salazar, and Kelly simply couldn't be here for every single second. She needed to take a break and recharge to keep her head clear in case something else went wrong.

She walked out the double doors of the NICU and stopped in front of the elevator. After giving it some thought, she decided to head down to the morgue first to see if she could speak with Dr. Hamilton. Her radar was on and it screamed there was something peculiar about Lupe's death.

The elevator doors opened, and she stepped inside. Kelly took her hair out of its elastic band, ran her fingers through, and pulled it back again, hoping she looked somewhat presentable. A quick glance in the mirrored button panel was far from reassuring. When was the last time she'd had a good night's sleep? Even when she had time for sleep, Kelly struggled to shut down her brain. In the scheme of things, sleep didn't matter as much as the lives of her little patients. Sleep could wait. What she really wanted right now were some answers.

CHAPTER FOUR

The elevator doors opened silently and Kelly stepped out. The stale, cool air hit her and she shivered.

In spite of the charming Dr. Hamilton, this was not one of her favorite places to visit. She generally tried to avoid it if at all possible. She was all about saving lives. Dead bodies were a grim reminder things didn't always work out.

The morgue hallway was long and dim. Four doors on either side led to various offices. Jake Hamilton's was the last on the right. Kelly tapped lightly, but there was no answer. She turned the handle. The door was unlocked, so she went in and waited.

Jake's cramped office was cluttered with stacks of files on the floor and half-opened cabinets. UCLA and Stanford degrees hung on the wall. The combined smells of mothballs, formaldehyde, and coffee stung her eyes. A photo of Jake's teenage daughter in a cheerleading uniform stood on his desk. All photos of his wife had been discretely removed, due to their recent divorce.

Jake stepped into the room. "Hey, you!" His green eyes sparkled. Those eyes, nice smile, and sun-kissed blonde hair gave him the air of a pretty boy. But there was a definite edge to Dr. Hamilton. A slightly crooked nose, the scar above his right eyebrow—they were just enough to make a woman wonder what sort of trouble he got into in his spare time. If Kelly had to guess, the scar was an old one, probably from a fall off of his bicycle when he was a kid. "I didn't expect you down here, but I'm happy to see you. What's up?"

"What isn't? Up, I mean." Kelly smiled, aware of the chemistry growing between them. They'd been colleagues and good friends for years, and it was clear he was interested in her. But he was fresh off a divorce and Kelly didn't want to rush into anything just yet.

"Oh, now you've piqued my curiosity. What brings you down to the depths of despair?"

"Curiosity."

"Oh, yeah? About what?" He crossed his arms and leaned back against the desk, eyebrows raised.

"You received a patient down here in the past hour. Lupe Salazar?"

"I did. I haven't had a chance to process her yet. Ty is prepping the body. I'm backlogged though. It's been a crazy week." He paused, tapping his fingers on the desk. "Why the interest in this girl?" He stood and walked over to his coffee machine and held up a cup. "Want some? I splurged and picked up one of those instant espresso machines. Delicious."

"Yes, thanks. Some liquid fuel would help right now, I think."

He fiddled with buttons and after 30 seconds of hissing, a freshly brewed cup of espresso streamed into a waiting cup. Jake deftly scooped a heaping spoonful of sugar into it, stirred, and then handed it over. She studied him for a second.

"You wondering how I knew how you liked your coffee?" She didn't respond. "Because I pay attention, Kel. We've had coffee together a few times. When you like someone, you notice things, file them away for future use." He smiled and raised his cup to her.

Kelly felt heat rise to her cheeks.

"Sorry. I didn't mean to embarrass you."

She smiled and took a careful sip of her piping hot, and perfectly sweetened, espresso. "No. Not at all. We're friends."

"Yes we are. So before I dig myself in any deeper, let's talk about this patient."

"She delivered one of my babies."

"Tough stuff, I take it?" He took another sip from the small cup.

"Yeah. Strange. She came in here not even three hours ago, and now she's dead. No family that we can locate. No boyfriend. Nothing. Of course, I start with the stereotypical train of thought, and I'm thinking she's a runaway caught up in some bad things. Brightman was the attending, and he gets on the scene and tries to go chief on me. We were losing the girl, and the baby's time was running out. I had no idea what we were dealing with since it all happened so fast the labs hadn't even come back yet. My gut was telling me she's addicted, got something running through her veins. It was the only thing that made sense."

"You're skilled, Kelly. If that was your guess, I'm sure it was a good one."

"I know. But I'm watching this girl, looking into her eyes, and all I can think is something is off. Lupe wasn't strung out, Jake. It would have made sense based on the way she was acting, but she wasn't. So the girl seizes, codes, and dies. Nothing was going to save her. I've never seen anything like this. From everything I can tell, we were dealing with a healthy teenager. Anyway, baby was failing. I had to get her out. We couldn't bring the mom back. She was gone, so I took over and did a C-section. I've got the baby now in NICU with all sorts of problems. I don't know what to make of any of this. I need that autopsy. Something is wrong here."

"What are you saying?" Jake asked.

"So far all her labs have come back inconclusive for drugs, which makes me wonder if there is something new on the streets we don't know about. She had no alcohol present either."

Jake's eyes widened. His left hand jerked suddenly, nearly spilling his coffee. He walked around to the back of his desk and sat down.

"Are you all right?" Kelly asked.

"Yeah, yeah. I'm fine. It's just what you're telling me sounds, well, unusual."

"Tell me about it," she replied.

"I'm not sure what I can do. I won't have a report ready on this girl for at least forty-eight hours, maybe longer. And you know how long tox can take." He absentmindedly picked up the photo of his daughter.

"Rumor has it this girl isn't the only one. In the last week, two other women came in, delivered, coded, and died. Both had stillborns. The baby I have upstairs is the only one to survive so far. I haven't had a chance to look into the mothers' backgrounds or anything, so I'm only going off what I've been hearing in the hallways. I need your help here, Jake. Did you find anything in the autopsies on those other women? It might help the baby in the NICU."

For a moment, Jake didn't say anything. He turned his head to the side as if trying to figure out how to respond. He brought his fist up under his nose and looked at her. His eyes closed for a second and then he sighed. "I don't know what to say. I don't think I can help in any way."

"Jake?"

He was quiet for a moment. "There was nothing odd about the autopsies. I mean, no strange chemicals or anything. I don't know. I wish I could help, but…"

"But what? You're telling me you don't know how those girls died? Come on. Of course you know. Were the mothers healthy or not, Jake? That's all I'm asking."

"I can't…I don't…"

Kelly didn't like the evasive tone in his voice. "Jesus, Jake. What is it? What the hell is wrong? You're freaking me out." She'd asked him a simple question, what was the big deal?

He reached across the desk and grabbed her by the hand. Out of instinct she pulled back. He held on tighter and pulled her close, lowering his voice to a whisper. "You have to drop this. Leave this alone, Kel."

She pulled back again, and this time he let go. "Jake, you're scaring me. What's going on?"

He put his hand to his forehead. He was visibly perspiring. "I can't talk to you about these cases. They're classified."

"Classified? Classified?! I've got a baby in my unit with a slim chance of surviving, but I certainly can't help her if I don't know what I'm up against. If you know something, you need to tell me. I *will* take this to the chief and the board if I have to."

He shook his head. "No. You can't do that. Please. I'm begging you to drop this. You could get hurt."

"What?" She was furious. And confused. And beyond disappointed. What the hell was wrong with him? He knew damn well she needed information from the autopsies in order to help the baby. It was his *duty* to tell her. This conspiratorial attitude of his was ridiculous. Not in a million years would she ever have imagined Jake acting this way. "This is insane, Jake. I'm going to save that baby's life, and you're going to help me do it. You know that's the right thing to do, rules or no rules."

He paused, breathing deeply. "Okay. I'll tell you what I know. But not here. It's too dangerous."

Now Kelly held his stare. She saw genuine fear in his eyes. *Oh my God. He's really serious.* There was something going on here, and it obviously involved the death of three pregnant women. But clearly she wasn't going to get any more information out of him here.

His assistant, Ty, tapped on the door. "Dr. Hamilton, I need a hand."

"Sure. Be right there." He looked at Kelly. "Tuscany's at seven-thirty. I really wish you would drop this. Trust me."

"I'll be there. And you should know me better than that." She walked out of his office toward the elevator, baffled by what had just taken place. Jake wasn't just afraid, he was terrified.

CHAPTER FIVE

After another sleepless night, Ryan decided to get up at 5:00 a.m. and head to the lab. If they were watching, they'd see how dedicated he was. And most importantly, they'd hopefully assume the brain washing had worked and he—good, all-American white boy—had truly joined their ranks.

He'd been watching his back. He had to. If The Brotherhood knew his background and his true feelings, Ryan knew what they could do. He had to act as if he had been converted.

How he hated these men and what they stood for. How he hated himself.

And they knew everything. They had him by the short hairs. Ryan sighed heavily with memories of his old life pervasive in his head. He pulled into the garage at Frauen Pharmaceuticals— a privately owned company based in Germany with headquarters in Los Angeles. Frauen had some very influential investors, and was an up and comer in the women's pharmaceuticals market. They produced pills for menopause, anxiety, depression; they were even working on a Viagra-like pill that would heighten sexuality for women. But Ryan didn't develop any of those drugs. Not by a long shot.

He parked the Audi and got out his card key. After getting through security, he went up to his office, and then into the lab where he stopped in his tracks.

"Good morning, Ryan."

It was Peter Redding. Redding was the CEO of Frauen Pharmaceuticals. He was also much, much more.

"Good morning, Mr. Redding. I didn't know you were flying in."

A crooked smiled spread across Redding's face. His blue eyes held an unpleasant light. Ryan was pretty certain the man was Satan himself. He was handsome, by most people's standards. Peter was of average height, but well built. He obviously spent a lot of time in the gym. Redding was probably closer to fifty than forty, but it didn't show. His salt and pepper hair sparkled under the fluorescent lights. "I came to see you. Only you. Come with me."

Ryan's stomach sank. They had found out. They knew about the e-mail.

"What's this about, sir?"

"I will explain in my office."

Ryan's stomach twisted. Wished he'd gone in and kissed the twins' cheeks goodbye that morning. Oh God. The twins. Jeanine! What if *they* were there now, with them? What if *they* were hurting his family? Killing them? The memory of Frederick

Färber holding a gun to his head while he witnessed the torture and murders of The Petersens vividly flashed in his mind. What if that bastard Färber was in his home? Sweat slicked his back. He thought he might throw up.

Redding opened two wide Mahogany doors and Ryan followed him inside. "Sit down," Redding pointed to a chair at the conference table and picked up a TV remote, turning on a screen in front of them.

Ryan closed his eyes for a second, knowing what was coming next. His stomach sank.

"Do you see this, Horner?"

Ryan opened in his eyes and a wave of relief hit. It was a baby hooked up to all sorts of IVs and monitors. He nodded and with trepidation answered, "Yes."

"And how about this?"

A young woman—a girl really—Hispanic…dead on a slab. "Yes."

Redding turned off the TV. "This is not what I fucking want! This is not what *we* want, Horner! We want aborted fetuses, we want sterile women. Dead women alert people. They make people scratch their heads and wonder why, why, why?! This is fucked up! Do you understand what we are doing here? Do you?!"

"Yes, sir." He tried to keep his hands from shaking.

"I am not sure you do." Redding turned the TV back on and now the screen showed his beautiful wife in their kitchen drinking coffee. Then it changed to show his five-year old daughters eating cereal in front of the TV in his family room.

"No," he whispered.

"No what?"

They had cameras throughout his house. Why was he even surprised by this? "Please don't hurt them."

"I don't want to, Ryan. I really don't. You have a lovely wife. Cute kids. I like you. I heard you were the best. That's why you got the job. And of course, Petersen turned it down." He frowned and it was obviously forced. Redding paused a beat, then his frown turned upward into a wicked smile. "Yes. I like you and I am going to give you another chance to make things right. Fix it. Fix the problem. I have a fucking race to purify, and I can't have people asking questions about dead girls. Isolate and fix the problem so you can continue to go home every night to your lovely wife and cute kids. Do you understand?"

"Yes, sir."

"Good. You have two weeks. Start testing those fucking rats and monkeys of yours and get me the results I want."

Ryan looked up at the TV as Redding turned it off. His wife. His daughters. Ryan would do whatever Redding wanted. He would find a way.

CHAPTER SIX

Jake glanced at his watch. He was running late to meet Kelly. *Shit.* Why was he so easy to read? He couldn't lie to her. She was so damn on top of it. It was one of the things he liked about her, but at this moment, her intellect wasn't making things easy. She was involved now whether she knew it or not, and he'd have to find a way to protect her.

Well, he could just not tell her the truth. That was one idea. But then what *would* he tell her? And how would he convince her he wasn't lying? Her bullshit meter was too sensitive for that. It was an impossible situation. There was one thing Jake knew for sure, though: the people behind all of this were bad. Really, really bad. What choice did he have? Kelly would be relentless until she got the truth out of him. He knew that. Hell, maybe he even needed her help. Letting her in might be a good thing. Maybe there was a way the two of them could work together, figure out exactly who these people were.

Figuring out what to do about it once they knew, however, would be another story entirely.

Jake picked up the picture of his daughter again and traced the outline of her face with his fingertip. "Oh Beth, what have I gotten myself into?" He remembered a time when his little girl had complete and total faith in him—trusted him implicitly. Daddy could do no wrong. But if she knew how much danger he had put her in, she'd hate him. No. He could not tell Kelly. He would have to think of something. Send her down a dead-end path.

He set the photo down, determined to come up with a story to pacify Kelly. He took his coat from the back of the chair and pulled it on. He walked across the hall to shut the lights off in the morgue. Ty had already gone home for the day. Jake glanced around the room to make sure everything was status quo and flipped the switch. "My briefcase," he said out loud. He couldn't forget that. His mind was not working the way it usually did. He was too consumed by the mess he was in. He had to find a way out of it. Get back on track. This place and this situation were going to eat him alive.

He had to find a way out.

He took another step back towards his office, totally unprepared for the blow to his head.

Jake hadn't heard a thing, but now a warm sensation oozed down his back, the pain immense as he collapsed to the ground. A groan escaped his lips. His head smacked hard against the cold floor with a loud thud. He tried to pick himself up, only to collapse again. The pain grew more intense with each labored breath. His vision blurred. He knew the warm blood trickling from the back of his skull would soon run cold.

They knew. God damn it. They knew he'd talked.

Oh God, Kelly.

His daughter!

He prayed someone would find him before he died. He had to get to her before they did. Impossible, though.

Footsteps along the floor, passing him. "Really fucking stupid. At least for your sake, we decided you are dispensable, my friend. If you weren't, I'd be killing your kid right now. Lucky for her."

Jake felt another sharp pang on one side of his neck that traveled in a deadly arc to the other. His throat had been cut. He attempted to bring his hands up to stop the bleeding. No chance.

He closed his eyes. An image of his daughter flashed through his mind.

Then nothing.

CHAPTER SEVEN

Kelly finished her Chardonnay and glanced around for any sign of Jake. She wasn't a big drinker, but after his strange behavior, she'd had a feeling the wine might calm her nerves. He was fifteen minutes late, and her patience was running thin. A voice inside told her something was wrong, but she pushed the thought out of her mind and took another sip of the wine. She would give him ten more minutes. She'd called his cell phone twice already, but it'd gone straight to voicemail. Jake almost always picked up so either his battery died or…something else had happened.

She thought about their discussion earlier. He was a straight shooter—not evasive and not one to play games. But this felt like a game to her, and she didn't like it at all. She would've never left the hospital to meet him for dinner if she'd known he was going to blow her off. It was so unlike him. And because it was so unlike him, she knew something was wrong. The sinking feeling in her stomach worsened. Five more minutes ticked away, and she decided to pay for the wine and head back to the hospital. Once in the car, she tried to reach Jake again by cell phone. She drove by his house, only a few minutes from the hospital. No lights were on and his car wasn't in the driveway. Good. Maybe he was still at work, and he could explain what was going on. She wasn't leaving until he told her everything. Whatever *everything* was.

She pulled into the hospital parking lot and scanned it before getting out of her car. Her days at USC had taught her one could never be too careful. Walking toward the building, she noticed several police cars out front. Must've been another gang-related shooting or something.

There was a noticeable buzz filling the halls. Something was out of whack. She spotted another policeman by the elevator. Kelly stopped a passing intern who was reading over a report on his clipboard. "Hey. What's going on? Something major happening in the ER?"

He studied her for a second, clearly trying to decide whether or not she was entitled to know. She flashed her credentials from the chain around her neck. His eyes widened. "Oh sorry, Doctor. I didn't realize you were staff." She nodded. "No. It's not in the ER. I don't know exactly what's up, but rumor has it there was a murder downstairs."

"What? Downstairs as in the morgue?"

"Yes."

Kelly's breathing changed, her body tensed. "Who?"

He shrugged and looked back down at his clipboard. "Sorry, I don't know. I have a patient waiting."

"Yeah, sure." Her racing thoughts took a giant turn for the worse. She tried hard to push them away, but they wouldn't budge.

She headed toward the elevator. Before she could ask the officer what was going on, the doors opened. A man with dark hair and piercing brown eyes stepped out. He glanced at Kelly, straightening his navy and teal striped tie against his button down.

"Excuse me, officer..." she said.

He looked at her. "Yes?"

"I'm a doctor here on staff." She showed him her ID. "Could you tell me what has happened?"

"Dr. Morales."

"Yes," she said.

"You're exactly who I've been looking for."

CHAPTER EIGHT

Kelly was now following the man toward a private room to talk. Following the *detective*. Tony Pazzini. Her heart raced and every nerve pumped adrenaline. He still hadn't told her anything other than he needed to speak with her in private. However, her gut told her what was coming.

This was about Jake. It had to be.

As they headed down the hall, they passed an orderly who dropped a handful of charts. Kelly bent down to help pick them up. The detective grabbed her arm. "I think he can handle that."

"I was only trying to help."

He touched her shoulder. "I understand but what we need to discuss is important."

She turned to him, arms crossed. "I'm not going any further until I know what this is about." She needed to know. She needed to hear it.

"Look, I just need to ask you some questions. I'd like to do it in private."

Anger, fear, and confusion stirred a vicious brew inside her. Kelly was terrified of what he was about to tell her. She nodded.

"Follow me."

Once inside the doctor's lounge, she turned and faced him, crossing her arms. "Okay. Now can you tell me what is going on?"

"Did you have an appointment with Dr. Jake Hamilton this evening?"

"I did. We were supposed to have dinner together."

"He didn't show up," the detective stated.

Kelly closed her eyes for a second. "No. I was on my way downstairs to see him when you came off the elevator." Beads of perspiration formed on her top lip.

"I am sorry, but Dr. Hamilton was found murdered about an hour ago."

Blood drained from her face as her stomach twisted into a knot that made her want to vomit, leaving a sour burn in the back of her throat. Her hands shook, and a cold descended upon her, chilling her whole body. The detective reached out and took her elbow as she collapsed onto the yellow sofa. She put her face in her palms, too stunned to cry. Too stunned to think.

Only one thought came to mind: *She was the reason Jake was dead.*

She knew this with the most painful certainty.

The detective poured her a glass of water. "Do you think you can answer a few more questions for me?" he asked. "I'm sorry to do this now, but it's necessary."

She nodded. "I'll try."

"Okay. Thank you. So, you planned to meet with Dr. Hamilton this evening?"

"I did." She was tearing up again.

"What time was he supposed to meet you?"

"Seven-thirty," she answered, barely audible.

"Where?" He jotted a note down on his pocket pad.

"Tuscany's."

"Was this a date?"

"No. Dr. Hamilton and I were friends." Her gaze fell to the ground. She didn't want him to know she had considered the possibility of being more, but now...

"So you were not romantically involved with Dr. Hamilton?"

She hesitated. "No. I just told you it wasn't a date." She took a sip of her water and ran her fingers through her light brown hair. He gave her a weak smile. "We planned to meet for dinner because we needed to discuss some patient cases we were working on."

"A dinner date to discuss business then?" He'd obviously decided to ignore the edge in her answer.

"Yes. Some patients, as I said."

"Did you plan on going home with him?"

She frowned. "No. That actually had not crossed my mind, Detective." Heat was rising in her face.

"Were you, um...were you intimately involved with Dr. Hamilton?"

She frowned, her eyes narrowing. "I am not that kind of woman, and I don't see the relevance to that sort of questioning. I told you, he was a colleague and a friend."

"I'm working a murder case. Everything is relevant. I don't judge what kind of woman you are, Doctor. Honestly. I am only trying to establish facts. Friends and colleagues can mean one thing to one person and a something else to another."

"What are you, a detective or a relationship expert?"

This got a slight laugh out of him. "Well, actually, in my line of business you become a little bit of everything, I guess."

She frowned. "I still don't understand your questions."

He paused for a second. "I'm gonna lay it on the line."

"I wish you would."

"When I have a murder case, I have to flesh everything out. I'm sure you can appreciate that. And the thing is, I can't discount anything. Many times these cases wind up being crimes of passion or at least the victim knew the assailant."

She crossed her arms, the frown on her face deepening. "Wait a minute, are you suggesting I murdered Jake?" She let out a soft cry. "Oh my God! As I said our relationship was one of mutual respect. I liked him. I liked him a lot." The tears welled in her eyes again. "He was an excellent doctor and a decent man. He was also my friend." She wiped her face with the back of her hand, and tried hard to contain her emotion. "We were not intimate. We've never been. I don't know where things were headed, Detective. But what I can tell you is there is no way in hell I killed Jake." She shook her head vehemently.

"Hey, I'm sorry if I offended you. I am only doing my job. What do you say we get back to the questions and I can let you go home?"

"Fine. Ask away."

"Where were you between seven-fifteen and eight-fifteen this evening?"

"I left the hospital, drove to the restaurant, and waited there for Jake. When he didn't show up, I came back here. I think you know the rest." She stated it matter-of-factly and wiped the last of her tears away.

"Can someone verify they saw you at the restaurant?"

"I assume so. A hostess seated me. A waiter waited on me."

"Okay, good."

"Are we finished? I would really like to go home now."

"Yes. I'll probably need to speak to you again. Some time tomorrow. I may have more questions."

"I will be here." She left, holding back more tears and convinced she had in some way caused her friend's death.

CHAPTER NINE

Redding sat back in the plush leather seat inside the chartered jet, waiting for take off. He swirled the ice around in his scotch and soda. He was headed back home, his work done in Germany. Hopefully. Something worried him about Horner though. He couldn't put a finger on it. Other than the chemist still hadn't produced what they wanted. They were on a timeline. Next year was an election year and it was vital to stay on schedule. Would Horner be able to get the job done? Redding sensed the guy was struggling. Maybe losing it. Peter sighed heavily. There were always going to be problems with a project like this. It was staying on top of the problems that mattered. Staying organized.

He remembered his father—George Redding. The Reddings had adopted him when he was three and George had loved him and been an amazing teacher. He was the one who had explained the order of things. "You have to keep your soldiers in line, Petie. When fighting a war—and trust me, we are fighting a war—you have your minions down on the bottom. Now they may not seem all that important. But they are. They're like fleas—they can be disposed of and most easily replaced within the ranks. But the problem is, they can also be broken down the easiest by the enemy. They will almost always talk when push comes to shove, so it's very important you have a solid foundation.

"Next are your henchmen. These guys recruit the minions. Minions do little jobs. You can control their minds. Henchmen do more difficult jobs. They have to be discrete, trustworthy. Then there are the helpers. They are your confidantes and partners. Then there's you—the leader, son. You are a leader."

Peter took a sip from his drink. "Yes, Dad, I am," he muttered. His cell phone rang. It was a henchman calling. A *very* important henchman with very important connections. Connections who put a lot of money into Frauen Pharmaceuticals and Peter's back pocket.

"Our little problem taken care of?" Peter asked.

"Yes, sir."

"Good." He leaned back in his leather chair and sighed. "And the girlfriend?"

"I don't think she knows any more than what we heard, but we can't be too sure."

"No, we can't. No loose ends. I want to know her every move."

"Anything else, sir?"

"No. Money will be wired to your account. Good work."

"Thank you, sir. Good night."

Peter hung up the phone. The jet engine roared down the runway. Hamilton. The good doctor. A minion. Not one who believed in the cause, though. A minion by force, just like Horner.

There were only a few of those who Peter kept a close eye on. They could ruin everything he'd worked so hard for. Everything his dad would have been so proud of. Men like Hamilton and Horner scared him, but he needed them—or guys like them. Hamilton was easy to dispose of. Dumb fuck should've realized his office would be wired. Horner was another story. Once the job was finished on the chemist's end, Peter would feel much better when they'd gotten rid of him.

He took another long sip of his drink. He didn't like setbacks and these bumps in the road were definitely setbacks. This Dr. Morales better not be a problem. He didn't want to have her killed, too. He didn't need a body count adding up. Body counts alerted cops and cops sniffing around anything was never good. The Hamilton case would never be solved. The henchman who had taken care of the doctor was good at taking care of problems. He'd proven it when he had been involved with the Petersen fiasco. The young man had orchestrated the whole thing. A job well done.

But God how Redding had hated all of that bad business, however, he'd soon realized when Andrew Petersen had blown him off, he would need to make a strong and definite impression on his next victim—Dr. Horner. Yes, the young man had done a nice job there, and now with Hamilton taken care of, he'd once again proven he had the stamina to get things done. Best of all, Chad Wentworth had connections…nice political connections. And to think Chad had been discovered guarding the double doors outside The Brotherhood meeting in Valencia only four years ago. He had come a long way.

"So fuck it," he said aloud. "Fuck it! This little setback is good for the character." However, Redding knew any setback—minor or major—was not good for this project. Peter hated problems and loose ends. Hopefully Dr. Morales would keep her nose out of things. She would be much better off that way. The lights flickered from the city below, growing more distant as the plane reached cruising altitude. The alcohol began to ease tension from his shoulders and his mind. But he couldn't relax completely. He knew too many casualties would quickly alert the calvary, and the goddamn calvary was not invited to this war, because Peter Redding was determined to win.

CHAPTER TEN

Mark Pritchett loved watching the pretty doctor. Everyone loved watching Dr. Morales. But he was by far the most skilled at watching without her ever knowing. Hell, he'd been watching her long before he'd gotten word only a few hours earlier to keep an eye on her.

That's who he was—a watcher.

He couldn't wait until he got the go-ahead to take care of her. They would want that, wouldn't they? The Brotherhood wouldn't just want him to keep an eye on her and then do nothing about it.

Mark wanted so badly to prove himself to The Brotherhood. He was tired of being a peon. He was worthy of so much more. He could *do* so much more for the cause. He knew he could. If only they'd give him the chance.

For now, Mark would bide his time. It wasn't as if his assignment was a bad one. Keeping an eye on certain doctors was easy, and he'd been doing a damn fine job of it. Watching them and reporting back in. Smooth as silk. He knew he should be happy they trusted him. There were not many of them who had been placed in a position like this. Out of all of the guys who could have been chosen, they'd chosen him.

There had been a handful of doctors on his list to watch, including Dr. Morales. He'd about split a nut. She was gorgeous. But an ice-cold bitch. Like they all were. Women. From his mother to his fat-assed sister to the ex-girlfriend he should have offed for being the most annoying, pain in the ass on Earth.

Then there was Dr. Morales. Kelly…

Damn, he would have loved to see her face when the bad-ass detective told her about Hamilton. Priceless. He wondered what Hamilton had done to get himself iced. One thing he knew for sure was when you fucked with The Brotherhood, they didn't mess around. Obviously.

Mark snuck inside a supply room and stuck his hand inside his elastic-waist pants, wrapping his palm around his already hard cock. He looked down. The tattoo above his navel made him smile —his identity.

Everything that swastika stood for, he stood for.

Thinking about the various ways he would handle Dr. Morales excited him. He tightened his grip and moved his hand faster. Little Miss Big-Shot Doctor. Now that would be something, wouldn't it? That would really be proving himself. Death. Murder. Yes. With the good doctor, he would look right into her eyes. He would make it slow and torturous. A begging-for-mercy kind of thing.

He thought more about Dr. Morales and what he was going to do to her. It was pure ecstasy. He leaned against the wall, slid down to the floor, and finished himself off. He couldn't wait much longer. But waiting was a must because Mark knew no matter how bad he was, the people he worked for were far worse.

CHAPTER ELEVEN

Georgia Michaels—Gem for short—ran her fingers through her pixie cut, wondering how many grays were hidden beneath the Clairol Golden Blonde she'd been using since she was twenty-one and first spotted one of those nasty buggers. That was eighteen years ago, and she had no doubt the stress of raising two teenage boys—not to mention the strain of her job—had turned her hair snow white by now. There was a time, before she'd had the boys, when she'd wanted to become an international correspondent. But her hopes and dreams of interviewing and producing stories for CNN were dashed when her first son came along. She'd taken mothering as seriously as she'd taken anything in her life, and although Austen hadn't been planned, she'd fallen in love with him at first site and enjoyed being a mom.

However, kids grow up, divorces happen, and finances dwindle. For the past few years, she'd gotten back into reporting and her dreams were alight again with possibilities for the future. Probably too middle-aged and not pretty enough to be on television, but she still had brains and brawn, and could sniff out a good story and hunt down information like nobody's business.

Gem stared at the computer screen in front of her. *Deadline, deadline, deadline. Jesus, it's just another homicide. Write the damn thing, and get it to Stu before he hunts you down.*

God it was hard getting back into the swing of things. Gem had just returned from a week in Puerto Vallarta. Finally! Vacation. With a handful of forty-something divorcees drinking a shit-load of margaritas and eating way too much good food. Five pounds heavier and craving salt, lime, and tequila…the last thing Gem wanted to do right now was her job.

Homicide, schmomicide. They were all the same. So-and-so was killed at such-and-such location, by whomever using whatever—if they even knew *that* much. At least this one had some intrigue to it. It wasn't the typical boy-meets-girl, fall in love, girl falls out of love, boy goes psycho and blows her brains out story. No. This time one of the top pathologists in the state had been offed right in the middle of County Hospital. *Whoever toasted this guy was a total nut job or at least had some real balls. Or was some kind of hired hand. Maybe the doctor owed the wrong people some cash? Could be anything.*

Gem was checking into the ex-wife. From what she'd heard, the split between Dr. Hamilton and his ex had been messy. The wife made off with most of his money and was living large. Of course the death of her ex meant those alimony checks were going to stop rolling in. On the other hand, if she had an insurance policy on the doc, or if he had failed to change his beneficiary over on an existing policy, well, then…that could certainly be reason enough for murder.

Or maybe it wasn't about money. Gem had done enough checking into this thing to discover Dr. Hamilton had eyes for a pretty pediatrician who ran the neo-natal intensive care unit at County—a Dr. Morales. Gem wondered who had instigated the divorce between the Hamiltons. The ex could have a whopping jealous streak.

She looked at the blank screen that stared unforgivingly back at her. One would think this wouldn't be a problem to write. This was her place, her people. Noises from the newsroom, people dashing about, crazed writers high on caffeine or nicotine (or both) typing away as their minds raced at a clip their bodies could certainly never keep up with, always poised to pounce on the next big story...Jesus, she should be able to write this story in her sleep.

Big story. This one had the feel to it, like a lion hiding in his den waiting to come out for the hunt. The photo of the guy was really all she had at the moment other than the usual rumor and conjecture from a handful of hospital employees—all filled with speculation. She had insiders at the police station, but the strange thing was, no one was talking. At all. The cops had given a brief statement, and that was it. Detective Pazzini, who Gem thought was a decent cop and a helluva good-looking one, told the media once forensics was finished investigating, the press would receive clearance from the hospital and get a detailed report. Great. A lot of good that did her right now.

Her phone buzzed and snapped her back to the here and now. "Yeah?"

"It's Goldman." She cringed. It was her boss, Stuart Goldman. "How's your story coming? About finished? It's a front pager. We have to go to press in a couple of hours."

"Just about. Without the police saying much, it's a little on the light side."

"Well, you have to give me something. This guy was an important member in the community. Loved and respected. Go on that."

"Right," she replied, holding out her hands and looking at the light pink, chipped polish on her fingernails. The call from the boss was the motivation she'd needed. Gem turned off everything else around her and went to work, pounding out the best story she could. Once finished, she opened up her e-mail and attached the story to send to Goldman. She buzzed his office and let him know it was on the way.

Before heading out for the evening, she figured she'd better take a look and see if she had anything interesting in her inbox. She really was back now. E-mails aplenty. Her numero uno rule while down in Mexico was no computer and no cell phone.

Ah. L.A. was too far from Puerto Vallarta.

She scrolled down and saw the typical story pitches, lots of forwards from her book club friends, who she had consistently asked to stop sending her those damn jokes and chain letters. There was a short e-mail from her mom reminding her to make reservations early for her and the boys to fly back to New York for Christmas. The usual stuff. Except…one e-mail caught her eye. It was from ChemMadderhorn@gmail.com. At first she figured it was one of those skanky ads for Viagra or Cialis. God knew she received a ton of those, even with the filters on, but it was the subject line that grabbed her. "Your Neighbor, Chad."

She opened the e-mail and read the short note. *Watch your neighbor. Three years ago, San Diego, Ca., Petersen family.*

"Oh my God," she heard herself whisper. "What is this?" She knew about the Petersen family. Everyone in Southern California and pretty much in the U.S. had heard of them. And Gem had met her neighbor, Chad. But there was no way he'd been connected to that grisly, horrible crime. No way. She went to delete the e-mail, thinking it was some sick joke, but something held her back—her gut, her instinct, her sixth sense. She wasn't sure what, but she closed the e-mail and opened her documents on the Petersen family.

CHAPTER TWELVE

Stunned, Kelly mindlessly flipped through the channels on her TV trying to find a distraction. But the only thing that seemed to help was her cat, Stevie T (short for Stephen Tyler). He was curled up on her lap, purring away. Kelly stroked the long yellow fur on the tabby whose only purpose in life was to sleep, eat, and soak up attention. She scratched behind his ears. "Wish I was you," she said. The cat opened his green eyes slightly and let out a soft meow, likely in protest that Kelly had spoken. "Sorry."

She finally settled on HRTV to watch some horse racing. Horses were in her blood. She had been around them all her life, and even had one—Sydney, a mare—that she kept at the LA Equestrian Center. She tried to ride at least three days a week, when her busy schedule permitted.

Kelly had been born in Puerto Rico where her father worked as a groom and breezing race horses in the hopes of becoming a jockey. An opportunity came along when she was three and Raul moved his family to Lexington, Kentucky. In Lexington, he was able to work his way up from grooming race horses to training them. Now he trained and managed his own small stable. With any luck, he could end up with a future winner in his barn.

As a teen, Kelly breezed horses on the track before dawn. She'd thought long and hard about vet school vs. medical school, but in the end, she knew healing humans would be easier on her than trying to heal animals. She'd always formed attachments more easily to animals than people. However, as she'd grown in her role as a pediatrician, she realized being a human doctor was as tough as she'd thought being a vet would be. Emotions were emotions and they could get the better of her if she let them.

This train of thought led her right back to Baby Salazar lying in the NICU, and then to Jake. She tried to focus on the race —mud flying everywhere under pounding hooves, spraying like bullets into the eyes of the jockeys and horses.

Jockeys were an interesting lot. They worked so hard to make weight. They did everything from working out, starving themselves, taking diet pills, and even using cocaine to sharpen their focus and reaction time. Cocaine addiction amongst jockeys was high. It was one of the things her father did not like about racing. He'd recently fired one of the best jockeys to come through his stable for drug use.

Addiction. It would have been so easy for Kelly to piece all of this together if Lupe Salazar had been addicted to something. Kelly could treat addiction. She would know exactly what she was dealing with and how to handle it.

She needed to figure out the missing pieces. But as the emotions of the day finally caught up with her, she began to shut down. As she listened to the announcer and pounding hooves on the TV, she dozed off. Tomorrow she would see what she could figure out. She would do what she always did when she needed answers—make an early morning visit to the L.A. Equestrian Center, and, if time permitted, take Sydney out for a short trail ride before work. Syd had a way of helping her see things in a different light. Now it was time for sleep.

CHAPTER THIRTEEN

Kelly locked the house up behind her and stepped into her Land Rover. She'd fed Stevie T and left a light on in the entry and kitchen since she planned to return late. Her shift would start at nine and go for 12 hours. Leaving at 6:00am would give her enough time to visit her horse, and maybe get some perspective out on the trail.

Thirty minutes later, the rich scent of earth, dew, and freshly cut hay hit her as she opened the car door. Nickers and whinnies echoed across the grounds from the equestrian center. It was breakfast time and the horses were definitely ready to eat. She knew her timing wasn't great, but it was either today or wait for the weekend.

Kelly let out a low whistle as she walked down the barn aisle. A big bay mare popped her head out and turned to face her. Sydney nickered a gentle hello. Kelly smiled. "I'm happy to see you, too." In fact, she was more than happy…she was relieved. Tears welled in her eyes. She was exhausted and reeling from Jake's horrible death. This was the only place she could come and find peace, even if only for a short while.

"Hey big girl." Kelly slid a hand down Syd's face. She reached in her pocket and brought out the apple slices she'd prepped at home. Syd took it eagerly. "I hope this makes you feel a bit better about being late for breakfast." Kelly knew it wasn't kosher to take Sydney off her feed schedule, but she'd only be an hour behind by the time she was finished with her.

She took Syd out, put her in the cross-ties, and quickly groomed her. After tacking the mare up and putting on her helmet and gloves, Kelly led her out to the mounting block and got on. A few minutes later, she and Syd were walking at a leisurely pace on one of the back trails behind the equestrian center. Tree branches reached across the wide path, leaves blowing gently in the slight breeze. The sun shone strong overhead with only a puff of cloud here and there, dotting the powder blue sky. For the first time in 24 hours, Kelly felt like she could breathe again. And, more importantly, think.

In the 30 minutes it took her to arrive back at the center, Kelly had analyzed her situation multiple times. She needed to get a hold of the charts on the two other women who died like Lupe Salazar. Unfortunately, Jake had been her primary connection in the morgue. She didn't know the other pathologists well, and she'd been out the days those two young women came in. She wished Dr. Pearson was around. He was a far more amicable man to deal with than Pierce Brightman. But Brightman had been OBGYN on both Lupe Salazar's case and one of the other young women. Amicable or not, Kelly knew she needed to have a chat with him. Would he have the same strange reaction Jake had with her? What if something happened to Brightman, or her, as a result? Paranoia was beginning to get the best of her.

And then there was Jake.

Kelly played her conversation with Jake over and over in her mind. She thought about Lupe Salazar and Baby S. and what the reports detailed. She would need to see if the other women and baby charts matched up in any way. Kelly sifted through her theories, most of which were conspiratorial and bizarre. But at the end of the trail, she was no closer to making sense of anything, leaving her frustrated and confused.

She put Syd away and headed toward her car, when she spotted a familiar face—Dr. Tamara Swift, her vet. Tamara was tall and thin with long blonde hair, which she always kept pulled back and tucked under a ball cap. She had warm hazel eyes and a golden glow, likely due to her time spent outdoors. If she hadn't been a vet, Kelly was certain she could've made one heck of a volleyball player. The moment Kelly saw Tamara, an idea began to form. "Hey Tam," she said, quickening her pace.

"Hey there." Tamara took a step back. "Wow, Kel. You okay? You look a little…"

"I know," Kelly said holding up her palms. "I can't go into it right now. But I, um, need a favor." Tamara had become more than Kelly's vet over the years, she was also a friend. In fact, Kelly had introduced Tamara to her husband who Kelly had interned with. She'd been in her wedding.

"Sure," Tamara replied.

"It's dicey."

"How do you mean?"

"I need some blood work sent in for a couple of tox reports."

"Something wrong with Syd?"

"No," Kelly replied.

"What do you need then?"

Kelly sighed. "I can't go into details here, but if I can get you the blood, can you help me?" For a second, she started to rethink her request. Could she get her friend into any trouble? Or worse, would she be putting her in any kind of danger? She shook her head. "You know what, Tam, never mind. It's silly. I never…" Kelly closed her eyes and fought back tears.

Tamara put an arm around her. "Hey, hey, Kelly…what's going on? It takes a lot to make you cry. Hell, I remember last year when you broke two of your ribs after Syd dumped you going over that double oxer." Tamara pointed to the jump arena. Kelly couldn't help but laugh. "No tears then, right? I mean you kept saying how you were fine and you could get right back on, until you nearly passed out."

"That hurt like hell," Kelly said, smiling.

"Okay, so what's this all about?"

"I don't really know to be honest with you."

"Let's start with why you want the tox reports."

Kelly knew if she was going to ask Tamara for help, she owed it to her to tell her everything she *did* know. She quickly shared yesterday's story with her friend…trying hard not to get upset all over again.

"So, your friend, Jake, the pathologist, he was murdered after he warned you there was something sinister about this girl's death?"

Kelly nodded, feeling drained. "Yes."

"What about the police? Did you tell the detective who interviewed you last night about any of this?"

"I told him Jake and I were going to meet to discuss some patient cases."

"I don't understand. Why didn't you tell him what was really going on?" Tamara asked.

"Because it sounds crazy, doesn't it? The detective was kind of, I don't know…not a jerk, but also not exactly gentle. I mean he was prying and asking things about my sex life."

"Why?"

"He thought I was hooking up with Jake, I guess. Look, I know I need to tell the police, but I needed a sounding board first to hear me out and let me know if this whole thing is as crazy as it sounds."

"It does sound a bit strange, but you're a grounded person, Kelly. You're a respected doctor. The police might find it odd, though, so I can understand where you're coming from."

"Do you see why I want some kind of proof there is something behind the deaths of these pregnant women, something Jake got killed over?"

"And you think the tox reports may show something more?"

Kelly shrugged. "After hearing Jake talk about this, I don't know if I can trust the tests that were already run, and I don't know if everything was done thoroughly. I mean, inconclusive doesn't really give me a whole lot of information."

Tamara nodded. "I'll do it for you."

"Please be careful. I have no clue what we're dealing with."

Tamara gave her a hug and said, "Hopefully, we'll find out."

CHAPTER FOURTEEN

Pazzini sat behind his desk, blinking eyes that had gone blurry. He attempted again to focus on the overload of paperwork. What a night. The murder at County was one he knew would be eating at him for a while. Bizarre cases always did. He suddenly felt much older than his forty-two years.

But being a cop was what he knew best. He lived for the job and his son, Luke. And the job took away from time with his kid. It wouldn't be so hard if Anna were still here. But she wasn't, and even with the help of his parents, he still felt he was in some way cheating Luke.

He took a large gulp of Coke and a sharp spear of burning acid shot through his stomach. Pazzini instantly regretted the decision to put jalapenos and onions on the hot dog he'd devoured earlier, after wrapping the hospital crime scene.

The stress of the job, plus the onions and hot peppers—which in all honesty, he could never get enough of—didn't do much for the ulcer his doctor had warned him about. The burning sensation in his gut never left him alone these days. This morning it was much worse than usual.

"Jeez, Pazzini, what'd ya do? Hit Cotija's Taco Shop last night?" Simmons taunted.

"Nah, wise ass. I had a dog with a heap of the good stuff on it." He looked up from the paperwork and smoothed down his slightly wavy black hair, thinking he should probably comb it. He winced when his palms hit the back of his head. He could've sworn there had been more hair there a few months ago.

"Oh, man, that'll do it every time. Wish I had some antacids for you. But I got a message instead." Simmons winked at him, smacking on the tobacco chew Tony swore never left the side of his cheek. His stained teeth substantiated that theory.

"What's that?" Tony asked, irritated by Simmons' twang, which could only come from a cowboy wannabe. Simmons swore he was Texas born and raised. It was his story, but Tony knew the truth. He was really from Nebraska. Tony stared at the idiot for a few seconds, his annoyance growing at Simmons' ridiculous overgrown goatee that was eons out of date. It wouldn't hurt if he trimmed his shoulder length hair and took the earring out as well. Freaking Rhinestone Cowboy. Please.

"Boss man wants to see you, dude."

"Dude? Seriously Simmons, you gonna catch some waves now?"

Simmons ignored him, "What d'ya do now, Paz?"

"Hey, *dude*, shut the hell up. Don't call me Paz. It's Pazzini. I can spell it for you if you like."

Simmons held up his hands. "Hey, man, sorry. You know, no offense. Didn't know it bugged you. Note to self."

Tony nodded and slid out of his desk chair, heading toward his boss's office.

"Dragging your feet a little, aren't ya?" Simmons laughed.

That stopped the exhausted detective in his tracks. He faced Simmons. "*Dude,* this isn't Texas, Nebraska, or Bum Fuck Egypt. This is L.A., and in case you hadn't noticed, it's you, not *ya*. And another thing, do you think you could lose the *look*? Your look? It went out with disco."

Simmons abruptly stormed out of the room lined with desks and detectives. The place reminded Tony of a classroom, except it was far more cluttered, and instead of sweaty kids, it smelled of sweaty adults and stale air. At the moment, only a few actual detectives were sitting at their desks, mulling over reports, doing the tedious work. They had all stopped to watch the scene.

"Oh come on, Pazzini, sure the kid is an odd duck but do you have to be such a hard ass?" Barkley commented. He was an older detective who had been on the force for thirty years and was inching close to retirement.

"I just think people should be who they really are. FYI, Simmons isn't even from Texas. He's from fucking Nebraska!" Tony yelled back as he reached the chief's office. Barkley was probably right. Maybe he was being too hard on Simmons, but he was exhausted and his nerves were on edge.

Standing outside Linden's door, he couldn't help the pang in his stomach, which he knew wasn't entirely due to his earlier lunch. Pretty much every time he stepped into this office, his boss had a bone to pick with him. Usually, Tony had to admit, the chief was right. He had a hot button and had been known to rough up a few dope dealers and scumbags here and there. Linden always covered his ass, but not before he tore him a new one. But Pazzini couldn't think of anything he'd done lately to warrant the usual warning…unless it had to do with Dr. Morales. He might have been a little rough on her, but he would have figured her too tough to call in a complaint about him. In any case, he'd just been doing his job. But had he pushed the doctor too hard? He didn't think she was a killer, but those questions had to be asked. Then again, beauty could blind people from the truth. And Kelly Morales was definitely good looking.

He turned the handle on the door and peered inside Linden's cramped quarters. The office reminded him of his grandfather's fishing cabin up in the Sierras. At least in the way it smelled—musty, old.

Linden lifted his head up off his desk. His blue eyes were bloodshot.

"Hey, boss. Simmons said you wanted to see me."

"Yeah. Sorry. I'm getting some shut-eye. Tired these days."
He rubbed his bleary eyes. "Think I'm fighting a flu bug. Carol is
home with it."

"That's too bad." Tony didn't buy the flu thing at all.

"Anyhow, I wanted you in here because I need to know
what happened at the hospital last night. I'm getting some heat
from upstairs and from the mayor's office. That sort of thing.
Hospital people are upset, and the CEO over there is going nutso. I
got some broad calling me every hour asking if there's any news. I
told her as soon as I know something, I'd give her a ring. And I
don't even want to talk about the media. That pain in the ass Gem
Michaels from *The Times* has been calling about a statement and
information."

Tony tried not to smile. Gem was a tough as nails reporter,
and she could be a pain but Tony liked her. She was honest. No
hype. Just the facts.

"Not good, Chief."

Tony sat down in the cracked vinyl chair across from his
boss. Kind of a joke, really. The only reason the guy still had any
real power was because his dad was good buddies with the
commissioner. It wasn't a secret Linden was burnt out. However,
he still did merit some respect. At one time, he'd been one of the
finest. He'd solved more homicides than anyone else on the force.
But then he was shot while on duty and now could walk only with

the help of a cane. That explained the ever-present alcohol—self-medication. He'd been put behind a desk and Tony knew it had nearly killed him.

"Any suspects?" Linden asked, the faint smell of whiskey wafting off of him.

Tony took note of the coffee cup resting on Linden's desk and wondered what was really in it. "Nothing out of the ordinary. I'm checking into the usual things. The ex-wife, colleagues, friends, anyone associated with him who might hold a grudge. Nothing stands out at the moment."

"No one saw anything?"

"No one coming forward, anyway. We're still questioning people, obviously. This is going to take some time, sir."

"We don't have time, Pazzini. You're telling me no one in that entire hospital spotted anything out of the ordinary? Some doc gets rubbed out in the middle of a busy hospital like County, and no one sees a thing?"

"He wasn't in the middle of the hospital, sir. He was in the morgue, and I don't think it's quite as bustling as the rest of the building. I'm working on it. If anyone did see anything, they aren't talking yet. Forensics is still over there this morning. I just received a roster of everyone who was working during those hours. But like I said, this is going to take time. We are questioning everyone. Then there were visitors in the building until eight o' clock. We need to look at the sign-in sheets. At this point, the killer could be anyone. Oh, and we're also checking all security cam footage."

Linden rubbed his eyes again. He looked wiped out…or very hung over.

"What we know, or can surmise at this point, is the suspect was alone and locking up for the evening. The morgue is on the bottom floor of the hospital. The perp came from behind and zapped him with a silencer. Then slit his throat. Our big problem is how many people are in and out of that place daily—dead or alive. DNA is *everywhere.* It's a hospital. The crime scene was contaminated before we even walked in the door."

Linden nodded and leaned back in his chair. He folded his hands together and placed them under his chin. "You spoke with a woman doctor." He looked down at some notes. "Dr. Morales? I understand she had a dinner date with the vic."

"Yes."

"Tell me about her."

"Her story checks out. She was at the restaurant waiting for him. Busboy confirms seeing her. She claims they had some patients to discuss."

Linden made a face. "What? This guy is the morgue man and she's in the NICU. What patients could they have in common?"

"I would assume an infant...or mom. It happens. Maybe she needed to talk pathology with him. I don't know. It seemed plausible to me."

"Guy is taking her to Tuscany's to talk business? He's gonna fork over that kind of cash on a business meeting? I don't buy it. He was looking to get a piece of ass."

"I think he might have been looking in the wrong place," Tony replied.

"Ice queen?"

"No. I think she's respectable, is all. I think they were friends. Seems like there was a mutual attraction between them and if the poor guy hadn't been killed, they may have wound up in a relationship. But at the stage they were at, it wasn't happening yet."

Linden studied him and clucked his tongue. "She must be a looker." Tony didn't respond.

Tony understood his boss's implications. "Please. I am a professional. Dr. Morales answered my questions and was cooperative. That's the bottom line." He sighed and thought carefully about what he was going to say next. He wanted to prove to Linden he hadn't been blinded by the doctor's good looks. "I did get the feeling, though, that she could be hiding something."

"Why do you say that?" Linden He picked up his mug and took a swig.

"Just a hunch, that's all."

"Yeah, well, you need to trust hunches. Sometimes gut reactions solve cases. Stay with her a little longer." He sighed and rubbed his eyes again. "I want an arrest on this, Pazzini. And soon. My oldest kid just got accepted at USF. Place is not cheap. My youngest needs braces, and my wife wants to go on a European vacation. She seems to forget I'm not Donald Trump. And between us, I am ready to retire from this place. But before I do, I need to go out on a high note, if you know what I mean."

"Right."

"Get back to me as soon as you have something. I'll make some calls, see if I can keep the politics at a minimum. You're working with Simmons on this."

"What?" Pazzini asked. "You're kidding, right? You can't do that to me. Come on…"

"Does it look like I'm kidding? You're going to need a partner on this one."

"I do my best work alone."

"Not this time," Linden said. "He's a good cop. He's a little different, but he's sharp. You can tolerate his idiosyncrasies."

Tony rolled his eyes and walked out of the office. "Damn," he muttered under his breath. He had a front-page homicide with no real leads, and now he had to work side-by-side with the urban cowboy.

CHAPTER FIFTEEN

Upbeat jazz thumped through stereo speakers. Champagne glasses clinked together as more bubbly was poured. Ryan smiled at his wife, Jeanine. She winked back. The Mueller's annual wine tasting party was in full force.

As much as Ryan hated being away from the kids, wondering what he *might* come home to, the timing of the party could not have been better. Ever since he'd sent that e-mail, he'd been driving himself insane. The visit from Peter Redding hadn't helped at all. Ryan had to find a way out. Any way out.

Then yesterday, Jeanine reminded him of the dinner party at the Muellers' home, and immediately he began to plan. For him to get out, for him to get his family out, would take some organization and risk. But he had no choice. He could not continue with The Brotherhood, with Frauen Pharmaceuticals, and with Peter Redding. He knew if he didn't get them out, it would only be a matter of time until he and his family wound up like the Petersens. He winced at the thought.

Ryan took another glass of champagne from the caterer and kissed Jeanine on the cheek. She flashed her pretty smile at him, her blue eyes sparkling. "I love you," he said.

She cocked her head to the side and brushed her blonde hair behind her shoulders. "I love you, too, sweetheart. Might want to slow down on the champagne, though. You're not exactly great at holding your liquor."

He waved a hand at her. "I'm fine. I think after working as hard as I do, I deserve a little drink." He waved the glass in the air, slurred a bit, and spoke more loudly than normal. Ryan was known for being a bit on the quiet side.

"Ryan," she said, giggling nervously.

"In fact, sweetie, I am going to get another drink."

"I, uh, I..."

Jeanine's friend Bärbel approached them. "Everything okay?"

"Just fine," Ryan answered. He headed to the bar and then to the bathroom where he poured the drink down the drain and sat on the edge of the bathtub. He was tired of this game. And he hoped what he was about to do would work. He hoped Jeanine would believe him and do everything he needed her to do to get them out of this. He took out a card he'd bought at a gift shop earlier that day, and wrote a detailed note inside. He had to be quick, but it was the only safe place he knew he could do this. He was sure they had some kind of surveillance in his car.

Redding may have had cameras installed in his home, but he couldn't have put them everywhere Ryan and his wife went. Certainly there weren't any inside the Mueller's home.

Someone tapped on the bathroom door.

"Just a second," Ryan said.

He came out of the bathroom and smiled at the woman who walked past him, as he apologized for taking so long. Then he walked over to the bar and got himself another drink. Ryan found Jeanine talking with a small group of friends, laughing and gossiping. He staggered a bit. "Honey, I think maybe we should go," Jeanine said, as Ryan stumbled into her.

"No, no. I want to take a walk. Let's go outside and get some air. I love their back yard," he said, trying to keep just enough drunkenness in his voice.

"Honey, really, you're tired. We should go."

"No, Jeanine. Please. Take a walk with me."

Jeanine glanced at her friends.

"Take him out for some air, darling. We'll be right here. I can have the caterer brew some coffee. That will help," Bärbel said.

"Um, okay," Jeanine replied.

Ryan hooked his arm through hers and said, "That's my girl."

They threaded through a group in the family room and out to the back garden where a few people mingled in the crisp night. "Ryan, you are drunk. We need to go," Jeanine said once they were out of ear-shot.

He took her by both arms, faced her, and looked straight into her eyes. "I am not drunk," he said, his tone low. "I am stone-cold sober."

She hesitated. "What? Then what the…"

"Come sit down on the lounge chairs with me. I have something for you that will explain everything. You're going to think I'm crazy…"

"No kidding. I already do."

He looked at her again. "Have I ever lied to you?" Of course she did not know their lives were now one big lie, but he was only doing it to protect them.

She shook her head and looked warily at him. "No."

"I'm not starting now. I am dead serious and we don't have a lot of time. Trust me. Sit down and act like you're pleased I gave you this card. Then do everything it says."

"Ryan?"

He raised his eyebrows.

"Fine."

They sat down on the edge of the chairs. Ryan put his coat over her shoulders. He handed her the card and watched her expression. She glanced at him a few times, a look of disbelief and dismay on her face. "This can't be true."

"It is." He wasn't sure she believed him. Not until she slapped him hard across the face, with angry tears in her eyes, in front of everyone at the party.

CHAPTER SIXTEEN

Kelly hadn't wanted to come into work. And she hadn't wanted to leave Syd. But Jake's murder had shaken her to the core and now she needed to find a way to get those blood samples to Tamara. She knew she could get blood from Baby S, but getting a hold of Lupe Salazar's blood-work would not be easy. And what was she testing for, anyway? Damn. Kelly knew it was a long shot, but she had to try everything. If she sat back and did nothing, she worried Jake's murderer would get away.

Since she'd last been there, the hospital had flooded with reporters and police making it difficult to get through the front doors. She threaded her way between officers and frustrated patients. The police were vainly trying to manage the media. Fortunately, by five o' clock the turmoil had quieted down. The reporters had filmed their footage, aired their stories, and left.

What happened? Why had Jake been murdered? He was in trouble, she knew that. Why hadn't she told the detective last night? Yeah, he was kind of a jerk, albeit an attractive jerk. He had been doing his job and she respected that. All the same, she couldn't help resent his line of questioning. Had she been sleeping with Jake? Jesus!

But when all was said and done, she knew she had to reveal the conversation between her and Jake to the detective along with her theories about foul play and what happened to the Salazar girl and her baby. Kelly couldn't help but suspect something sinister was underfoot where Lupe Salazar and Baby S. were concerned. She couldn't help wondering what similarities there were between Salazar's death and the recent deaths of those other two moms. She needed to get a hold of those files. She also needed to get at least one vial of Lupe's blood.

She walked into the NICU and spotted Eric filling out a chart. He glanced up, a concerned expression on his face. "You okay?"

"Just tired, I suppose."

"I am sure you are. We're all a bit shaken, I think."

A monitor sounded from down the hall, and Kelly remembered why she'd come into the unit. She walked over to the Salazar baby. Her little eyes were closed, opalescent lids shut tight. Her tiny body heaved with each machine-assisted breath. "Hi, sweet one." Kelly put gloved hands through the incubator's hand holes, and skimmed Baby S's back with her finger. The baby flinched slightly. She removed her arms and hands, not wanting to over-stimulate her. It didn't make any sense, but something told her tiny Baby S. held the key to Jake's murder.

She also knew the child's life depended on those answers. She took out a tube from her lab coat and performed a quick blood draw, gently inserting the needle into the infant's heel. She'd done this so many times during her intern days, babies rarely even felt it. This one was no exception. She glanced around, knowing it was a bit risky. The docs rarely drew blood and she didn't want to be questioned. No one seemed to take note as she slipped two vials of blood into her coat pocket. "Please help me find the answers, little one," she whispered. "I think I'm going to need all the help I can get."

CHAPTER SEVENTEEN

It was one of the most heinous and grisly murders in San Diego history. Known for its pristine beaches and moderate climate, the city was totally unprepared for a crime of this magnitude.

San Diego was only two hours south of Los Angeles and the Petersen murders had been a huge story well beyond the city's borders. Gem covered it for *The Times.* It was a seemingly senseless crime and people wanted answers. They needed someone to blame. The only thing the police could dig up was Petersen's tenuous link to the Mexican drug cartel. No arrests were ever made, but they connected his wife, Selena, to the cartel via a cousin involved in drug running. He'd been found dead only a week after Eric and his family were murdered. Some figured it might have had something to do with Petersen's job as a chemist for a San Diego bio-tech firm. It was believed Petersen had been developing a new kind of drug for the cartel, or possibly supplying them with Percocet, Vicodin, or some other pharma narcotic they could resell for top dollar on the street. The police assumed something had gone sour and pissed off cartel leaders, and the family had been brutally murdered as a warning to any other "risk takers." But even now, it was hard to know the truth. When it came to the Mexican cartel, there were few informants, and many suspected drug money padded police pockets on the U.S. side of the border.

The story had been awful and Gem was happy to put it behind her. But now…this e-mail. It got her thinking again. She reread it at home. Went back over all her files on the Petersen family.

Gem got up from her desk and went to the fridge to pour herself a glass of Pinot Grigio. She took the glass of wine outside and sat on the patio. The sky had transformed into a myriad of different hues—purple, red, yellow. It was a gorgeous sunset. But its beauty didn't take away the feeling she was missing something. Something big. She could not get the images of the Petersen family out of her mind. The photos sat on her desk. They showed a happy family. They were well-off and lived in the well-to-do Scripps Ranch suburb. How no one in their neighborhood saw or heard anything the night of the crime still baffled Gem, but she'd let it all go once the cops said the cartel was responsible.

Gem stood and moved an overgrown hanging fern out of her way. There didn't seem to be anyone home at her neighbor's house tonight.

Three years ago she'd noticed her very handsome, younger neighbor in the townhouse across from her place in Studio City. She wasn't sure if he owned or rented. What she did know was how much she enjoyed watching him sun himself on the patio when the weather was warm. Yum. But no women ever seemed to visit. At least not any Gem had seen. No men either.

She'd only actually exchanged words with him a few times. But although the guy was handsome, something in the way he spoke to her gave Gem the creeps. However, creepy or not, she could not see Mr. Clean-Cut, all-American involved with the Mexican cartel. Then again, stranger things had happened.

Gem went back inside and poured herself another glass of wine, her nerves on edge. She sat down again and read over the story she'd written about the Petersens. She looked at the photos again. She tried to send Chemmadderhorn@gmail a reply, but it bounced back. Of course it did. Maybe this was all a hoax. But why?

Gem went up to her bedroom and into her master bath, hoping a bath would relax her. She turned on the tub, poured in some lavender salts, and then walked toward her balcony to open the door and let in some fresh air. She couldn't help looking over at Chad's place. As the tub filled, her mind wandered. An idea grabbed her. It was crazy and might not result in anything, but she felt compelled to try.

CHAPTER EIGHTEEN

Pazzini was late. He'd gotten caught up in more interviews with folks who'd known Dr. Hamilton. This guy seemed to have no enemies whatsoever except for his ex-wife. Interestingly enough, she was overseas in Monaco, of all places. He couldn't help but wonder how she could afford that kind of vacation on alimony. Sure, doctors made a very good living, but not the kind that afforded the items the ex-Mrs. Hamilton seemed to have. At least not these days.

The ex had to have moved on to something, or someone, bigger and better—someone with a substantial bank account. Simmons was still trying to reach her. Pazzini had a few pointed questions to ask. A woman with that kind of money could easily hire out a hit. But then why bother? She was divorced, clearly well off...what was the motive?

Then there was the teenage daughter. She was staying with friends while her mother was cavorting in Monaco. Tony had yet to speak to her, but she could be an excellent source of information. He'd had one of the female officers break the news to her about her dad, and take a statement. However, Pazzini figured it would be vital that he also have a word with the kid. From what he heard, she was pretty distraught, and even more so because her mother was incommunicado. Another odd thing…if the ex-wife was out of town, why was the sixteen-year old daughter staying with friends and not her dad? That didn't add up. Nothing was adding up for him with this case. Maybe the doc could provide more insight.

Dr. Morales met Pazzini at a Starbucks around the corner from the hospital. She gave him a slight wave and a tentative smile when he came through the door. It appeared she'd forgiven his heavy hand from the evening before. Her face was drawn with exhaustion but she still looked lovely.

"Sorry I'm late," he said as he sat down.

"It's fine. I got you a coffee. Black. Didn't know if that was okay, but…"

"Live off the stuff. Thank you. Black is perfect."

She smiled again, erasing some of the fatigue from her face. "I grabbed a sandwich…this is my dinner break," she said. "Hope you don't mind. If you want something, I can wait."

"No. I'm good. Hoping to get a home-cooked meal tonight."

"Your wife is a good cook, I take it?"

He didn't respond for a moment. "Actually, my mother. She takes care of my son while I'm at work. My wife passed away a few years ago. Cancer."

"Oh! I am so sorry. I didn't mean…" She shook her head, looking chagrined. "I would love a home-cooked meal. I really should eat better. Doctors' schedules and all."

"We all should….eat better, that is. And you don't need to apologize, but thank you." She had lost the anger, but seemed jumpy, anxious—something was off. He clasped his hands together. "You called, which is good because I wanted to ask you some more questions."

She took a sip from her coffee. "Ask away."

"Why don't we tackle what you wanted to talk to me about first, Dr. Morales. Maybe we can kill two birds with one stone."

"Sure. By the way, you don't have to call me Dr. Morales, Detective. Kelly is fine."

He hesitated for a second. Yes, there was a definite edginess to her, which put him on alert. "Okay, then, Kelly. Please call me Tony." If she wanted to try and make things comfortable, he'd follow her lead.

"You may think I'm a lunatic—and I may be, I don't know —but, here goes. I think that Jake's murder ties into something more sinister and complex than a revenge plot, crime of passion, or whatever the police might think is going on."

"Really? I don't know that anything of the sort has been concocted. What are you getting at?" How had she come up with an idea about revenge? She knew more than she was letting on.

"I believe someone wanted Jake dead because he knew something that…that someone didn't want him to talk about."

"What do you mean?" He set his cup down on the chrome table, and leaned back watching her every move—her eyes, her hands. All of her. He was looking for any tell-tale expressions or movements that would show she was lying.

"Have you looked through his most recent case files?" she asked.

"Of course we have. I can't go into details, though. Why?"

She crossed her arms and sat back in her chair. "I went to speak to Jake yesterday about a patient. A young mother, Lupe Salazar, came in for an emergency delivery. She was a runaway but was really concerned about her baby. She told me she had been doing all of the right things, as much as she could anyway, and was even being seen at the local clinic. She was living at the shelter on East Fifth. The whole thing was strange. The girl had a wild-eyed look to her, and it crossed my mind she was using. Lupe flat out denied it, but she was frightened. These kids come in and think if they give us any kind of information about using, we'll have them hauled off to juvie after they deliver. Anyway, I didn't get much time to get any history from her, and neither did the attending O.B., because she seized, coded, and died in a matter of minutes. We had limited time to attempt to resuscitate because of the infant." Kelly finished telling him the details of Baby S's delivery. She told him about the inconclusive reports and possible connection to other recent deaths with pre-term mothers. "This isn't normal. Three young women die in labor and delivery in one week, presenting the same symptoms…I don't know what to think. It's what Jake and I planned to discuss over dinner."

"I'm confused how all this relates to Dr. Hamilton's murder, though. Granted it sounds strange but what's the tie in?"

She frowned and leaned towards him, lowering her voice just above a whisper. "Jake got nervous…I mean, not just nervous, but he seemed terrified when I asked him about Lupe and the other girls. I asked to see the autopsy reports. He told me to back off, told me I could get hurt. He wasn't acting at all like his usual self. He was…he was really scared, and kept trying to get me to drop the whole thing. When I kept insisting, he agreed to meet me for dinner and tell me what was going on, or maybe what he thought was going on. I don't know. I am wondering if my insistence on getting info out of him got him killed."

Tony wasn't sure he believed her. It didn't make much sense. Was she trying to feed him a line to make him think Dr. Hamilton was caught up in some rotten deal? She was sounding a bit too "conspiracy theorist" for his tastes. Street kids died every day from drug overdoses and other causes. Maybe she was a crazy and covering her own tracks? And why hadn't she told him this last night? She'd had twenty-four hours to concoct a story, but why? "So you are saying the deaths of these women and their children are tied to Dr. Hamilton's murder?"

"Yes. Exactly."

"How? Why?"

"If I knew, I would tell you, and then some bad people would be behind bars." She took a bite of her sandwich.

"Why didn't you tell me this last night?"

She shrugged. "I don't know. I was in shock and I guess after seeing the fear in Jake's eyes, it had me spooked. I'm sorry. I should have said something."

"Yes, you should have. I don't mean to patronize you, Doc, but I have to be honest. This sounds a bit far-fetched. I am not even sure where you're headed with this." He raised his hands in confusion.

"Here is what I think…"

Uh oh. He watched as she shifted from cagey and anxious to annoyed and angry.

"I think there's a new street drug out there and it's flying under your radar. It's potent and hard to detect. And it kills."

"Wouldn't there be other deaths?" he asked.

"I assume so. Maybe you could start looking into it. I know drug overdoses happen all the time, Detective, but not the kind where there's no detection of a drug in the system. No explanation of why a seemingly healthy person would die. I think Jake discovered this drug in the autopsies, and someone killed him because he knew too much."

He shook his head. "If there is a new street drug available, the guys making it could care less who dies and who doesn't. They only care about the cash in their back pockets. Eventually this stuff gets found out."

"Okay, how about this? You and I know there have been plenty of sickos throughout history who have done things like plant poison in meds. Look at the Tylenol and Excedrin cases. Those seemed off the wall when they happened, but they were real situations. Plus, we're always hearing things in the media about the possibility of terrorists poisoning our food or water supply. Heck, there are documentaries about how genetically modified foods will eventually be our demise. I don't know." She leaned forward again, her face red. "*I don't know*, and I don't care if you believe me. But what I can tell you is some type of poison I can't put a name to is in a helpless baby's system. She is lying in her incubator, fighting for her life. I want to know what's killing her, and I want to know before it's too late."

The doctor certainly had passion and if she was selling him a story, she had herself convinced of it, or seemed to anyway. "Okay, so say your theory is correct, how did this person or persons know Hamilton was onto this thing?"

"You're the detective, you figure it out." With that, she stood up and walked out the door.

CHAPTER NINETEEN

Time was a major factor and Ryan didn't know how much he had. He knew The Brotherhood goons would be watching *and* listening. So, the morning after the fight with his wife, he called her cell phone from the house and left a voicemail.

"Jeanine, I love you. I love you and the kids very much. I'm sorry. I was a jack-ass. Please come home. At least call me, and tell me where you are. I just want to hear your voice. Please call. I love you." He clicked off his phone and sighed heavily. This had to work. If Jeanine was following his plan, and hadn't turned back, hadn't decided he was insane, or hadn't been caught…he closed his eyes at the thought. God, please let them be safe. Assuming they were, the next steps his wife took would be the most important ones.

Thank God through some stroke of luck, Ryan had sent his parents on a cruise for two weeks in Alaska. He assumed they'd be safe on the boat. But what if The Brotherhood found out what he was up to, and went after his folks? Did they know he'd purchased those tickets? Did they know his parents were on that cruise? Fuck! They seemed to know everything.

Ryan forced himself to stop thinking about it. He knew he was taking a big risk and he hoped in doing the right thing, he wasn't putting his family in any further jeopardy than he already had.

CHAPTER TWENTY

Kelly knew it was a risk to discuss her theory with the detective, but she thought he might be a bit more supportive or accepting than he'd been. In fact, he hadn't been open to her theory in the least. She could see it in his dark eyes, which seemed to grow even darker when she told him her thoughts. Or maybe she was just being paranoid. Her theory did sound far-fetched. New drug? Pregnant girls? *Murder?* She shook her head. It sounded idiotic. But one thing was for certain—Jake was dead. He had been brutally murdered, and she wanted to find some answers. If the detective was going to ignore her story, maybe she would see what she could find out on her own. Tamara had been by the hospital earlier that day to pick up the blood samples from Kelly. Unfortunately, she had not been able to obtain a sample from Lupe Salazar.

As she pulled into the parking lot, Kelly knew she needed to regain her composure before going back into the unit. She straightened her blue linen blouse and headed in. She knew, though, the minute she saw innocent Baby S., her thoughts would revert back to Jake and wondering what had gone wrong.

The unit was unusually quiet. It was feeding time, and the little ones who were not eating, were sleeping. It was a rarity. She passed by the receptionist who smiled at her. "Hi, Dr. Morales. All is quiet on the western front."

"Quiet is a reprieve, my friend. We both know it won't last long."

"True. By the way, it appears you have an admirer. There are some flowers in your office."

"Really?" Maybe they were from her dad. He did that every so often. Sent flowers or a card, sometimes a small gift to remind her he was thinking of her.

A large vase of dark pink tulips sat on top of Kelly's desk. They brightened an otherwise dull room, whose only other adornments included her degrees, a picture of her with her dad back in Kentucky, one of Syd, and one of her and her mom the year before she'd died. That had been the last happy summer of her childhood.

She opened the small envelope and took out the card. It read: *Hope you're having a nice day. I'll be watching you.* A prickle of foreboding crept up her spine. *I'll be watching you?* She shook her head. Some of the docs she worked with had a twisted sense of humor but after what had happened to Jake, she couldn't help be on edge.

She headed back to the receptionist's desk. "Jo, did you see who delivered the flowers?"

The receptionist shrugged. "Some delivery guy."

Kelly sighed and rubbed her temples. She went back into her office to call her dad and find out if he sent them. It would be like him. The note, however, would not. Maybe the card was meant for another delivery? Maybe she received the wrong flowers?

No sooner had she left word on her dad's answering machine then her pager went off. It was coming from the unit. Kelly flew out of her office. As she turned the corner into the NICU, she saw a handful of nurses working on Baby S.

"She's seizing, Doc!" Eric yelled as he adjusted the various tubes plugged into the baby.

A knot formed inside Kelly's stomach. The tiny infant shook violently, turning shades of gray. Kelly tried hard to keep her emotions in check.

I can't lose her now.

"Someone get the ultrasound. Call a tech up here. She may be hemorrhaging," Kelly shouted. "Get me neurology, too. I think Jessop's on call tonight."

The knot in her stomach began to loosen as she went to work on the baby, all her focus on keeping her alive.

The tech arrived just ahead of the neurologist.

Kelly took the baby's vitals again and attempted to stabilize her with Eric and two other nurses. Baby S. looked like a creature from another planet, her eyes rolling back into her head, veins popping out on her translucent skin. Fortunately, the seizure ended almost as quickly as it started. The baby's eyes' glazed over, and she lay lethargically inside her sterile world.

"She's having trouble breathing. Let's increase the IMV unit," Kelly ordered.

Eric turned the respirator another degree so Baby S. didn't have to do any of the breathing on her own.

"She's too exhausted to work very hard right now. Okay, let's get the transducer in place and see if we can locate a bleeder anywhere."

The neurologist Dr. Jessop entered the unit. His long legs carried him brusquely to the incubator. "What's the situation?" he asked. His salt-and-pepper hair matched the gray tie he wore underneath his lab coat.

"I think she may have a bleeder. I'm hoping it's not high grade. She's already been through a lot for someone so small"

"Let's take a look," he replied in a gruff-sounding voice. He reminded Kelly of one of her former professors—strict, conservative, but likeable all the same. Jessop was a doctor she held in the highest regard. He'd saved many lives during his career, and he maintained considerable compassion for his patients.

The tech handled the baby gently as she ran the transducer over the brain, head, and neck areas.

All of them huddled around the screen, trying to see if they could find anything.

"There it is!" The tech was the first to spot the bleeder.

"Good job." Jessop complimented her as he studied the picture for a few seconds before making a judgment. "Looks to be a grade two. But let's go ahead and get some more pictures and measurements. I'll have a closer look then. It doesn't appear to be too major so it shouldn't be too difficult to treat. You know what to look for, Morales, but I'll keep checking in."

"What are the chances of this progressing into hydrocephalus?" Eric asked.

Jessop clucked his tongue. "That's tough to call. You know how it is with these really tiny ones, how quickly things can change. I mean one minute it looks like they are on an upswing, and the next minute…everything crashes. All we can do is wait. Make certain her head doesn't begin enlarging too rapidly. If she has any more seizures, we may want to consider putting a shunt in place."

"God, I hope not," Kelly said, knowing cerebral hemorrhages could lead to all sorts of neurological problems, including cerebral palsy.

"Me, too. Want me to speak with the parents?" Jessop asked. "Let them know what we've found?"

"She doesn't have any."

"Ah. I see. Well, there isn't a lot we can do for the time being. Monitor and make sure we aren't seeing major growth in head size."

Kelly looked down at the baby in the incubator and said a silent prayer the baby girl would survive. And not merely survive, but would not have to suffer for the rest of her life.

God damn you, Kelly thought. *God damn whoever did this.*

She took Eric aside and asked him to meet her in her office.

He walked in behind her and commented, "Oh, you have a friend, Doc?" He pointed to the flowers.

"You got me. No name with them and the card is strange. Here read it." She handed it to him.

"Ooh, kinda creepy."

"Agreed."

Eric sat down in the chair across from her desk. "Watch your back, Doc. Some weird shit is going on around here." He tossed the card back to her. "But this is probably from one of those interns around here who eyeball you all the time."

She rolled her eyes at him and got up to close the door. "So I called you in here to ask you about those two girls you mentioned."

"I assume you're talking about the pregnant women?"

"Yes. You worked on both those cases. I mean you were there for the babies."

"Yeah. We were standing by for the babies."

"At what point did you make it down to ER with each case?"

"I think with the first girl, um, her name was…" He looked down. "Naomi Williams! The team got in there fifteen minutes before she started to deliver. The girl came in by ambulance. I guess she'd been found by a friend in the tenements."

"I can only assume she was doing drugs?"

"That's what we thought. She never was conscious the entire time, and just like Lupe Salazar, she had a seizure and coded. Pearson did like you, delivered the baby, but it died within a minute or two. He was tiny and blue. There was no way he would have survived."

"And then, the girl's body was moved into the morgue." She knew Jake had performed the autopsies.

"Do you know anything else about the girl? Family? Friends? Anything?"

He shook his head. "I'm sorry, Doc. What are you thinking?"

"What about the other girl?"

"Desiree Jones. I remember her clearly. She was in a lot of pain just like Lupe Salazar and thrashing around. I was only in there for a short while before everything went down just like the

Salazar girl. The next day I was off, but when I came back, I heard Pearson took off on an extended vacation."

Kelly sat back. "I can't help but think the deaths of those three girls are tied into Jake's murder. Even you said it was a bit strange and coincidental."

"I need to tell you something," Eric said.

"What?"

He leaned forward across the desk. "I'm good at reading people, you know that. I considered Jake a work friend—we had coffee and lunch sometimes."

Kelly nodded. She had introduced Jake and Eric the year before and the three frequently dined together. She knew there had been a few times when she couldn't join them, or wasn't working the same shift.

"Jake was scared of something. Then, the day before he was murdered, I saw him heading over toward Howard Mason Medical Center. I thought it was a little out of the norm. I mean, what would he be doing in the cancer treatment center? I actually started to worry he might be sick or something. But then I don't think that was his final destination anyway."

"What do you mean?" she asked. The cancer center was a half-mile from the main hospital. It would definitely be weird for Jake to go over there.

"I called out to him, but he didn't hear me. Now here's the weird part. I watched him cross the street and get into a limo. That's strange, right? And it wasn't like he was dressed to go out. He was still in his scrubs and from the way he approached the car, he seemed hesitant or reluctant."

"Have you told this to the police? You know they're asking anyone with information to come forward." Kelly tried to shove the rising fear back down.

"I planned to tell the police, but I left before they finished packing up. I thought I could call the detective on the case and mention it."

Kelly frowned skeptically. "You expect me to buy that?"

He shook his head. "I am likely as paranoid as you, Doc. There was something up with Hamilton that day. Limos and shaky nerves on a pathologist known to be as level headed as they come —I don't like it at all. Don't get me wrong, I liked Jake, and I want to see justice served, but I really think he was in over his head with something. It's a bit scary."

"I have to agree with you. I just wish I knew what it was."

"Well, whatever it was, it wound him up on a cold slab. I don't have any plans to join him." He leaned across the desk. "And you shouldn't either."

CHAPTER TWENTY-ONE

Jeanine Horner took hold of her five-year-old twins' hands. She still could not believe what she was doing, and she was struggling as to why she was doing it at all. The card Ryan gave her was in her purse. She'd read it over and over again on the train. He hadn't had much time to explain. None really. And she didn't completely understand. No. She didn't understand at all. But she knew by the way Ryan looked at her that he wasn't lying. They were in trouble.

The girls had been asleep when she'd arrived home by taxi from the party. She paid the babysitter and said her husband had been delayed. Then she called her best friend back in the states. It was only six a.m. in New Jersey. "Mel, it's me Jeanine."

"Jeanine? You okay?"

"No." She started to cry.

"What is it, honey?"

"Ryan. Ryan and me. He's cheating."

"What?!" Melanie shouted into the phone.

"He said it was only a one night thing and he never meant for it to happen," she sobbed.

"Oh my God. That bastard."

Jeanine sobbed even louder.

"Honey, what are you going to do? I just can't believe it. Ryan? You guys been having problems?"

"No. Not that I knew of. I mean, he works late and it's hard here in a new country, but I've made friends. The girls love their school. I was even looking into a job."

"I am so sorry, honey. What are you going to do?"

"I don't know," she said.

"Come home. Come stay with us for awhile until you figure it out."

"No. Thank you, but we can't do that. I need a few days to think. That's all. I don't know. I might take the girls to France or Italy. Maybe Switzerland for a few days. Get my head together. I love him, Mel."

A brief silence on the other end. "I know you do. Yeah, well, maybe it's best if you take a few days away from home. The girls are little and they need their mom and dad. Maybe you guys can get past this. Get some counseling."

"Maybe," Jeanine replied. "I don't know. I'm going to go stay in a hotel for the night though. I don't think I could stand to see his face right now, and he could come home any minute."

"Okay, but remember the offer still stands."

"Thank you." Jeanine hung up the phone, wiped her tears away, which were not all fake, and went to her closet where she changed out of her cocktail dress and into a pair of jeans and a long sleeved t-shirt. She threw some items into an overnight bag and went into the girls' room where she did the same thing. Twenty minutes later, she woke them up and told them they were going on an adventure. They protested sleepily until she whispered Disneyland Paris in their ears. They didn't question the time, or where their daddy was.

Now they were in the center of Disney Village in Paris, and Jeanine was calculating her next move. She bought the girls lunch, and they sat down at a picnic table to eat before heading back through the Magic Kingdom. She took the card from Ryan out of her purse and read it again.

The people I work for are killers and they're watching us. You need to 1. Have a fight with me here. 2. Go home, call Mel, and tell her I'm a cheater. 3. Go to another European city. Somewhere with lots of people. Stay there for a day. 4. Leave on an early flight to the states. 5. Go to the cabin and wait for me. 6. Change your looks. Do not use your cell once you leave Europe. EVER. DON'T use it to book flights. 7. Call a journalist at the L.A. Times named Georgia Michaels. Tell her to look into Peter Redding, Frauen Pharma, and her neighbor. Make sure you use the words neighbor and . 8. I'm sorry. Be careful and keep eyes open at all times! These people are powerful and they can be anyone and anywhere. I love you.

"Mommy, I want to go back to Peter Pan," Taylor said.

"Yeah, Peter Pan." Chloe clapped.

"Okay. Finish your sandwiches and then it's back to Peter Pan." She tried to laugh for the twins' sakes. "And then on to never, never land," she muttered under her breath, wondering what the hell her husband had gotten them into.

CHAPTER TWENTY-TWO

When Kelly entered her home on the edge of Laurel Canyon, it was just after eleven o'clock. She hadn't heard anything from Tamara about the blood samples, but she knew it took time.

She started to turn off the alarm on the wall behind the front door. But when she punched in the numbers, she realized it wasn't on. Jesus. What was wrong with her? She'd forgotten to turn it on again? She'd had the alarm installed about six months earlier when a Peeping Tom had been reported in the area, but she often failed to set it while heading out to work in a hurry. She was pretty sure she'd done it that morning though, especially after Jake's death. But maybe she hadn't. It wasn't too difficult to imagine it had slipped her mind, considering all that had been going on.

She double bolted the front door and headed into her kitchen. Putting the kettle on the stove to heat up some water for tea, she opened up her pantry and took out a box of kitty food to signal to Stevie T it was time for dinner. She shook the box—a ritual that would normally have him bolting from wherever he was sleeping—and called his name. "Stevie. Stevie T! Here kitty, kitty, kitty." She poured the food into his bowl. But he didn't appear. Again she called, "Stevie, here kitty, kitty." Nothing. That was odd. He lived to eat. Her stomach fluttered. What if he was sick somewhere? He was getting on in years. Her voice, now frantic, kept calling his name as she searched the house.

Kelly reached her bedroom, still calling, when she heard a soft meow. Where was it coming from? Outside? She opened the slider off her room and Stevie T strutted into the house. "What? Where have you been? How did you get outside?!" Then, "Oh my God."

The flutter in her gut grew into a knot of anxiety. Every nerve ending vibrated. There is no way she would have left a door or window open. She lived too close to a main street, not to mention the coyotes in the canyon who would love a plump cat like Stevie for dinner. She picked him up, happy he was alive, but confused and a little scared.

As she held Stevie T close to her, anxiety slowly changed to terror. Her eyes focused on her nightstand. Someone had been in her home and left her a present.

CHAPTER TWENTY-THREE

Gem noticed details. She also had a photographic memory. As a journalist, this came in handy. As a human being, it could, on occasion, be a nuisance. Tonight though, it was all good.

One thing she'd noted over the last couple of years was her neighbor, Chad, went out in the evenings. More precisely, he went out every Tuesday and Thursday evening. The weekends and other days were sporadic, but on Tuesdays and Thursdays, her handsome, creepy young neighbor was usually gone from the time she walked through her front door, poured her Pinot Grigio, and plopped her ass down on her deck chair…until about the time she'd poured herself a third glass of wine and was watching Late Night with Dave.

She also knew the next-door neighbors, Martin and his wife Patty, screwed on Friday nights at almost nine o'clock precisely. Every Friday, Martin's mother would come by and pick up their seven-year-old son who Gem babysat on rare occasions. Martin always came home with a gift in hand for Patty. Usually it was a bouquet, but on occasion Gem noticed he might also have a gift box in hand.

Once the kid was gone, the flowers in a vase (or the gift opened), and Patty was parked on the patio with a martini watching her balding but sweet husband grill steak or fish, the two of them spoke in hushed tones. Gem could not help the twinge of jealousy as she watched them. After dinner, candles burned out, they would go back inside, turn up some music, dim the lights, and, well, it didn't take a brain surgeon to figure out what happened next. Saturday morning Martin Jr. would be promptly returned home by Grandma at ten o'clock

Details.

Second glass of Pinot down, a grilled cheese in her stomach, and dressed in black, Gem knew what she was about to do next was reckless and could likely get her into hot water if she were found out. But she would never have become a successful reporter if she hadn't learned to take a few risks.

She opened up her desk drawer and found everything she needed. Then she stepped outside and, after a glance around, walked through her patio gate across the garden over to the wide sidewalk where her neighbor Chad's gate faced the walk. She took another quick glance around and noted there were no dog walkers or night joggers out. It was after ten o'clock. She was giving herself thirty minutes and if Chad was following his pattern, he would be home about an hour after her mission was complete. *Mission? Who am I, James Bond?* Gem laughed softly and then got down to business.

First she pulled a small switch-blade and screwdriver from her backpack. The blade would probably work. It had done the trick for her the few times she'd locked herself out of the house. Hopefully Chad didn't have an alarm. She knew he didn't have a dog.

In less than five minutes, Gem was inside. Her heart racing, she could feel the adrenaline pumping through her. It felt sneaky and wrong, but at the same time her gut told her she was making the right choice. If she could get a life-changing story out of this or one that could right wrongs, it was worth the risk. It was why she'd brought some tape recorders, phone bugs, and wire tapping instruments along for the ride. This was the one and only thing— aside from their wonderful sons—she could feel genuinely grateful to her ex for. Dennis had been nothing to write home about, but he'd been a decent private investigator and had taught her a few tricks of the trade. She'd even helped him back in the day— typically with adultery cases. But this thing with neighbor Chad was way past that.

What *did* scare her was the Mexican cartel. If, in fact, Chad was somehow connected to the cartel underworld and she got involved in a story that led in a direction the narcos did not want it to go, she could find herself taking a dirt nap. The kind she knew she'd never wake from. For now—her blood racing, nerves tingling—none of it really mattered.

Gem was proud she managed to set up two separate wire taps and two phone bugs in less than 30 minutes. She placed them in the guy's bedroom and family room.

Now it was time to leave. But she paused to take quick note of her surroundings. Clean with modern furniture, a lot of plants, some art—mostly ugly and mundane—and one family photo. She picked it up and turned on her pen light to get a better look. The photo appeared to be of a family reunion—lots of people in it from little kids to a few elderly people and even one guy who appeared ancient. The man standing next to Chad looked like someone Gem knew. But it was dark and without better lighting, she was having difficulty making out who he was.

The piercing ring of a cell phone froze her in her tracks.

Details.

The ringer sounded just like Chad's. She'd heard it before, and knew she was majorly screwed when a key slid into the front door lock.

Everything slowed down. *Dead journalist walking* flashed across her mind's eye. Survival mode kicked in.

Details.

Chad was living in a third-floor plan. What the sales agents referred to as The Optimum. Back in '06, nearly half a million dollars purchased The Optimum. Gem hadn't been able to afford that floor plan. But she sure had dreamt about it and studied the hell out of the plan in the little brochure they handed out at the sales office. Thank God for that. She had about fifteen seconds to bolt the hell up those stairs to the third floor guest room/loft. In it, she found a day bed. She silently thanked God for her petite frame and quickly shoved herself beneath it before Chad walked through the door.

Her heart didn't settle into her 5'1" frame for at least an hour. She listened as Chad fixed what she could only guess was something with garlic in it—a lot of garlic. She also heard him uncork and pour a bottle of wine. Then the TV went on. A pause. Gem's heart skipped a beat. And then, words and phrases—just a few she could make out. Words and phrases that most certainly didn't add up if this guy was somehow associated with the Mexican cartel. Phrases like "Hitler's ideology of eugenics was a correct one. The timing for a new change—a right change, is now," and "The white race…the *real* American race…is the pure race. It is time for us to stand up for what is right. For what we believe in." Gem's stomach turned. Maybe the guy was watching some kind of documentary. Dennis had lived for the WW II programs on the History channel. But what chilled her to the core was when she heard Chad say out loud, "Heil, Hitler."

What the hell?! Seriously, was this guy for real? Maybe he was some kind of bizarre history re-enactor. Or maybe he took part in community theater? Because if not, the only other conclusion she could draw was Chad was missing a few screws, quite possibly a major sick-o, and she needed to get the hell out of his place, pronto.

She had to keep her cool. Losing it would be a major mistake. She could feel the heavy beating of her heart and hear the blood rushing through her ears. And she had to pee on top of it all! The way she saw it, she had three options. None of them terribly appealing. One, she could lay in wait until morning and pray he never found her and left to wherever he might be going. No way. Her bladder would not hold out that long. And how did she even know when and if he might leave the next day? She didn't!

Oh God, her hands were starting to shake. Keep cool! *Details*. Think. Second option was Chad shared a common wall with his neighbor. Gem knew she was an elderly woman whose husband had died a couple of years ago. She was hard of hearing. There was an air duct. Maybe she could get it open, get through it, and shimmy into granny's place. No way. First off, she may have been petite but her ass had always been akin to Jennifer Lopez's. Getting the butt through an air shaft would be impossible and even if she did, she could wake granny up and scare the poor thing to death. No real option there. The only one left then was to wait until the freak fell asleep. Gem would have to go out the same way she had come in.

She waited for almost two hours. The television had gone off. She thought her bladder might explode. Her heart still raced at a clip that made her certain she could have a heart attack at any moment. She'd heard him clamor up the stairs, run water in his sink, a toilet being flushed, and then the click of a light being turned off. And then she waited some more, praying she timed his REM sleep pattern just so.

Two hours into it, Gem knew she had to take that chance. She slowly and as quietly as possible, with the knowledge that her, life could very well be on the line, slid herself out from under the day bed. She stood steadying herself on the wood side of the bed. She took a deep breath.

Three steps down the stairs a creak rang out under her the foot she had just stepped down on. She sucked in her breath and listened. Nothing. She took each step with measure and caution. What felt like an eternity she finally reached the bottom step and stood downstairs in Chad's family room. She heard movement upstairs and threw caution to the wind. As quickly, carefully and quietly as she could she made it to the sliding glass door, slipped the lock and got outside where she sprinted across to her home where she went around to the front door where even if Chad was up he could not see the front door of her place. She'd been wise to leave all of her lights off. She reached underneath a potted plant that she kept to the side where she had an extra key. She slid the key quickly into the door and made it into her place where she turned around and bolted the door.

She dropped to her knees and felt the tears wanting to come. She had made it out alive! A few seconds later she finally made it to the bathroom without ever turning on a light and she peed like a freaking race horse. She walked back into her kitchen, and hands shaking, she grabbed the entire bottle of Pinot. Screw the glass! She marched upstairs into her darkened room and sat back against the headboard of her bed where she took several swigs off the bottle of wine until her heart finally stopped racing.

CHAPTER TWENTY-FOUR

Before Tony could get both feet in the door, his mother asked where he'd been all night. "Your papa fell asleep an hour ago, and you don't answer your phone. That phone is hooked to you like glue. Why didn't you answer?" Her clipped Italian accent was thick with worry and frustration.

"Oh, Mom. C'mon. I'm sorry. We have had this discussion…I don't know how many times. If I'm not answering your calls, it's because I'm on a case."

"How do you know it's not an emergency when I call? How do you know Papa isn't in the hospital or Luke isn't hurt?"

"Mama…" Tony sighed. "I am tired."

"Hmmph." She straightened out her long, silver-streaked hair. Her large brown eyes flashed in anger. He gentled his voice. She was, after all, his mother and deserved respect.

"Mom, no one needs to wait up for me. It's after midnight. Come on. I am a big boy." He glanced over at his father, snoring open-mouthed in his leather recliner, the television blaring. His mother's poodle, Franco, lay on the old, green shag carpet Tony kept promising he would replace on one of his weekends off. His parents needed so much done to the house. A stab of guilt hit him. The duplex smelled of his mom's wonderful veal Marsala. Likely now tucked away neatly into the refrigerator. "You should be in bed, Mom."

She tossed up her arms. "I worry."

"I'm a police officer. I think I got this down.

"No, You know what I do worry. Don't ignore me."

It was coming. The same talk they had on a monthly basis. "I do know why you worry, but this is my job. This is what I do. This is how I make a living for me and the kid, and help you guys out, too. I don't want to talk about it again. Not tonight. I'm tired."

"I'm going to say it one time and that is all. Luke, he got one parent. One. He loses you, he got none. That's it. Then when your papa and I gone, he got no one. Orphan. Is that what you want?"

Tony sighed and walked to the fridge, where he grabbed a beer. He needed to get Luke upstairs and into his own bed. Tony would make himself a sandwich later and insist his mom go to bed. There was so much irony here, but he didn't want to ponder it. He'd moved his family into the upstairs of his parents' duplex to help them out. His father, in particular, was showing signs of aging. Now Tony's wife was gone, and he was the one getting help from his mother. She mothered Luke as best she could, but a grandmother was not a replacement.

"I'm gonna say one more thing."

Of course she was. Tony took a slug of beer and tried not to roll his eyes. "I know what you're going to say."

"And you know I'm right. That baby in there needs a mama."

He walked over to her, gave her a kiss on the cheek. "I love you, and I love that you worry and care so much. Luke and I are fine. We are good. If you need help, I will hire some."

She slammed her hands onto her wide hips. "I don't need no help! That is not what I am saying, Antonio."

Oops. He had pissed her off. She'd used his full name.

"It's time for bed, Mom." He gave her his most charming smile.

"Leave Luke here. He's asleep. You gonna be tired tomorrow morning, and I know you, you gonna work late again. I will take him to school."

"I love you."

She waved a hand at him, and he started down the hall. "Now don't you go in there, Tony, and wake him up."

"Aw, Mom, I just want to see him before I go upstairs."

She sighed and gave up the fight, and instead went over to his dad's chair. She nudged him gently and told the old man to wake up and get into bed. Tony headed down the hall, into the small guest room they'd turned into a room for his little boy. He looked down at Luke. He was beautiful, like his mother had been

—so much like her. His hand grazed Luke's face, causing him to stir slightly.

Tony stayed with him for a few moments, even considered lying next to him, he was so tired. But he knew if he did, neither of them would get a good night's rest. So Tony reluctantly left his son sleeping.

He locked the front door behind him and started upstairs to his place. His phone rang. For a split second he thought about not answering. At this hour, it could not be good.

"Pazzini."

He was surprised. It was Dr. Kelly Morales. And she sounded scared.

CHAPTER TWENTY-FIVE

Night two without Jeanine and the girls had passed. It was a little after six a.m. when Ryan made another frantic phone call begging her to come home. He was still staying in their home, going to work, doing everything as if all that had occurred in his life was the departure of his wife and kids. But he was biding his time, and he knew the clock was ticking faster. "If you don't call me back, I will be forced to call the police, Jeanine. We have to talk. You can't just take the girls and go like this. Please call me. I love you and I'm sorry. I have to go to work soon. You can call me any time, but please do." He hung up the phone, and wiped away real tears. If she followed the plan, she would call within two hours. And he knew The Brotherhood was listening. He'd found a bug inside his room under their bed just three days ago. He'd left it there.

Once the call was made to Jeanine, it wouldn't be long before either the truth would be exposed—that is, if anyone would believe him—or, he and his family would wind up dead.

He was just getting into his car when his cell rang. It was Jeanine. "Honey! Where are you?"

She responded in a distant, angry tone. "Listen, Ryan, don't threaten me with the police."

"I'm sorry. I just, I…well, I'm desperate. I can't live without you. Please come home."

"I'm not ready to come home."

"At least tell me where you are. Please," he begged.

"Italy. The girls and I are in Italy."

"Where? Let me meet you. Let's talk."

"No, Ryan. Plus, you have work to do, I'm sure. I'll call you in a couple of days and maybe then I will be ready to talk. For now you might want to consider a decent lawyer. I'm not sure I can forgive you for this. Good-bye."

Ryan heard the phone on the other end click off. He thought she had added a nice touch by throwing in the line about the lawyer. But what if she was telling him the truth? He couldn't blame her. What if Jeanine never forgave him?

CHAPTER TWENTY-SIX

The headlights shining into Kelly's front window belonged to the detective's off-duty car. She watched him from behind the closed curtains, ashamed at the surge of relief she felt. She was no longer angry with him. She just wanted to feel safe.

"Thanks for coming over," she said after opening the door. "I'm really sorry to bother you so late."

"You said you thought it was important."

"Yes, but...maybe I should have waited." After she'd called him, she had gone around her entire house with the gun she kept. She'd learned how to shoot from her dad back in Lexington. He'd wanted her to know how to defend herself before sending her to the City of Angels. She'd turned on all the lights in the house. No one else beside herself was in the home. That much she knew. But someone had definitely been there.

He frowned and gave her an odd look. "You know, it's after one o' clock, and you don't exactly strike me as the kind of person who calls a detective in the middle of the night for no reason at all. What gives?"

She nodded. "Follow me."

While he followed her back into her room, she relayed the entire story to him. "So you see, the flowers were delivered to my office, and then they disappeared before my shift was over, and showed up here." She pointed to the vase on her nightstand. The bouquet's ominous presence chilled her.

"The flowers disappeared from your office?"

"Yes. I figured it was the cleaning crew. I didn't know."

"I need to get a team over here to dust for fingerprints. I think it's important to check into this. It could be connected to your friend's murder."

The same thought had crossed her mind.

"This note is a pretty serious threat, and we have to treat it as such. With Dr. Hamilton's murder hanging over our heads, we have to treat all of this as possibly being related."

She nodded. "Can I get you some water or coffee?"

"Water. I'll call this in."

Pazzini made a call to the station. "Yeah, and I'd like to get a twenty-four hour watch on Dr. Morales for protection. Thanks."

When he hung up the phone, Kelly said, "Do you really think I need protection?" Her eyes widened.

"I think considering what happened with Dr. Hamilton and the two of you were friends, yes, it's a good idea. Don't worry though. I know you're busy and have a job to do. No one will be in your face. I assure you. These guys are pros. We know how to do our jobs. You won't even notice him most of the time. You can do your rounds without him hanging with you. And it is likely I will be taking the late shift."

"I don't like any of this."

"It'd be strange if you did," he replied. He turned and glanced out the front window. "Looks like my guys just pulled up. I'll go down and let them in."

She hated the idea of being under police protection, but she was scared and the detective's points were valid. What was even more unsettling was it looked more and more likely—to her at least—that Jake's murderer was someone who worked at the hospital. The thought that she might know Jake's killer, maybe worked with whoever it was on a daily basis, sent a chill down her spine. How could her world have been turned upside down in such a short period of time? Maybe Jake had been right when he'd told her to mind her own business.

Maybe if she'd listened, he would still be alive and she wouldn't be in this mess.

CHAPTER TWENTY-SEVEN

Peter Redding did not like waking up to the shrill ring of a telephone—especially before six a.m. It usually meant there was a problem. He didn't like problems. "Yes," he said, trying to shake the sleep out of his voice.

"Sir, this is Frederick Färber."

"Yes, Färber? This better be important. Do you know what time it is here?"

"I do, and I apologize, sir. I think it is important… possibly."

"Think? And possibly? Not sure how I feel about those words, Färber."

"It's Dr. Horner."

Peter sat up in bed. "Horner?"

"Yes, sir. His wife left him."

Peter sighed and snapped his fingers, then tapped his companion on the shoulder. She'd been taught well, and knew what to do. She immediately rolled out of bed, her bare and very nice ass swaying as she walked out of the bedroom and headed into the kitchen to pour him a fresh cup of coffee. "This is a concern because?"

"It's a concern because Horner left work early and we have lost all contact with him."

Redding shifted uneasily. "What do you mean you've lost all contact with him?"

Färber cleared his throat and paused before responding. Redding was not a stupid man, and knew Färber was choosing his words carefully. "I mean, sir, our surveillance isn't working. The GPS has been disengaged. His cell phone is out of service. The taps in his car are not picking up anything. His home surveillance is still working, as well as in his lab. But he isn't home and he isn't in the lab. He's gone, sir. It's possible, though, he went to Italy to find his wife and kids."

"What?" Redding was trying to digest this information.

"The last call we picked up was with his wife. I have the recording. I just listened to it. She is very angry with him. Maybe he went to find her, and it's possible he is out of range. That does happen."

Redding sighed heavily as his naked partner sauntered back into the room and set his coffee on the nightstand. She quickly retreated. "Get me all his tapes from the past two weeks. I want all surveillance. Horner is not headed to Italy and his wife and kids are not there either. Find them. Find all of them and kill them. Track credit card records, cell phone calls, bank account withdrawals, all of it. Put people at all of the airports and train stations. Find them, Färber."

"Yes, sir."

Redding hung up the phone and knew he'd fucked up. Big time.

CHAPTER TWENTY-EIGHT

Gem was on her fourth cup of coffee. After last night's escapade she was exhausted and truth be told, still a bit shaken.

Now she stood in front of her boss Stuart, and as delicately as possible told him her story.

"You did what?! Who do you think you are, Catwoman? This isn't a movie or comic book, Gem. You could have gotten yourself arrested or worse!" He was pacing back and forth in his office. Never a good sign. "No. No! Leave this one alone, Georgia. The Petersen murders were put to rest a long time ago and the last thing you need is to dig into anything involving the cartel." He dropped back into his chair emphatically.

"But what if it wasn't the cartel who was responsible for those murders? And what about that email from Chemmadderhorn?"

Stuart rolled his eyes and pushed his chair away from his desk. "Oh come on, Gem. There are a lot of twisted, sick people out there looking to get off on this kind of thing, and whoever this guy is who sent you the e-mail, he's a joker, and you are his goddamn punch line."

Gem put her hands underneath her seat to keep from biting her fingernails—a nervous habit she had when she was agitated. Her boss wasn't the easiest guy in the world, but he liked her and was a friend. If she could just convince him to do a little more sneaking around, find a few more answers…

"Listen to me." Stuart raised his eyebrows. "Just listen. Say my neighbor isn't tied to the narcos. Okay fine. And say he wasn't involved with the Petersen murders…but here's the thing, the guy is a racist. I mean, talk about hate. I heard the rhetoric he was listening to on his TV and his salute to Hitler." She shook her head. "Jesus, it may sound trite, but that shit sent a serious chill down my spine. I mean I'm half Jew."

"And I am a Jew all the way, so I get it. But come on, Gem. What your neighbor does in the privacy of his home is his bit and *none* of your business."

"I know. I know that. But there is something more here, Stuart. I feel it. I have watched this guy now for three years. He's odd. He's handsome and charming enough when I've passed by him, but he's *odd*."

"So what? Ninety-nine percent of the human race is odd."

She glanced up at the ceiling and paused for a few seconds as her brain pulled something out of nowhere. *Details.* "He's Lawrence Wentworth's son."

"What?"

"Yes. I saw a photo of him and his entire family and Larry Wentworth had an arm around him like he was his father."

"The senator from Texas? That Lawrence Wentworth?"

She nodded. Her brain had finally put a name to the face.

"He only has daughters, Gem."

Gem tossed up her arms. "Okay, well, they are related. That much is obvious."

"Is it? People take photos with famous folks all of the time. It certainly doesn't mean they are related." Stuart shook his head.

"Point taken, but maybe they are. Let's play the "what if" game. Say this guy, my neighbor, is a bad guy of some sort. I know for sure he's a racist, and I can only assume he is related to the senator who we all know has plans to run for the presidency."

"Assume, Gem? Remember what it means when we assume…"

She waved a hand at him. "Come on, Stu. I know the saying, but I promise there is a story here, and when I find it, there is no way it will make an ass out of you, or me." She leaned forward in her chair and put her elbows on his desk. "It would be super juicy if the senator has a relative with racist ties, and even more so if we find a completely different story behind the Petersen murders. How would you like to break that news story?" Stuart eyed her carefully. Gem smiled and pointed at him. "Aha. Cat got your tongue and I have your ear now, don't I?"

"Maybe. It's out there, Gem Michaels. It is out there, but I trust you. But here's the thing: let's say this neighbor is a bad-ass racist. Man, those guys are rotten dudes. They could be as bad as any cartel member and you could be putting yourself in just as much danger. And what if the guy isn't related at all to the senator? The race thing has been done before. It'd be hard for me to convince others that Senator Wentworth has those kinds of ties."

"I'd be careful. I would be fine."

He eyed her. "What makes you think they won't hurt you?" He picked up a dart and aimed it across his office, hitting the bull's eye on his dartboard.

"No way. I'm too street smart not to be able to talk my way out of trouble, especially after all my years working homicide. I have a hunch. After last night, I have a major hunch about Chad."

Stuart cocked his head. "A hunch? The race card, discrimination, hatred, all of those stories have been done thousands, millions of times. Is anyone even going to care? Don't you think this country is past that? We have a black president in The White House. Per capita in this state there are more Hispanics than whites. We are a blended community, a melting pot. How much racism is left?"

Gem laughed. "Are you serious? Come on. The right is getting more conservative. The left more liberal. Our nation is more divisive than it has ever been. People may not always say what they are thinking about one another, but racism is out there. Every day, hate crimes are being committed. You've got people against gays, against Latinos, against blacks, against Asians,

Muslims, whites. You name it. You may like to think we have it all figured out, and we are one big, happy melting pot, but don't deceive yourself. I don't think the country should be deceiving itself either. I think hatred is something that should always be addressed. Always looked at square in the eye and spoken about. It's when people become complacent that this kind of evil sneaks in through the back door, and before long, what you were afraid to look at has now become something so awful you couldn't control it if you wanted to. Let me expose these bastards, Stuart. And if the senator has ties to any kind of racist group, isn't it our responsibility as the media to expose the truth?"

Stuart didn't respond right away. He just studied her and tossed another dart toward the bulls-eye. "Wow. You're good." He let out a long, low whistle and then sighed. "How can I say no after that? Just get the guy's last name first and find out if he is tied to the senator. Start there. Start slow. And be careful."

She smiled. "I won't let you down. Slow and easy, I promise."

CHAPTER TWENTY-NINE

Kelly had just finished a stint in the O.R. with an infant born with his intestines outside his body. The baby was now stable and Kelly was confident there wouldn't be any complications.

As she headed into the break room to change out of her surgical gown and cap, she nearly collided with Dr. Brightman. She'd planned on confronting him at some point that day, but wasn't sure how to go about it. There was no time like the present. "Brightman." She smiled. "I wanted to talk with you."

"Kind of in a hurry, Morales. I've got a patient in maternity with pre-eclampsia."

"I just need two minutes of your time."

His handsome face creased into a frown. "What's on your mind?"

"A couple of patients you saw in the ER a little over a week ago. One was a Naomi Williams and the other was Desiree Jones. I wanted to see their charts."

"What's this about?" Brightman crossed his arms.

Kelly wasn't sure how much to tell him. "I don't think Lupe Salazar's death was caused by drug addiction."

Brightman held up a hand. "Why does any of that concern you? And I'm sorry, but you need to refresh my memory because I have a heavy patient load."

"Lupe Salazar was the girl brought in here just a couple of nights ago. I delivered her baby. You oversaw her case. She passed away."

"Okay."

She forged ahead. "The thing is, the labs I am getting back on the baby are inconclusive. I also read over Miss Salazar's chart and it's the same thing."

He cocked his head to the side. "Again, Morales, I am not sure what you're asking." He glanced at his watch. "And I need to get going."

Kelly put up a hand to stop him from leaving. "From what I understand, Desiree Jones' and Naomi Williams' deaths were very similar, but unlike Lupe Salazar, their babies did not survive. I asked Dr. Hamilton about the deaths. This hospital has had three very similar cases in a short period of time. Three women died and only one baby survived. That baby is in my unit now. I have not been able to read over the charts on all three girls yet, but my gut tells me they are somehow linked. I would think since you were also on all three of these cases that you might be a tad concerned, Doctor."

"I'm sorry, Morales, but you are not making a lot of sense. All three of those girls were probably runaways and living on the street. In fact, if I remember correctly, one of the kids was living in the tenements and another at the shelter. Who knows what they were into. You and I both know lab reports aren't always on the money. Focus on the baby in the unit. I don't think you'll find anything where the women are concerned. There is nothing linking them except they were poor, uneducated, and homeless."

"Maybe it's true, but even so, they were human beings and their deaths should not go unchecked. That would be wrong."

"Hey, call me an asshole, call me amoral. Whatever. What I do know is I have to go. I have other patients. I think you're wasting your time and frankly, I don't know what you are looking for. Good luck with the baby, Morales."

With that he turned and walked away. Kelly's jaw dropped. She most certainly would call him an asshole…and more. But then she started to wonder…did he know more than he was telling her? Was his nonchalance an act? Was it possible Dr. Brightman murdered Jake or was somehow involved with Jake's murder? The thought made her cringe. Maybe she shouldn't have shown him all her cards. She could believe Brightman was an ass, but a killer? That really did not add up for her. Then again, she would have never believed her friend and colleague would be murdered in cold blood in the same hospital she worked in.

Kelly changed quickly and decided to go find the officer assigned to protect her at work. It was time to call it a day. But before she did that, she checked back in with Eric.

"Hey, Doc, about ready to head out?" Eric called out as she approached Baby S's incubator.

"I am. Everything good?"

"Yeah. Take a look at our little one here." He pointed down to the baby who lay sleeping inside her simulated womb, the fluorescent lights still beating down on her bare back. "The bleeder seems to have stopped."

Kelly noticed how peaceful she looked among all the tubes. "Excellent. She looks to have quieted down in the last few hours. I hope she keeps improving. Have social services been by?" she asked, knowing Baby S. was now likely a ward of the state, unless a father or grandparents could be located.

"Not that I'm aware of. If she keeps this up over the next few days, we'll be able to take her off the IMV and put her on C-Pap. What do you think?"

"I'd think it's a possibility. Wouldn't that be a blessing?"

"Sure would." Eric's emerald eyes lit up.

"Keep an eye on her, and if she continues improving, then we know we're on the right track. I wish to hell we knew what drug her mother had been using."

"You still think a drug did this?

"My gut does."

"Gotta trust that. Labs came back inconclusive again?" he asked.

"Yes. I confronted Brightman about the cases he was on. He was a dead end. And with Pearson on vacation, I don't think I will find any answers there. It seems awfully coincidental, or at least a bit strange, that the people I want to speak with are either out of town or think I am wasting my time. Maybe I'm being paranoid or overly sensitive. I don't know. What do you think?"

"I think it's pretty strange. And, no, you're not being paranoid or sensitive. Hey, I did get a hold of the charts you asked for on those girls. They're on your desk."

"Thank you."

"I think you'll be disappointed," he said.

"You take a look?"

He nodded. "But I could have missed something. From what I read, nothing stood out. The labs came back the same as Lupe Salazar's."

"Damn."

Eric put an arm around her and they both stood watching over Baby S. "We will save her. She's doing great." He looked down at the sleeping infant and smiled.

"I have to believe that's true. But what if more girls come into this hospital and die in the same way? What if we lose more children? If we can find out what's going on, get on top of it, we can at least treat those patients."

"I think you need some rest. And whatever I can do to help, I will," Eric said.

"Right now the best thing we can do is keep a low profile. I'm going to keep nosing around. I think I will take those charts with me and look over them tonight at home. I have to wonder if someone isn't tampering the charts. Do you know very many people in the lab? "

"A few, but I can't imagine any of them doing something like that." Eric shook his head.

"I hear you, but I can't imagine Jake being viciously murdered right here in this hospital. Someone here knows something about it. I guarantee it."

"I don't know what to say, Doc. Call me if you need to talk."

"I will and vice versa." Kelly smiled. She didn't want to tell him about the police protection. It would only worry him more.

"I assume you're going to Jake's funeral tomorrow?"

Kelly's hands began to shake. She'd been trying hard all week to forget the funeral. She nodded.

After a few seconds he said, "You know I'm here for you. I want to help you find the answers you're looking for."

"Thank you." Kelly glanced at her watch. "I better get going." She knew Officer Simmons was waiting to hand her off. She headed to her office, grabbed the charts, and found Simmons in the family waiting room. He folded up his newspaper and stood. She had to check in with him hourly, unless she was in the O.R. or dealing with an emergency.

"Hey Dr. Morales, looks like it's quitting time. Pazzini should be here soon. You did say you got off at seven, right?" He rubbed his goatee.

Kelly discovered Simmons was a pretty decent guy when she popped her head into the waiting room and spotted him joking around with a few of the mothers. Getting parents of a sick child to laugh was no easy feat. He'd earned her respect. "I guess we'd better go."

"Yes, ma'am. I'm needed at my sister's wedding rehearsal. Frankly, I'm surprised Pazzini even let me off."

She shook her head. "Can I ask you something?"

"Shoot."

"Is Pazzini a jerk?"

Simmons was rubbing the goatee again, his mouth puckered, eyes squinting. "Nah, not really. He just takes his job real serious. He's a good guy. A lot better than most of the guys down at the station." He shrugged. "He's got a tough guy exterior but he's soft on the inside. That's my take anyway."

"I think it's going to be an interesting evening," she commented.

He laughed. "I can't argue with that. One thing I do know about Pazzini…he is an interesting guy. Never know what you might learn."

"I can't wait." She smirked and the headed down to the lobby.

CHAPTER THIRTY

Ryan drove to Copenhagen, shaved his head bald, and got his ears pierced four times in one ear and six in the other.

***

Jeanine landed in New York and took a bus to the Bronx. She rented a car from some shady car rental place and headed to New Jersey. She knew this was not Ryan's plan. But this was her home territory and she needed to ground herself before heading to their cabin in the Catskills. She just needed to be in her hometown, if only for a little while.

The twins complained and then mommy put on their favorite dvd and they sang silly songs from The Wiggles. Soon they were whispering to each other and after another fifteen minutes, they were asleep.

***

Ryan went to a tattoo shop and had a cross tattooed on his right shoulder and the initials J, C, and T on his left shoulder. It hurt like hell.

***

Jeanine wanted to call her husband and scream at him. What the hell had he gotten them into? What had he done? Her hands were shaking as she held the cell phone. She was supposed to toss it before she left Europe. He'd been explicit about that. But goddammit, didn't she have any say in this? Her thoughts and memories now plagued her. She thought about calling her best friend, Melanie, and going there instead. Tell Mel the truth, and not continue with this ridiculous story about Ryan cheating on her. Maybe Ryan was insane. At that moment she didn't know anything, anything at all.

***

Ryan stopped at a pawn shop and purchased a hunting knife. He needed some kind of weapon on him. Just in case. He then bought a few groceries, including a bottle of Vodka. After he rented a room on Reventlowsgade. He ate a bag of potato chips and a banana and then leaned against the head board in the filthy motel room and fought back an urge to sob. He'd come this far. He had to go the distance. There was every possibility The Brotherhood had figured out he'd gone MIA and Jeanine and the kids had disappeared. He counted his money. He'd been secreting cash away in small amounts for months so The Brotherhood would not notice. He'd put away almost 970 euros. Hopefully it would be enough.

***

Jeanine sat at the edge of the double bed, flipping through the TV channels—the girls, thankfully, asleep with a Happy Meal in their stomachs and tired from the long flight. She was exhausted. She'd known the second she'd looked into Ryan's eyes that night at the party…they were in trouble.

***

Ryan jumped at every noise outside his motel room. He was anxious and tried to focus. He needed to plot out his next steps. He tucked his money away and opened the bottle of Vodka and took two swigs hoping it would calm him. It didn't. He contemplated his sanity and if he would ever see his wife and daughters again.

CHAPTER THIRTY-ONE

Gem was on the phone with her sixteen-year-old son, Austen. He was complaining about his dad's rules and how badly he wanted to move back home and live with her. "Come on, Mom. Dad is such an ass."

"Sorry, Austen. If I remember correctly, I was the ass not long ago. You boys always think the person asking you to help with the yard or wash the dishes is an ass. It's Dad's turn now, bud. I like being the fun parent for a change."

"You're no fun if you don't let me come home."

"Yeah I know. I like totally suck. Whatever. Listen, sweetie, I love you very much. But, I think you forget that you and Kurt begged me to let you move. You both laid a heavy guilt trip on me about not spending enough time with your dad, and how I raised you, and should I go on? I let you go. It wasn't easy but I wanted to do the right thing for you boys. You know, let you get to know your dad. Now you guys made your choice and as much as you both may not like it, it is what it is. You changed schools to do this. I don't want to switch back and I don't want to make the forty-five minute trip twice a day."

"I'll have my license soon."

Gem looked upward at the ceiling. The kid was incorrigible. As she was trying to figure out how to say no to him (not easy for her), she heard a voice coming from upstairs. The hairs on the back of her neck stood up. What the hell? "Hey, I gotta go. Um, I'll call you later."

"But, Mom…"

"Later, bud." She hung up the phone before he could respond any further. The sound of someone's voice still carried on in her bedroom.

It took her about thirty seconds to figure it out. It was the wire tap from across the street and the voice she heard was Chad's. She bolted up the stairs, sat down behind her desk, and began listening intently.

"Yes, sir. Yes, I understand. I am flying under the radar. I promise. Yes, I will be at the meeting tonight. I'm leaving in about fifteen minutes." Gem wished she'd had the technology and time to install a wire that would allow her to hear both sides of the conversation. But that would have taken more time and included hardwiring, which her ex-husband had never taught her. However, Chad's end of the conversation continued and it didn't take long for her to start piecing some of it together. "Of course I understand how important this is. Okay. Yes, sir. Give Aunt Elizabeth my best. I will let you know. Thank you. Good night."

Aunt Elizabeth! Elizabeth Wentworth! So *that* was the connection! The senator was Chad's uncle. Ha!

Gem began to scramble. Car keys…car keys…on the kitchen counter. She ran back down the stairs, grabbed her camera bag from the entry closet, slipped on her tennis shoes, and headed out to her car. There was only one way in and out of the townhouse community and knowing Chad was headed to an important meeting of some sort—one where discretion was of the utmost importance—Gem figured she'd better follow him and see exactly where he was going and, if possible, find out what he was involved in.

She got behind the wheel of her navy blue Chevy Malibu and squealed out of her garage. She beat the light, left their gated complex, and parked across the street. Chad drove a sleek, silver Porsche 911, and she waited until she saw its gleam at the light. There was no mistaking him.

She plugged in her IPOD and dialed up some Bob Marley, hoping the tempo and upbeat lyrics would calm her. Her heart was pounding as she pulled into traffic three cars behind Chad.

A moving truck got in her way as they headed south on the 101. Gem switched lanes and lowered her speed. She doubted her neighbor had any idea what kind of car she drove, but thankfully the sun was beginning to set. Right now, darkness and anonymity were her friends.

Minutes later he exited off of Lankershim. She stayed with him, keeping four cars in between them. He turned east, and the further he went, the more desolate it got, and the more she had to back off so she wasn't spotted.

Out of caution she slowed down and lost sight of him as the sun dipped below the horizon. Then she spotted his car far ahead. And saw where he was going. There were no other headlights, but she could see a line of cars heading up a long, steep drive, behind a heavy iron gate. The place appeared to be a ranch of some sort. She drove by slowly. A guard stood outside, and she passed by on the main road without so much as an inquisitive glance in his direction.

Gem pulled her car off to the side of the road about a half-mile past the gate and grabbed her camera equipment. The heavy weight tugged on her short frame. She hiked back toward the compound, ranch, whatever it was, staying low in a ditch between the road and an open field. She got closer. Tumbleweeds shielded her from the cars pulling into the ranch. Maybe some kind of party? From her vantage point, though, she couldn't see any women. Nice cars, too. Mercedes, a Jaguar, Maserati, and a couple of BMWs.

From what she could see with her close-up lens, the men entering the palatial villa were white and varied in age from thirty to sixty years. It was difficult for Gem to tell exactly because she couldn't get too close without being spotted, plus she had no idea what kind of security system the place had, but if she had to guess, she was pretty sure it was locked down tighter than Fort Knox. There were also a couple of uniformed guards walking around with Dobermans. She was sure those guard dogs would be straining at their leashes if they had even the slightest inkling she was there. She froze when she noticed one of the beady-eyed canines looking her way. It started to bark frantically. She sunk onto her belly next to a small boulder praying the dog's nose wasn't working well. Man it was uncomfortable—dirt and little pebbles digging into her body. She was pretty sure she felt something crawl up her shirt. She wiggled in an attempt to smash it.

One of the guards yelled an order at the barking dog who immediately stopped. Gem let out a sigh of relief but realized she was far from safe. She waited several minutes before lifting her head again. The sun was descending rapidly in the west and she had little time, if any, to gather more intel. She could make out one man at the front door, his shadowy figure vaguely familiar. Gem smiled at the realization that it was her neighbor, Chad. "Gotcha!" She snapped a photo. And then began taking picture after picture. She wasn't entirely sure what she was photographing or how good the photos would come out, but she felt they were important and would eventually help tell the whole story.

Once all the men were in the house, she used her zoom lens to scan and shoot the cars parked inside the compound, trying to get as many license plates as she could. Soon darkness took over and blanketed the valley with only the lights of the compound and estate to illuminate the empty hills. Gem's adrenaline rush had reduced to a slow simmer and she knew it was time to get the hell out of there.

She made it back to her car. She was anxious to get back to her place, so she could develop the photos. Something told her she was about to give her boss the story of a lifetime.

CHAPTER THIRTY-TWO

Tony pulled up in front of the hospital and parked his gray sedan in the loading zone. He got out and approached the thick glass doorway. The panes slid silently open for him.

He went inside the lobby and sat down in the waiting area. He picked up a National Geographic, thinking he should get a copy for Luke, who loved the glossy photos of wild animals and foreign cultures.

Everyone else seemed to be focused on a gameshow on TV. Pazzini glanced up and saw Simmons and Dr. Morales come out of the elevator. She looked worn out. Pretty, but tired.

They approached the lobby. "How's it going, Doc?" Tony asked.

"Okay, considering." She tucked her long, dark hair behind her ears.

"You ready for a great evening?"

"What have I got to lose?" she smiled.

"Hmm." Tony wasn't quite sure what to make of her. Was that sarcasm he detected, or was she being nice? He'd never been great at reading women.

Simmons broke into a wide grin. "Ah, she's a sweetheart once you get to know her."

Kelly frowned at Simmons. "And here I thought you had my back," she said. "I like *him* though." She pointed at Simmons.

Pazzini covered a hand over his heart. "Oh, so you don't like me? Ouch! I'm only doing my job."

Simmons glanced from Kelly to Pazzini and quickly stepped in, "Hey, so thanks for covering me, boss. I'd really hate to miss my little sister's rehearsal dinner."

"No problem." Pazzini smiled. In the past couple of days Simmons had grown on him. And as far as the doctor went, he couldn't deny there was something about Kelly that intrigued him. She was the first woman since his wife, Anna, who provoked any kind of response from him other than a purely sexual one. This lady had already made him angry, feel sorry for her…hell, whether or not it had been her intention, she'd even made him smile a time or two. After Anna died, Luke was the only one who got any kind of smile out of him.

Tony noticed Simmons wink at her and she smiled back. He coughed. "I think we'd better get going."

They left the hospital and got into his car, driving silently for a few minutes before Tony blurted out, "So, you and Simmons hit it off, I see?"

She turned to face him, her almond-shaped eyes darker than before. "He did his job. I did mine. He stayed out of my way. It worked."

"I'm trying to do my job, too."

"Stop provoking me, then. And what are you looking at?"

"You. Trying to figure you out."

"Don't you think you should be keeping an eye on the road?"

He focused back on the freeway, slamming on the brakes as the rush-hour traffic began to slow to a standstill.

"Look, this is likely only for a couple of nights. I think we should make the best of it, okay? See if we can't get along. Is that a problem for you?" he asked.

For a moment she didn't respond. Finally she muttered, "No. I guess not."

"Good. I hope you're hungry because I'm famished. Why don't we go have a decent meal, try and make nice. I'm actually a good guy. I know you probably think I'm an ass…"

She shrugged. "I don't know why I would think that."

He shook a finger while keeping his eyes on the road. "I do detect the sarcasm in your voice."

"You *are* the detective."

"Funny. Cute really."

"Not trying to be cute," she replied.

If they were on a date…*if*…shit. How could he even think like that? But how couldn't he? He was after all a man. But a detective first. No. A man first. A man doing his job. His mind was going all stupid on him now, because he knew *if* they were on a date he would have told her she wasn't even close to cute. She was goddamn hot. Well, maybe he wouldn't have said those exact words, but he'd at least tell her she was beautiful. He tried very hard to erase that thought from his mind, knowing it went against every professional and ethical code grilled into him. He decided to try and get back to being completely irritated by her. She was irritating. She was damn irritating. Gorgeous but still irritating. Smart but irritating. Damn!

"Oh you're not cute. Not at all," he said keeping his tone as monotone as possible.

"But you just said…"

He gripped the steering wheel. "Okay. So let's get something to eat and then we'll go back to your place. You can go about your business and I'll handle some paperwork I need to catch up on. You won't even know I'm there." They turned off Fairfax, and pulled into Canter's Deli. "Is this okay?" he asked, thinking maybe he should have taken her somewhere nicer, an upscale pizza place maybe? She struck him as the white wine-type who enjoyed pizzas with artichokes and goat cheese, or some kind of fancy shit that didn't belong on a pizza. Not a *real* pizza, anyway.

"Fine," she replied.

Fine! Fine. Good God. Well then, it would have to be *fine.* Yep. Irritating. He shook his head. Got out and waited for her. He wasn't about to open the car door though.

No sooner were they in the door of the restaurant when the hostess—who'd been there probably as long as the deli itself—approached them. Her eyes lit up when she turned to the doctor. "Hello, Doc. Long time no see. How are you?" she asked, her Brooklyn accent thick and loud. "Is this your new man?" Her lips covered in coral-shaded lipstick puckered as she eyed Tony up and down in obvious approval.

He couldn't help but be surprised and amused when he saw a blush rise in the doctor's cheeks. He wanted to laugh but stopped himself.

"No. He's, uh, he's um…he's just a friend."

Friend. He was working hard not to laugh.

"Oh a friend, huh? Nice looking *friend.*" The waitress winked at him and turned to show them to a booth.

The doc was in front of him and he tapped her on the shoulder. She glanced back. "Friend? Nice. Good call." He smiled widely.

"What was I supposed to say?" she said, trying to keep it down. "This is the cop shadowing me because some creep is out there sending me ominous messages and breaking into my house? Oh yeah, and he may have murdered a friend of mine. Sure."

"Good point." He smiled all the way to the booth.

"Enjoy, kids," the hostess said as they slid into the pale pink seats. This was one of those old-school delis…pastel colors on the walls, Formica tables and counters, fantastic sandwiches.

Tony ordered a Reuben; the doc a turkey on sourdough and a beer on tap. She rubbed her eyes, which were red and tired looking but still sparkling with energy.

She broke the silence. "Did you find out any more about the note and the flowers? Do you have any more leads? And what about Jake? Is what happened with me related?"

He smiled sympathetically. "We are still investigating."

Her shoulders slumped and she stared down at the table until the food arrived.

Tony watched as she guzzled down the beer and ordered another before taking a bite of her sandwich. "Might want to go easy there, Doc."

She frowned. "It's been a rough week."

"Trust me, that won't help."

"Probably not, but it might for a little while."

"Not long. I speak from experience." He grew silent. The doc shifted uncomfortably in the booth. He weighed his options and decided he really didn't want or need to elaborate. He was simply keeping the doctor safe, and finding her friend's killer. He shut his emotions down. He finally looked back up and noticed her studying him.

"You okay?" she asked.

"Yep. Just tired. Long days."

"I can relate to that," she replied.

"I'm sure you can. I don't know how you do it."

"Do what?" she asked.

"Your job. I mean you must see some really tough stuff."

She laughed. "There's the pot calling the kettle black! How about you? You're a homicide detective."

"Good point. But you have to deal with babies all day long. Sure, I have a lot of awful things that I see and deal with, but I couldn't deal with sick or dying babies. How do you manage?"

She finished the second beer. "It's not easy. Not at all. But I try not to let myself think about it much. I became a doctor to save lives and it's what I do. There are far more babies who started out with me and grew up into healthy, happy kids than ones who die under my watch."

"You have a difficult job and it's got to be hard. I admire what you do. Believe me. I couldn't do it." He had the utmost respect for doctors.

She didn't say anything at first. "You know what? I'm sorry. I didn't mean to snap at you. You actually seem like a nice guy and I know you're trying to do your job here. You respect me, I respect you, and now I think it's probably time to head out."

He sighed. "Okay. Oh, um…do you mind if we stop off at a bookstore? I know there's one on the way to your place. I have to pick up a book for my son."

"Sure. How old is he?"

"He's six."

"That's a fun age," she said. "So much going on with their little brains. I love kids."

"You want some of your own?"

"Sure, I think. Someday. Right now I'm so focused on my job I haven't even made any time to meet anyone, much less think about starting a family."

He nodded, not really knowing what to say. She was intelligent, attractive, a bit edgy, which he liked so it was hard for him to understand why she didn't have someone in her life. "You know that you can have both?"

"What?" she asked.

"A career and a family."

"Of course I know that, Detective. I just haven't met the right guy yet."

"You will. I'm sure you will."

She sighed. "Maybe I'll get myself a book, too. Something to take my mind off of things."

"You like to read?" he asked.

"When I get a chance," she said. "I like anything where I don't have to think too hard. A good thriller, adventure, that type of thing."

"You haven't gone the way of the electronic world like everyone else, you know with a Kindle, Nook, or iPad?"

She smiled and it did strange things to his insides. That feeling could not be butterflies. Ridiculous. "I have an e-reader. I mean, who doesn't? But there is something about the printed book I don't think I will let go of completely. You know, holding it and smelling the ink. I don't know…it's appealing in a weird way. God, I think I'm buzzed. I sound stupid."

"No, not stupid at all. I agree. About the books. I like the feel of a printed book myself."

She smiled again and it threw him off-kilter. Again. Time to get the check and leave. But as they were walking out the door, he couldn't help but smile. Who knew…maybe the night wouldn't be so bad after all.

CHAPTER THIRTY-THREE

Mark watched them leave the hospital together. He'd noticed the cowboy dick hanging out with her all day and it made him real nervous. He'd been in and out of the lab, making sure he'd covered his ass with the files of those dead chicks, and their kids. It had not been easy though. He'd been able to get into the computer system and make some hasty changes once those girls had died, but he'd had to get a hold of hard copies to be certain nothing got lost in the shuffle.

He needed to talk to Chad and tell him what was going down. Mark was supposed to let him know what was going on with the doctors on the payroll, and with Dr. Morales who may or may not know something about them thanks to that dumb-fuck Hamilton. Chad could at least give him kudos for keeping an eye on the lab results. Maybe they could get together and have a beer over that.

Back to the problem at hand. The doctor. Little Miss Too-Good-For-Everyone-Else must be scared out of her mind to get the cops all over this. Now she thought she needed a big protector. All the pretty little doctor needed was him. Dammit. Mark couldn't tell Chad he had a thing for the doctor for a couple of reasons. First of all, Dr. Morales was a Mexican…or something like that. Mixed relationships went against all the codes and rules. But it wasn't like

Mark was in love or nothing. There were other things the doctor could be used for. The other reason was if Chad knew about Mark's little obsession and that he'd been semi-stalking her outside the parameters of what his job entailed, he might get into a bit of trouble with The Brotherhood. He definitely didn't need or want that. He had to get his shit together…be more discrete.

Mark wasn't too worried about the dipshit with her now. Some protection the cop was. Big asshole. Hell. He hadn't even noticed Mark following them from the hospital. He'd screamed at him while in his car watching them go into Canter's. "You're a big fucking bozo, cop!"

That detective was no match for him. Hollywood had its perks. Like good costume shops with all sorts of great masks, make-up, and everything you'd ever need in order to change yourself quickly and effectively.

He wanted to get closer to them. See what they were doing. He put on a UCLA sweatshirt, a pair of sweats, and a baseball cap. Glasses, too. Made him look brilliant, which he obviously was.

"Yeah. Perfect." He opened the car door and slung a camo back-pack over his shoulder for an added touch. He laughed.

Mark walked through the door and spotted them right away. Now why would a cop who was supposedly protecting someone take her out to dinner and then to a bookstore? What, were they in, some sort of dipshit book club? He chuckled at his own joke. But really, what the hell was going on here?

And what if she recognized him? Nah. Fat chance. She hardly glanced at him in the halls at the hospital. She wouldn't recognize him. He worked for The Brotherhood and they didn't hire idiots.

All he had to do was keep his special feelings for Dr. Morales a secret. She'd be his soon enough.

CHAPTER THIRTY-FOUR

Peter stepped out of his silver Mercedes Coupe and strolled to the mansion his organization used for meetings with prominent backers. The ten men of The Brotherhood who financed the Covert Reich Project. The top echelon.

He stood in the doorway, his ID ready for inspection. It was a silly formality at this point, but one they followed per the parameters set forth with the initial creation of the program. Peter flashed his ID, and gave Chad Wentworth his password. How ironic was it the senator's nephew was a simple minion?

Peter liked Chad. The kid really believed in their cause. Peter wasn't as certain about the senator, but facts were facts. And the facts were politicians liked money and power. They tended to be greedy bastards, more like whores than anything else. Most would sell their souls if they thought it would get them what they wanted—money and power.

Money guaranteed men like Wentworth certain positions of power in life. He would be an easy puppet to control. Chad could be an asset, and he could one day be in the power seat just as his uncle surely would—controller of the free world. Chad could continue the legacy of purity. He had scored big points with Peter when he'd done the Hamilton job. A job well done. Efficient.

"How are you, Chad?"

"Very well, Mr. Redding. Thank you for asking, sir," he replied.

"Good to hear it." Peter walked inside the mansion, an exact copy of an eighteenth-century French chateau. Within a few minutes, the rest of the men entered through the front door, and joined Peter in the large library. Priceless artwork adorned the walls. The smell of cigars and scotch combined into an intoxicating haze of luxury and wealth.

The compound, as Peter referred to it, could also be used as a temporary residence for visiting dignitaries whenever they came into town. It was fully staffed for those whose needs were sufficiently important for the organization to pamper, such as Senator Wentworth. All the members, however, had funded both the grounds and the building itself.

Peter walked to the front of the room, a fireplace behind him. He took his seat at the head of the table.

"Greetings, gentlemen," he said as they were milling around, slowly taking their seats. The room grew quiet, and all eyes were on their leader. "I'm glad you could all be here." Everyone knew full well no one was allowed to miss a meeting. The only valid excused absence was death.

Peter made a point of nodding his head to all of his out-of-town guests. One was from New York, a few from Dallas, San

Francisco, the Beltway, and even Europe. They all nodded in return and murmured greetings.

"I think it only appropriate to address the most important topic at hand, which is the purification of our country and eventually the world." He nodded his head toward the members from London and Germany. "You will be pleased to know I have looked over the numbers you gave me at the last meeting regarding our project. Things are proceeding smoothly and efficiently. However, we are going to require a little more funding for this vital project. Mr. Shaw will explain the reasons. As you are well aware, Mr. Shaw is the CFO of Frauen Pharmaceuticals." He gestured for Bill Shaw to speak.

Shaw stood up in his glacially methodical way. He was in his early sixties and very old school. His snow-white hair was carefully coiffed. The shadows around his dark eyes revealed an early life of hardship. Peter knew Shaw had worked his way up, just as Peter had, and he had the utmost respect for the man. The Brotherhood had been around for nearly seventy-five years. It had started as an off-shoot of the KKK. But unlike that organization, the men of The Brotherhood were more educated, more esteemed, quite a bit wealthier, and kept a much lower profile. Such a low profile, in fact, that they flew under the radar of the government except those who were in their ranks, which there were a handful of very wealthy and powerful men.

The KKK and other factions of the Neo-Nazi movements weren't always the best and brightest. They gloated. They enjoyed the limelight. They shouted at protests and committed hate crimes that many times they got caught committing. Not the members of The Brotherhood. Sure, there were a few loose cannons out there. And at one time, some of the men who were considered brothers weren't working with full decks. Once Redding took over the program a few years ago, he'd made every effort to rid The Brotherhood of just that type of riff-raff. Purity meant purity, and that meant the best of the race.

"Thank you, Peter. I am going to get right down to facts, gentlemen. The drug is not resulting in the necessary spontaneous abortions. In a few cases, yes, but in others, it is merely causing more defective newborns to be brought into a world already overrun with undesirables. Now, we know we must rid our society of precisely these types. We certainly don't want any *more* refuse. Therefore, we need more funds in order to proceed. Hitler was correct when he developed his eugenics program and we will continue to pursue his original plan. Only this time, we will succeed where he was unable.

"I think this drug will be ready for mass production in ten months time. Of course, we will continue with our experimental research. We have to expect problems like this with *any* new product. I know we are all in agreement that the sooner we rid ourselves of these welfare cases, the better off the whole country will be."

Peter stood. "Thank you, Bill." He gazed across the table of men, making earnest eye contact with each member.

"I know we are behind schedule, but for our plan to work as smoothly and efficiently as possible, we can't afford raised eyebrows over a handful of cases that may cause the authorities to take a second look. Fortunately, our asses are all well covered."

Craig Johnson stood up and pointed an accusatory finger at Peter. "We've all put a lot into this thing. Research costs, distribution expenses, the usual bribes, and now funding for the senator's forthcoming presidential campaign. How much more are you expecting us to shell out? And what do you mean "our asses are covered?" Are you going to cover my bank account losses, Peter?"

A loud murmur raced through the group.

"Look Johnson, we all knew what we were buying into. We all knew the costs, and we knew they could escalate," Peter was trying to keep any edge out of his voice. "I think we agree we have enough individual finances to keep food on our tables." Johnson started to protest. Peter slammed both hands down hard on the table in front of him and then held up a finger, "But let me ask you," He pointedly looked at each man. "Do any of you truly believe when your grandchildren get to an age where they can appreciate the finer things in life that they will be able to? Do you really think private education, good upbringing, nice families, and trust funds will provide for them? No! No fucking way! And I will tell you why. Entitlement. Our grandchildren may feel it. Hell, our own children likely have a sense of it. In fact, it's my personal belief the majority of this fucking nation has an abnormal sense of entitlement. It's despicable and disgusting. Let good Old Uncle Sam pay for the masses. Let John and Sara Brown..." he looked at Harold Brown whose grandson John just married, "...take care of Jamal and Manuel and Saddam and all their goddamned children. Why? I will tell you why. Because even though your well-educated, gentile offspring enjoy certain entitlements, the undesirables want what we and our children have for nothing! They want their Blue-rays, their vacations, furniture from some faux high-end store, their Target purchases—they want it all, but without having earned the right. They want to do it on the dole, and your grandchildren will be paying for it.

"We can make a change in this world. It's within our reach. It may not seem like it now. But it is. Let the undesirables go back to where they came from. Once we weed them out, once we destroy their offspring, we can take back our country. Now, Johnson, do you understand the importance here and why we need to get our checkbooks out?"

"Yes, Peter," he muttered. "However, what about this chemist you hired? The best chemist in the world? I heard in just the past few hours that Dr. Horner is missing."

"That's absurd!" Peter yelled. "Horner is in the lab as we speak doing exactly what he is being paid to do!" Peter felt the blood rising to his face. "Where did you hear something so ludicrous?"

"You are not the only one with sources, Peter." Johnson looked at him calmly. The others looked from Johnson to him and back again.

A silence shrouded the room. Peter held Johnson's stare. "You're wrong and so are *your* sources. Now, *Mr. Johnson*, kindly sit down so we may proceed," Peter demanded. His eyes narrowed as he stared at Johnson, who returned his hostile gaze but reluctantly took his seat. Peter looked back at Bill Shaw. "Please continue."

"Thank you. We need an additional five million dollars. A distinct bargain considering the impressive results we are already seeing in our experimental trials."

Johnson muttered something, but Peter shot him a look, abruptly silencing him. Shaw ignored the interruption and loudly continued speaking.

"The money needs to be ready next week, deposited into our Swiss bank account. Come, gentlemen. A half-million apiece is

172 | P a g e

loose change. Let us remember the noble goal within our reach. A pure America. A pure world. As Peter mentioned, this is for our children, our grandchildren, and generations to come. This is our purpose, gentlemen. This is for our country. For the God we believe in."

"Thank you," Peter said, silencing him. Shaw was a good guy, but he tended to go off on religious tangents as he was fundamentalist to the core. "Our experiments will continue to be carried out in South Central, Los Angeles and downtown, as well as our project in Harlem. The next cities to purge will include Detroit and D.C., Miami, and then, of course, all the shantytowns below the Mason-Dixon line. Most of the people in high-crime and high-poverty locations are already addicted to drugs, so it will be relatively easy to get them hooked on a new one. For street purposes we're now calling it *Pure.* We are working diligently on making Pure effective for both men and women."

"Eventually, we will discover how to sterilize these people completely, so future pregnancies will not be a concern. As you know, the drawback to our current experiments with pregnancies is the involvement of private physicians and hospitals. We have to pay a great deal to cover these expenses for our security. Fortunately, we have only had to pay out expensive bribes in a few instances. Most of these lowlifes don't seek medical attention at all. However, we *have* taken care of those situations that caused concern."

"How do you know they won't talk? That these doctors and other professionals you are paying hush money to won't say anything?" Johnson interrupted.

"We have ways of dealing with that problem. And you must remember much of what we have done so far has gone undetected. Doctors can't look for something if they don't know what they are looking for, which in most instances is the case." Peter replied coolly.

He concluded the meeting by asking all of them to leave their latest numerical reports for the organization's ongoing research. He didn't like to do anything via e-mail. It wasn't safe.

Once they adjourned, the only woman allowed into the compound served coffee and drinks.

Peter breezed past Johnson. He could've sworn he heard Johnson mention the late, great Dr. Hamilton. Anger rose in Peter at the thought of Johnson discussing Hamilton's murder here. He wondered how he had ever wormed his way this far into their organization. He obviously was not the best of the best.

He walked over to Chad. "Chad, can you come by my house this evening?" Peter asked.

"Certainly, sir." He nodded.

"Good." Peter sucked back his drink and eyed Johnson. *Loose lips sink ships*. He shook his head. Peter could get rid of Johnson easily enough. The rest of The Brotherhood would understand why he'd done it. The bigger problem remained... where was Dr. Ryan Horner and his family?

CHAPTER THIRTY-FIVE

Back at her house, Kelly glanced over the charts she'd brought home. Eric was right. Nothing stood out. It was discouraging. Maybe she'd been wrong all along and Baby S. was just another sick infant in her unit and Lupe had died from natural causes. Same as the two other teenagers. It sure didn't feel right though.

Tony finished his paperwork. Although it seemed awkward at first, they'd agreed to be on first name basis. "Would you like a glass of water, Tony?" she asked.

"Sure. Thank you. I'm actually going to give my son a call. It's getting close to his bed time."

She nodded. "I've got some laundry to do." She also saw it as an opportune time to call Tamara.

She handed him the water and started down the hall towards the laundry room.

"Hi, Mom. How are you?" Kelly heard him say. "Good. Everything is fine. I'm just working. As I said I won't be home tonight. I know. I'm sorry." There was a pause. Kelly felt guilty listening to his conversation. She didn't know why she was eavesdropping. His call was none of her business, but she didn't move. "I love you, Mom. Yes you are the best mother in the world. I will. I will. I will be home this weekend and cook with you. Promise. Now can I please talk to the kid? I said please." He laughed. "Because I'm scared of you." He laughed a little more and Kelly found herself smiling. His laughter was robust and warm. Great. No way in hell was she attracted to the detective. How stupid. Hadn't it only been a few hours ago she thought he was teetering on jerk status? She had to admit though she had gone back and forth on that verdict.

"Hi, bud. You treating grandma okay? Good." Kelly turned around and watched him from the hallway. She could see his face, lit up with a tenderness she hadn't seen before. Something flip-flopped in her stomach. *Behave, Kelly!* She turned and headed determinedly to the laundry room, shoved a pile of whites into the washer, and took out her cell phone.

Tamara answered on the second ring. "Dr. Swift."

"Tamara, it's Kelly."

"Oh hey, I'm glad we connected. So, I got some results back for you and I don't know what the hell you're up to, or whose blood this was, but you said it belonged to a patient of yours?"

"It belongs to a baby girl in my unit."

"She has traces of Ketamine in her system. No one picked up on that in your labs? I didn't think you guys used that any longer. Did she need anesthesia?"

"Ketamine? No, it isn't used often. Sometimes in pediatrics, but this baby was not anesthetized at all. And her mother wasn't either. We didn't have a lot of time to control her pain anyway. She passed away."

"My guess is her mother took it. That is the only answer. But you're also lucky your little one is alive in the unit, because she has Testerogen in her system."

"What? I don't know what that is."

"It's a relatively new drug out on the market. It's proven effective in sterilizing mares. Obviously we don't use it much because there is some controversy around its use. But there are some horses I have given it to. What I can't understand is why a human patient had it in her system."

"I don't know either." Kelly was perplexed by everything Tamara was telling her.

"I can also tell you we can't give Testerogen to pregnant mares because it can cause spontaneous abortions. The drug is given to horses if a vet spots a problem early on in an ultrasound or through fetal tests, in order to abort the fetus."

Kelly was stunned. The only noise was the soft whoosh-whoosh of her washing machine. "Hey Doc, you okay?" The detective called out. He'd obviously finished his phone call.

"Tamara, I have to go."

"What is going on? This is strange stuff, my friend. Talk to me."

"Listen, I can't talk now," Kelly replied. "I'll call when I can and explain it to you. Thank you." Kelly turned off her phone and called out to Tony. "Uh yeah. Fine. I was just adjusting the washer. It can be a bit difficult."

He came into the laundry room. "Oh. Want me to take a look? I can be handy sometimes." He squeezed past her. "What's the problem?" He grazed her hand with his arm, and she couldn't help feel a bit of heat rise through her.

"Oh nothing." She waved a hand at him. "It's fine. Sometimes the spinner comes loose. I fixed it. Maybe once the wash goes through, you can take a look." She was totally full of it and hoped he didn't know that. She needed to make sense of the information Tamara had just given her and then figure out how to tell the detective…Tony…about it. He hadn't thought her theory valid before. Would he now? And would he follow through? Check into things? Or would the pendulum swing the other way again and he'd think she had concocted some story to cover tracks she didn't need covering? She shook her head and sighed because she knew ethically, she needed to let Tony know what she'd learned.

"There's something I just found out about Lupe Salazar," she said.

"The girl who died in the emergency room, right?"

Kelly nodded. "The one whose baby is in my unit now, and, well, I don't know what it means."

"Okay. Why don't you tell me and I'll see what I think."

"Can we go in the other room?" The quarters in the laundry room were tight and that warmth that she'd been feeling had intensified. She needed an iced tea and some space between the two of them.

"Sure."

Once they were seated in Kelly's family room, she took a deep breath. "I got some lab results back on Lupe Salazar's baby. There are two drugs in her system that shouldn't be there."

Tony leaned in closer.

"Ketamine for one."

"Ketamine? Don't doctors use it for anesthesia?"

"We do, but not as much as we used to. And the baby has not been under a general. The drug had to have come from her mother."

"That might be your answer, then. She must have died from an overdose of Ketamine. Unless she was given it in the emergency room."

"No. We wouldn't have, because as you are probably aware, there is a hallucinogenic quality it induces and it would not have been our first choice with a pregnant woman."

Tony sighed. "I do know there is still street use of the drug. It's mainly produced in Mexico, and we still see it in batches of ecstasy at times, so it is out there. I think you can't rule out an overdose."

"I agree, but there was also a second drug in her system." Kelly told him about the drug used on horses and how it caused spontaneous abortion.

"Now that is odd. But maybe the girl changed her mind about having a baby. It does happen with these young girls."

"She was 32 weeks pregnant. The delivery was only eight weeks premature. I don't think this girl wanted to get rid of her baby. She seemed concerned and wanted to care for the baby."

Tony leaned back into the couch and didn't say anything for a minute. "Okay. Okay, let's say your theory about a new street drug is possible. New drugs and variations of old drugs pop up all the time. But you also said you thought this girl's death was related Dr. Hamilton's murder."

"I don't know. I really don't. I do think Jake was in some trouble and it got him killed. I don't know if it is all related but it feels awfully coincidental to me. On top of that, I don't know why the Ketamine did not show up in the labs. I get the other drug. If it's not something we ever see, I can understand reports coming in as inconclusive, but Ketamine should have been detected. I have to wonder if the results were tampered with." She looked down at her hands, which were clasped tightly together. "I hate to say this, but I wonder if Jake did it."

"Would he have had the time?"

She shrugged. "He might have scrambled after I went down and spoke with him. He was so scared, Tony. I mean really frightened of something. Maybe he was covering his tracks."

"Maybe. I'll tell you what. I will find out where Lupe Salazar lived. I'll go ask some questions, and see if I can get some more insight into what she was like. Someone could have drugged her. Possibly the father of the baby."

"Thank you," Kelly said. But her gut said Lupe Salazar didn't want to kill her baby, and no boyfriend or father of the baby tried to kill the girl. There was something way bigger going on.

CHAPTER THIRTY-SIX

Jeanine couldn't stand it any longer. She and the kids were holed up in some podunk, crappy motel off the interstate. The girls were whining. She'd just cut off a good chunk of their hair after she'd cut and dyed her own. She'd bought cheap clothes at Wal-Mart and dressed them like boys, telling them they were playing a game.

"This game is stupid, Mommy," Taylor whined.

"Yeah, stupid," Chloe agreed. "I wanna go back home. I wanna see Daddy."

"Soon." She knew she needed to call this Gem Michaels person. How Ryan knew her, Jeanine didn't know. And on top of that, would the journalist think she was a total nut? Probably. Her instructions were to tell Gem her husband was Chemmadderhorn. Then she was supposed to tell her to look into Redding and Frauen Pharma. It was already past six in California. Jeanine had made a couple of attempts to call the woman when they checked in. The bad news was the motel manager required a credit card to make phone calls. Jeanine thought it safer to use her cell phone.

"Mommy! I hate it here. It stinks."

"It does stink," Jeanine said and lifted Chloe up off the bed. "You know what, let's get out of here."

"Yay!" The twins clapped their hands.

She shoved the few belongings they had into her backpack and left the motel. She knew where she was going. It was only a couple of hours away. Ryan would not be happy about it, but the further she was from Ryan, the more she began to doubt his sanity, and her own. She needed a sounding board—a reality check. She gave Melanie a call.

CHAPTER THIRTY-SEVEN

Peter sipped his just-poured scotch. He loved having money. He'd married an extremely wealthy—albeit fairly neurotic—bitch. He gave a quick thought at how insane she'd become. Had he made her that way? Not that it mattered much now—she was no longer his problem. She currently resided in a private psychiatric hospital in Vermont. Beautiful place, really.

The day Peter had her committed was rough but he'd had no choice. She'd been screaming and carrying on to the medical staff that he'd made her lose their child—that he had deliberately killed their unborn baby. Okay, so maybe he had, but Jesus, bringing up some sniveling brat with a sense of entitlement didn't appeal to him in the least. He hadn't been about to allow a fortune to slip away through his fingers—which is exactly what would have happened if she'd given birth to the heir she'd so desired. Ah, poor Evelyn. Such is life.

Peter had never liked children. He hadn't even liked himself as a child. He'd been born into a family where children were everywhere. Nine of them, to be exact. He never liked his siblings. With nine kids around, toys were scarce—clothes, food—all of it scarce. His father left the family when Peter was about four-years-old, and he couldn't blame him. His stupid mother became a drunk and a whore and the kids were eventually spread out amongst foster homes.

Peter was so happy when he wound up with the Reddings, who had the right social connections and were good people. Mr. George Redding taught Peter everything he possibly could about purifying the human race.

He remembered his nightly talks with George, very clearly.

"Son, who is it we don't like?" he'd ask little Peter every day while drinking his highball and scanning his newspaper.

"Niggers, spics, dagos, Jews, Indians, towel heads, chinks, and beaners."

George laughed. "There's a few more, but you forgot a very important group."

"Oh yeah, faggots."

"Good boy. No, we do not like homosexuals at all."

"Who do we like, Dad?"

"Good, God-fearing, white people, of course—the people who built America. Now what do we need to do in order to make this country a great place again, in order to rule the world?"

"Purify."

George smiled and nodded. "That is right, my boy. You are learning everything correctly. One day, you will be running this great country of ours, and we will take it back again. This will be the place it was meant to be."

"We're not so far off," Peter whispered aloud. "It might look like it to some, but I promise you, Dad, we are not far off." The doorbell rang and his on-and-off-again companion, Susan, quickly appeared showing Chad into his office. The kid stood between the mahogany double doors of the library. "Hey. Come on in!"

Chad stepped into the dimly lit, elegantly furnished room. "Sit down." Peter motioned to one of the chairs opposite his desk. "Would you like a drink?"

"No thank you, sir."

Peter got up and poured himself another drink, then came around and sat next to Chad.

"You wanted to see me, sir?"

"Yes. There is a little matter that needs your attention, and it's delicate. That's why I asked you to come here. I know my home is a safe place to discuss matters at hand. Not that the compound isn't, mind you, but this is the kind of matter that must be handled in a certain way because it concerns a *brother*." He clucked his tongue. "I am afraid Mr. Johnson is causing us some difficulty and I'm troubled. I don't like to be troubled. I think we to need to be certain Mr. Johnson doesn't concern us any longer. Understood?"

Chad nodded. "I do." He hesitated. "Here's the thing, sir. I'm in a very tough position."

"Why is that?" Peter could see Chad begin to perspire.

"It's my uncle, sir."

"What about the senator?"

"Um, you see, he gave me some clear orders and one of them was I was not to get involved with…" he lowered his voice "…any dirty business." He sat back in the chair and crossed his leg.

Peter clasped his hands together. The kid thought he could pull out his uncle's name and get out of a job? This was truly amusing. Where did Senator Wentworth think his continual cash flow was going to come from? Peter chuckled. "I'm confused, Chad. Isn't everything we're involved in "dirty business?" Wouldn't taking care of Dr. Hamilton be considered "dirty business?"

Chad uncrossed his legs and shifted uncomfortably in the chair. "Yes. That's true. My uncle does not know I did that. I…he *just* had this conversation with me. I get you. Trust me, I do. I want to do everything I can to further The Brotherhood and the Covert Reich project. But I'm in a difficult position. I want to avoid upsetting my family further…especially if they found out the extent of what I'm doing for you…"

"For me? This isn't simply for me, Chad. This is for you, for the country, for your uncle who is positioning himself to be the ruler of the free world. There is a higher purpose here."

Chad hung his head.

"Tell you what, I will find someone else to take care of this, and from now on as your uncle wishes, I will make sure your position within The Brotherhood is maintained at a level the senator is comfortable with."

"Thank you, sir," he muttered.

"You're welcome. You may go." Peter watched as Chad left the room. He heard him shut the massive front doors as he let himself out. Peter stood, sighed, and poured himself another drink. He'd liked Chad. He really had. But it was time to send Senator Wentworth a very strong message.

CHAPTER THIRTY-EIGHT

Mark felt a sharp kick in his ribs. His eyes opened wide as he looked up at two burly dudes—guys he recognized from The Brotherhood. Mark immediately pulled his knees up to his naked chest, blubbering, "Hey, man, what the fuck?"

"Get up, asshole. It's your lucky day," one of them said, a German accent clipping the end of his words. He was bald, big, and ugly. Mark recognized him. He'd led a few of the local Brotherhood meetings.

"What do you mean?" Mark eyed him, full of suspicion.

"What he means, shit for brains, is you just received a promotion and now you have to earn it," The other guy was taller, skinnier, with plenty of hair—all slicked back with light blue eyes that bore into Mark. He wasn't as big as the other dude, but he looked meaner. "Get dressed. We have a job to do. Orders came all the way down from the head brass, so you can't fuck this up."

"Whose orders?" Mark asked, not entirely convinced what these guys were telling him was true.

"I don't really think that matters. What does matter is you get your ass up, dressed, and ready in two minutes. Something tells me if this job is done right, you'll be a very happy man." Baldy gave Mark one of those, *I fucking mean it* stares, and Mark decided it was probably in his best interest to do as they suggested.

Twenty minutes later they were parked in front of Chad Wentworth's townhome. Mark had been there once before. His boss. His brother. Chad seemed like a decent guy. He wasn't an asshole like these dudes. He'd treated Mark with respect. They'd even had beers together and shot the shit. Of course, it was all very hush-hush because everyone knew Wentworth had major family connections. That's why Mark was surprised Chad would be going with him and these goons to do any kind of job. Chad didn't *do* jobs. He gave orders. Except Mark suspected Chad had been the one to do Dr. Hamilton. So, maybe he was going with them. Maybe this was kind of like a final acceptance thing. Maybe he was graduating into the big league.

"Hey, I thought you guys said I wouldn't be meeting with the boss until all was said and done." Mark chuckled nervously.

Baldy, whose real name was Thomas, turned around and faced him in the backseat of the Mercedes sedan. "You will."

"Then, why are we at Chad's place?"

Now the scarier and skinner guy, whose name was Connor, turned and shook his head. "Chad has apparently been a very bad boy, and we're here to punish him."

Mark squirmed in the plush leather seat. "What? No! He's a good guy. He's one of us!"

"Shut the fuck up!" Thomas said. "Look here, Chad may have been your boss, but my boss is *the* boss, and what he says goes."

Mark didn't respond.

Connor clapped a hand on his shoulder, "The first rule to getting ahead, *brother*: Do not ask questions. Ever. Do you understand?"

Mark nodded slowly.

"It's easy really…" Thomas sat up front loading a gun. Mark swallowed hard. "We just follow the orders and we get paid a lot of money for moving our cause forward." Thomas placed a silencer on the gun.

"We're going to shoot him?" Mark heard the quiver in his voice.

"No," Thomas said and grabbed the handle of the door. "He's going to shoot himself." Thomas held the gun up to his temple. "Pow," he whispered, a scary little smile spreading across his face.

Mark swallowed heavily. "Nah. Come on. No way."

"Here, take some of this," Connor handed Mark a silver flask. "You'll see how it works. We like to make it clean. Murder is so nasty. Give the guy an easy way out."

Mark brought the flask up to his lips and took a long, hard swallow. The taste of whiskey hit his tongue. It was good stuff. It burned going down, and then quickly warmed him. Sweat dripped down his back. He took another swig from the flask. The guys... his *brothers*...laughed.

"I don't get it. Chad shooting himself, I mean. How's that gonna go down? No way in hell Chad...is going to shoot himself."

Thomas opened his door and Connor followed suit. "That's where you come in, *brother*." Thomas winked at him and Mark wished he'd taken a third hit off the flask.

The three men entered Chad's place through the French patio doors.

Chad was asleep on the couch. A near-empty scotch glass sat next to him on the floor, and the credits of a late-night movie rolled by on the TV. Thomas bent over and gently shook Chad awake. He sat up quickly, rubbing his eyes. Mark recognized fear immediately. Hell, hadn't he felt the same way less than an hour earlier? "What are you guys doing?" Chad asked, his voice shaking.

Thomas and Connor sat down on either side of him. They wore thick black gloves and scowls on their faces. Mark stood over them, the gun Thomas handed him pointed at Chad.

"What the hell is this all about? I don't get it," Chad said. "Come on guys, I don't like jokes, especially not in the middle of the night."

"No joke, brother," Thomas said. "Seems you upset the boss a bit."

"What? Redding? No. No way." He shook his head emphatically. "I just met with him and we were good. All good."

"You know this is nothing personal, right? We're simply the messengers," Connor said.

"Doing a job," Thomas added. "Right, Mark?"

Mark nodded and tried to keep his cool. "Right."

Chad looked at Mark pleadingly. "You're really with these clowns?" Chad's voice was rising. "Do you fucks know who my uncle is?"

"Yeah man, we know, but that won't help you. In fact, here's the thing…okay, first get the fuck off the couch and move your ass up the stairs into your room."

"No." Tears welled in Chad's eyes. "No man. Fuck you!" He struggled as Connor took one side of him and Thomas the other.

"Alright, if you don't do what we need you to do, a few things will happen. None of them pretty. We will torture you. Or we can make this painless and easy. You're going to die, no matter what." Connor said. The blood drained from Chad's face. "As I was saying, we can do it your way, which will be painful and ugly and there will be repercussions. For instance, the entire world will soon learn Chad Wentworth, nephew of the senator, was a criminal and a racist. How do you think that will go over? I think it would certainly break your mother's heart at the very least." Connor looked at Thomas who nodded in agreement. Mark didn't move.

"That's bullshit. Redding and all of you need my uncle to move forward. You know that. You do. Don't do this!"

"I don't know anything other than what I have been told to do. I also know no matter what, I would want to take the easy way out. Oh and I might add we know your parents' address, your sister's address, and the address of that girl you been banging up on Mullholland. Nice piece of ass. I would hate to see something so pretty and sweet wind up ugly and dead. In fact, I got a guy waiting there right now for, uh, what's her name? Melissa, Maryanne?"

"Marissa," Thomas chimed in. "Be a shame if you didn't do your part and she had to suffer for it."

"Real shame," Connor added.

"You're sick," Chad sucked back a sob.

"I've been told that," Thomas said, laughing. Then he grew serious. "But apparently, I understand what needs to be done to make this work—make this country—a better place. Make this world a better place. But you must have made a bad decision. I don't know what happened and I don't really care. As I said, this is not personal. Up the stairs. Oh, and where's your cell phone?"

Chad pointed to the kitchen. Connor walked over and picked it up off the counter. He stepped in front of Chad. Mark put the gun into Chad's back as he had been ordered to. Thomas came up behind them as Chad staggered up the stairs. They reached his bedroom and went in.

Thomas looked around and whistled, "Nice digs, Chad." Then he glanced back to Connor. "Hand the man his phone." Connor did. "Now send your soon-to-be-president uncle— who will be oh so sad and earn sympathy points—a text message telling him you love him and know he will be a great president."

Chad did, his fingers shaking. Thomas leaned over him as he typed. "Good. Press send. Okay. Clock's ticking. Mark…first wait." Thomas and Connor pulled out their own guns and pointed them toward Chad. "You're screwed no matter what, buddy. If you try and shoot any of us, you're still dead and, like I said, anyone you love or have ever loved, will be too. Mark…"

Mark held the gun to Chad's head. It was all he could do not to puke on himself. He took Chad's hand and fingers and wrapped them around the gun.

"Any last words?" Connor asked.

Tears streamed down Chad's face. "Yes. Tell Redding he will never get away with this. Tell him I will see him in hell."

Thomas and Connor laughed and nodded at Mark who pulled back Chad's finger on the trigger. There was a soft thwump from the gun. Chad's body jerked back and then fell forward. Mark looked away.

Thomas said, "Boys let's pack up. We got one more tonight."

Mark stared at the floor in front of him, not wanting to see the blood and brains splattered across Chad's bed and wall. He did as he was told. He knew one thing for sure, he'd do whatever they wanted if it meant he never had to end up like Chad.

CHAPTER THIRTY-NINE

It was almost eight a.m. and Gem was running late. She poured her fourth cup of coffee and stared blearily into the steaming cup. She'd been up half the night, developing photos. Granted, they didn't really show her a whole lot more than what she'd seen while taking them—rich, white guys driving nice cars and heading inside a fancy house. What she did see more clearly were the men's faces —none she recognized off the bat, but her gut told her it wouldn't be too hard to put names to those faces.

Gem set her mug in the sink and headed back up the stairs to her room to get her shoes on. The doorbell rang. Great. She chose to ignore it, figuring it was either a Jehovah's Witness, or worse—her neighbor in a bind with the kid and in need of a sitter. No time today. The doorbell rang again, and then someone pounded at the door. What the…?

She turned around and trotted back down the stairs. "Okay, okay," She peered through the peek hole. "Oh my God," she muttered. Gem opened the door, knowing the man on the other side was just as shocked to see her, as she was to see him. "Pazzini?!"

"Georgia Michaels." He shook his head in disbelief.

"Well, yeah, the last time I checked that was still my name." She smiled. "To what do I owe this visit?"

"Your neighbor—caddy corner…"

"Yeah?" She already wasn't liking where this was going.

"It appears he took his life last evening."

"What?! Oh my God. Chad, Chad... Shit. I don't even know his last name. I don't believe it!"

"Last name was Wentworth and, um, he came from a pretty high profile family."

She nodded. She didn't let on she knew he was a Wentworth in some fashion. "I guess that's why they brought you in? I mean, they don't usually bring in the detectives for a suicide, do they?"

"No. But there may have been some funny business."

Her ears perked up. Now that she could buy. "What do you mean?"

"Your neighbors, next door. The wife was up in the middle of the night. I guess their kid was sick or something. Anyway, she claims at about two a.m. she looked out the window and saw three big guys walking quickly up the walkway toward the parking lot, their heads down, dressed in black."

"Did she call the police?"

"No. She says the kid started crying and she went to take care of him."

"Who found the body?"

"A cleaning lady. Guess she comes a couple times a week and he was in his room."

"Wow."

"Did you see anything? I know most people aren't awake in the middle of the night, but you're a reporter..."

Gem laughed, "And what? Reporters don't need sleep? Or do you think we spend our nights spying on our neighbors in the hopes of grabbing a big story?"

Of course that wasn't far from the truth at all. She'd been awake, but hadn't heard or seen anything. She'd been too focused on the surveillance pictures. Gem stood in front of Pazzini. He was a good cop. A decent guy from what she knew. Working the homicide beat as a journalist, one typically got to know these guys pretty well and although Pazzini could be rough around the edges, he always allowed her to do her job and they shared a mutual respect for one another.

"Truth is, I wasn't awake, so no, I didn't see anything." That part was true, at least. However, Gem knew she was onto something big, and letting Pazzini in on it too soon could ruin everything. First, she needed real proof. She needed that story.

"Okay." He nodded. "Did you know the guy?"

"No." She shook her head. "I didn't really know him. He was quiet, kept to himself, you know...one of those neighbors who you could live next to for years and maybe say hello a few times. It's L.A."

"Okay. This thing is going to get huge soon. Once the press…" he winked at her, "…gets wind of this and discovers who he is related to, this condo complex is going to be a nightmare. You might want to get on it before everyone else does."

"Get on it?"

"The story."

"Ah. You want to let me in on who he was related to?" Gem was kicking herself for not being up front with him. Here the guy was cool enough to hand her a story before anyone else was getting it, and she was keeping secrets that could affect his investigation.

"Wentworth. As in senator and, according to the rumors, planning to run for President."

"No shit?"

"The kid was his nephew."

"Crazy. Can I ask how he did it?"

"Shot himself. In the head."

She shook her head. "My God. Why? Did he leave any note?"

"No note. But he sent his Uncle a text right before he did it saying he loved him."

"That's it?"

"That's it."

Gem let out a low whistle. She had a feeling her story had just gotten much bigger.

CHAPTER FORTY

What a morning. After Tony wrapped up the Wentworth situation, he decided to try and track down Jake Hamilton's ex-wife again. Hamilton's funeral was that afternoon, so he was hopeful she was back in town to escort their daughter to the service.

Susan Hamilton had moved out of the residence she'd lived at with the doctor. Oddly, at least to Tony, she'd agreed to allow Dr. Hamilton to have custody of their daughter. It was pretty unusual for the mother to voluntarily give full custody of her child to her ex-spouse.

He knocked on the double wooden front doors of Susan Hamilton's secluded beach house overlooking Malibu. An attractive, tall, blonde woman answered the door. "Yes? May I help you?" She was dressed in a tight fitting black dress.

"Susan Hamilton?"

"Yes."

He introduced himself. "I just want to ask you a few questions about Dr. Hamilton."

"I don't really have time, Detective. I'm taking our daughter to the services soon."

"I understand. This won't take long."

She sighed and opened the door. "We can sit in here." She walked into a family room and sat down on a small love seat. The back of the room was lined with floor-to-ceiling windows, giving an impressive view of the Pacific. "What can I do for you?"

"You and Dr. Hamilton had a pretty rough divorce."

She crossed her legs. "I don't know about that."

"You took him to the cleaners," Tony said.

She raised her eyebrows.

"Why did you divorce?"

"Irreconcilable differences," she said.

"No cheating? On either side?"

"No."

"Then why make it so ugly?" he asked. "You share a daughter together."

"Listen, Detective, if you are here to ask me if I killed my ex-husband, I did not. I was in Monte Carlo when he died."

"Yes. However, given your bitter divorce, I can't help but wonder if you'd simply had enough of him and decided to have him removed from your life. Permanently."

Her eyes widened. "That is preposterous."

"Is it?"

"I think our little talk is over." She rose quickly from the small sofa. Tony didn't move.

"One more question. Why was your daughter staying with friends when your ex was killed, and why did he have full custody of Bethany?"

"Because my mother can't stand me."

Tony turned around and saw a pretty, but very thin, teenage girl walk into the room.

"Bethany!" Susan Hamilton said.

"It's true. I don't care. When all this is over, I plan to have myself emancipated from you. You've never been a mother to me. I loved my dad and he's gone now. Maybe you did have him killed, I wouldn't be surprised.

"That is enough, young lady!" Susan turned sharply towards Tony. "It's time for you to go, Detective."

He ignored her and looked at Bethany. "Do you think it's possible? That your mother hired someone to kill your dad?"

"I don't know. She didn't love him. I don't think she's capable of loving anyone. She's a gold digger and even though my dad was a doctor, he didn't make enough to keep her happy."

Tony smiled. He liked this kid. She was smart.

"Get out! Get out of here, Detective. I will call my attorney. I did not kill Jake, nor did I have him killed. My daughter is distraught about her father's death."

Bethany shot her mother a cold look and turned back to Pazzini. "To answer your question about why I was with friends when he was killed, it was because he had some important cases he was working on that were keeping him at the hospital later than usual. He didn't want me to be alone in the house at night. It was only supposed to be for a few days." Tears welled in her eyes and she wiped her face.

Tony nodded. "I am sorry for your loss, Bethany."

"Thank you."

"I'm calling my lawyer!" Her mother shouted.

"Go ahead. You may need one."

Tony walked out of Susan Hamilton's home knowing the woman was hiding something.

CHAPTER FORTY-ONE

Gem wasn't buying that Chad had offed himself.

She had a friend who worked 9-1-1 dispatch. On the chance she had been working last night, Gem gave her a call.

"Hello," Linda answered her phone on the second ring. Her voice sounded gravelly and tired.

"Hi Linda. Did I wake you?" Gem asked.

"No. I just got in. I worked dispatch last night and then had some errands to run when I got off work. I'm going to bed after I eat, so if you're calling for a coffee break, I can't do it."

Gem smiled. "No. I actually wanted to ask you about a call that might have come in while you were on this morning at about seven."

"Crazy night last night. What call?"

"Would have been a suicide."

"Had a few of those last night. Full moon."

"This would have been near my place in Studio City. Actually in the same complex—caddy corner to me."

"I knew I recognized the address! I took that call. Housekeeper found him. Why are you asking?" Linda asked.

"He was my neighbor. He's also a pretty high profile guy as far as his connections go."

Linda paused on the other end of the phone. "Wait a minute, he's a Wentworth as in Senator?"

"Yes."

"You're doing a story, aren't you?" She let out a low whistle.

Gem laughed. "You know me well."

"Two peas in a pod. That's why we're friends. Hey, how are the boys?"

"Good. Teenagers. They want to come home, of course." Gem met Linda in Lamaze class while pregnant with Austen. They'd become fast friends, raised kids together, and even divorced around the same time.

"Mine too. So, this story sounds like it could be a juicy one, huh?"

"Could be," Gem replied.

"I might have another for you, in case you haven't already heard."

"Oh yeah? What's that?"

"Craig Johnson.

"Who?"

"The really rich guy who made all his cash in textiles and then in software? The one who has been quoted off and on for saying politically incorrect things?"

"Yeah?" Gem's ears perked up. "He's a real asshole. Gay basher and misogynist."

"I think he was also a racist pig."

"Was?"

"Yes. Chad Wentworth isn't the only one who took the easy way out last night," Linda said.

"Oh my God. Johnson, too?" Gem replied.

"Yes."

"Whoa. That *will* be a big story. Wonder which one will be bigger?"

"You tell me, reporter lady. Coffee next week?" Linda asked.

"You got it. I'll call you."

Gem hung up the phone and raced back to her office, lunch half eaten. If she didn't know better, there was definitely a scandal brewing. Wentworth. Johnson. Both racists. Both with money and connections. If Gem could find the common denominator linking the two of them together, a big story was only the beginning.

Huge story.

Big time.

CHAPTER FORTY-TWO

Jake's funeral was everything Kelly expected it to be: a depressing and horrible experience, reminding her of her mother's service when she was only seven.

She shifted her dark sunglasses on the bridge of her nose. Eric stood on one side of her, Dr. Jessop on the other. She'd asked Simmons to stand away from the mourners a bit, as she didn't want anyone to know she was being shadowed by the police.

Kelly couldn't help glance at Jake's daughter who stood in the front row with her mother. From Kelly's vantage point, there wasn't a lot of love lost between mother and daughter. Tears streamed down the girl's delicate, pale face and her mother didn't put an arm around her, didn't grab the girl's hand—nothing. Susan Hamilton's face was stone cold behind her oversized sunglasses. It made Kelly wonder if the ex-Mrs. Hamilton killed Jake.

As the priest gave a quick eulogy, Kelly brushed away tears. Eric squeezed her hand. He leaned over and whispered, "No wonder Jake divorced her."

Kelly nodded.

Once the service was finished and the mourners began dispersing, Kelly found herself drawn to Jake's daughter. Without giving it much thought, she headed over to her. The teenager had long, blonde hair and intense blue eyes.

"Bethany?"

"Yes?" the girl replied, her voice barely audible.

"My name is Kelly Morales. I was a colleague and friend of your dad's." Bethany stared at her. "He was a wonderful man and he loved you dearly. I am so sorry for what happened. I know he will always be looking out for you."

"Thank you." Bethany tried to muster a smile, but instead the tears pooled in her eyes again. Kelly wondered if she shouldn't have said anything to her.

"Excuse me, but we really need to be going," Mrs. Hamilton interrupted. She looked at Kelly with obvious distaste and distrust.

Kelly watched them leave and had the nagging feeling Mrs. Hamilton was not totally on the up-and-up. But she pushed it out of her mind because right now, all she really wanted to do was mourn her friend—a good man who had tragically lost his life all too soon.

She walked back to the gravesite and picked up one of the white roses placed in a bucket of water. She took the rose and set it gently on Jake's coffin. "I promise you whoever did this will pay for it," she whispered.

She stood and turned around, nearly bumping into the man behind her. "Oh, excuse me," she said.

"No problem," he replied.

Kelly walked off toward Simmons who stood leaning against an old oak. There was something weird about the guy she'd run into. She knew she'd seen him before, but couldn't place exactly where. She figured it had to be at the hospital. She turned around, feeling his eyes on her back. There he was. He smiled at her and then turned away and placed a rose on the casket. Unsettling. She was being paranoid. That was all. It was the day, the turmoil, the sadness—all of it. And the fact that whoever had murdered her friend was still out there.

CHAPTER FORTY-THREE

Mark was flying high. Sure, last night had been rough. Killing Chad had not been easy. Yeah, he hadn't really pulled the trigger and had watched the poor SOB do it to himself. But that was all okay, because he was moving up the ranks now.

After killing Chad, he, Connor, and Thomas had gone to some guy's yacht. His last name was Johnson and all Mark learned was he was one of the power players. They played out the same basic scenario as with Chad only this time, they forced their victim to hang himself. It was brutal and ugly and yet in some deviant way, Mark realized he'd enjoyed every second of it.

Smug and feeling pretty damn good, he'd taken a chance and had gone to Hamilton's funeral where he'd seen his lady love. Oh so sad.

Leaving the service, he got a call on his cell from Thomas. "Hey brother, looks like it really is your lucky day. You have a meeting to go to. Here is the address. Be there in an hour. Give the guard your name and you can go on in."

An hour later, Mark found himself in the foyer of an amazing estate waiting for whoever he was supposed to be waiting for.

Nerves knotted his stomach.

After a few minutes a good-looking guy came through a set of double doors to the left. He was tall, blonde, tan, fiftiesh, what could only be called distinguished. Mark stood. He was happy he had on his only suit. The man reached out his hand. "Mark Pritchett. Nice to meet you. I am Peter Redding."

Mark was speechless. He had hoped. He had thought maybe he would be meet Redding. Not many people knew who he was. But Mark knew. He'd been close enough to Chad to know. He sputtered, "Nice to meet you, sir."

"Follow me, Mark." Mark did and Redding offered him a drink, which he eagerly accepted.

Now *this* was more like it. This is exactly what he had been waiting and hoping for.

"I understand you did a good job aiding a couple of other soldiers last night."

"Thank you, sir."

Redding nodded. "I know it was not an easy task. Many times in the line of duty we will have to do things that are, simply put, not easy. But you did it, and you did well. I heard from Chad you had been doing a good job for us. What with surveillance on the doctors and reporting in about Dr. Hamilton." Redding took a sip of his drink and tskd, tskd. "Weak and dumb on his part. Which leads me to Dr. Morales. Kelly Morales. I know you had been reporting to Chad on her comings and goings and, well, with his unfortunate demise, we need to replace him. You will now report directly to me."

"Yes, sir. Of course." Mark took a deep gulp of his drink.

"Now that we have put the old business to bed, what can you tell me about the good doctor?" Redding pulled a photo of Dr. Morales out of his desk. "Pretty thing. Too bad she's a Latina. Isn't that the politically correct term?" He laughed. "Tell me about her. What does she know?"

Mark tried to keep himself from showing any nerves. "You know, sir, there's not much to tell. I mean, she doesn't know anything, really. It's more what she suspects. Or what I think she might suspect."

"Go on."

"I'm only theorizing." He was going to do his best to impress this man. "However, the cops are now shadowing her every move. She seems to be watching her back a lot. She's asked questions and caused some anxiety. You obviously heard the conversation Hamilton had with her, the one that got him iced. I think she's smart and afraid."

Redding leaned back in his leather chair.

"You know what I think?"

"Sir?"

"I think it's time for me to meet Dr. Morales." He handed Mark a card. "Bring her to me."

"You don't want her dead? Wouldn't that be easier?" Mark asked.

"Not necessarily. In spite of your recent…work…I don't care much for murder. It attracts the police. Dr. Hamilton's situation needed to be handled quickly, so the steps we took with him were unfortunate but also necessary. And, the other deaths, well, those were a necessity. But this Dr. Morales may actually be useful to us. Call this number when you have her and I will give you instructions. But don't hurt her." He shook his head.

"I, uh, wow, sir. I don't know if it's possible. She's got security twenty-four-seven."

Redding sighed heavily. "Mark, you witnessed first-hand what happens to people who can't get jobs done correctly. Correct?"

"I did, sir."

"Good. Then you will figure out how to bring Dr. Morales to me." He smiled. "Quickly. And I suggest you not screw it up."

"No, sir."

"Good. Oh and you no longer work at the hospital. You have just been promoted."

"Thank you, sir."

Redding stood and walked around his desk. He put his arm around Mark. "You're welcome. Now go get our girl."

CHAPTER FORTY-FOUR

Ryan wished he hadn't told his wife to ditch her cell phone. Yes it had been for her safety but now he had no way of knowing where she was and if she and the girls were safe. He knew his wife well. Jeanine did not always like being told what to do and she had now had some real time to think about things and what they might be up against. What if she hadn't listened to him and gone straight to their cabin to wait for him? He'd wanted to get his family out of the country first. Give them a head start. Now, Ryan realized what a selfish bastard he truly was. Sending his wife and kids on this mission had been cowardly. But he hadn't known any other way at the time. In fact, he still didn't. If he had abruptly left Frauen, Redding and his freaks would have definitely gone after his family. At least this way, they had a chance.

Ryan knew his wife was resourceful. She was also brave, funny, and sweet. As he tried to close his eyes and sleep, he could hear the jarring street sounds from below. His thoughts went back to Georgia Michaels and the chance encounter he'd had with her three years earlier.

He'd liked Georgia. When The Brotherhood employed him, after scaring him to death and blackmailing him, they decided to wine and dine him.

They flew him from New Jersey to Los Angeles where he was introduced to Chad Wentworth. The last name hadn't meant much to him then. He certainly hadn't connected Chad with the senator at the time. Wentworth took him to a fancy restaurant, offered to buy him expensive hookers, which he'd had zero interest in, and handed him oodles of cash. He knew all of it came with a price and he was being watched—always.

He met Ms. Michaels briefly. Chad asked his driver to swing by his condo. He'd forgotten something—something that turned out to be a Rolex for Ryan.

While Chad was inside, Ryan rolled down the limo window, badly in need of air. A petite blonde woman approached the car. "Hey, can you ask the driver to move? I need to get my car out and you're in the way."

"Sure. No problem," Ryan replied. The woman stuck her head in the window. "Sorry. I'm a reporter for the L.A. Times. Just thought I'd see if there was someone important or famous in the car. It's my job." She winked. "So?"

"So what?" Ryan asked.

"You important or famous?"

"Nope. Just a chemist."

"Ah. Right." She stuck her hand through the window. "Georgia Michaels. Gem for short. "A chemist, huh? Cool. What's your name?"

"Dr. Horner. Ryan."

"You work on anything interesting, Ryan? Like, I don't know, genetics, cures for cancer? Something I could write a good story about? I am always looking for a decent scoop."

Of course he couldn't tell her the truth. "No. I don't do anything very interesting at all."

"Well, if you ever have something to share, here's my card. Call me or shoot me an e-mail. I never forget a name or a face. I'm into details. Have a good evening!" She handed him her card, flashed him a smile, and waved good-bye.

After that brief meeting, Ryan decided to see what types of stories she typically wrote. He was shocked to see she'd been the lead reporter on The Petersen murders for *The Times*. Eventually he decided to reach out to her. For some reason, he felt if anyone could help, it would be Georgia Michaels.

As he closed his eyes, he prayed Jeanine had already spoken to the journalist and she'd begun to put two and two together. Maybe if he made it to the States, the story would be out and Peter Redding would be in jail, along with his cronies. Maybe.

CHAPTER FORTY-FIVE

"Let me get this straight," Melanie said. She took a sip of the Chardonnay she'd just poured for herself and Jeanine. She read Ryan's note again and looked up at her old friend. The twins were playing in the family room, while the women sat in the kitchen drinking wine. Melanie's nine-month-old son was upstairs, sleeping. "You two were at this party and Ryan was getting bombed, or so you thought…"

Jeanine nodded.

"Then he handed this to you?"

"No, he took me outside and handed it to me."

"Holy shit." Melanie drank some more wine.

"Yeah."

"Okay, honey, either your husband has gone completely bonkers, which I have not ruled out, and neither should you…" She pointed a manicured finger at her, "Or something horrible has happened to him, or could happen to the family. That's why he told you to leave."

"Yes," Jeanine replied softly and brought the wine glass up to her lips. She could see her friend was trying to register all of this, just as she had been doing for the past two days. "I know it sounds crazy. I do. That's why I came here. After leaving Germany, going to Paris, cutting the girls' hair, my hair, doing all of this crazy stuff, I started thinking maybe Ryan has been losing it." She shrugged.

"I'd say."

"But, you should have seen his eyes, Melanie. He was so scared and, I don't know, but I really believed him."

"What about this journalist, Gem Michaels? Do you know how he knows her or what the story is there?"

"No. Just that I was supposed to get a hold of her. I called the paper and left her a message."

"What did you say?"

"That I was married to Ryan Horner and it was urgent I speak with her. I left her my cell number, but as I told you, Ryan said I was supposed to get rid of the cell. I don't know. I have no idea what to think. I mean, how am I supposed to communicate with anyone, if I get rid of the cell phone? Say we are in some kind of trouble, wouldn't that have all been left behind when I left Europe? I started thinking maybe that's why he sent me so far away."

"I don't know. I think you should call the police," Melanie said.

"And tell them what? My husband has sent me on a wild goose chase from Germany to New Jersey, and I am supposed to contact some journalist in LA., and tell her to look into my husband's company that he works for?"

Melanie raised her eyebrows. "You have a point. Look, maybe all you need is a good dinner, some more wine, and sleep. In the morning, try and give Ryan a call and demand to know what in the hell is going on."

Jeanine sighed. Maybe Melanie was right. The further away she got from Ryan and Germany, the less and less any of this made sense.

"Robert won't be home until late tonight. He's taking some clients out for dinner. Maybe we should go out ourselves."

"Oh, I don't know. What about the kids?"

Melanie waved a hand. "Bring them. Oliver is a good baby and he should be up soon."

"I don't know if I can say the same for the twins."

"Don't worry about it. We can go over to our tennis club. They have decent food and a play area."

"Really?"

"Yes. Now come on. Something tells me you need to do something to feel normal."

Jeanine agreed.

Two hours later, the friends were full, a little buzzed, and Jeanine was pretty convinced her husband had gone off his rocker, which bothered her even more than the idea that they were in some kind of trouble.

"Hey, would you drive home? I think I had too much of that sangria," Melanie said.

"Sure." Jeanine had noticed her friend drinking more glasses than normal. Likely it had to do with the bizarre story.

As they got closer to the house, the twins started whining about not getting dessert. "Girls, that's enough," Jeanine said.

"Oh, hon, let's take them to Cold Stone, it's only a few blocks from my place. I don't ever get to see you guys, let me spoil them. I have some coupons on the fridge. Swing by the house and I'll grab them."

"Please, Mommy," Chloe called from the back seat.

"Sure. Yes. Let's go have ice cream!"

A few minutes later Jeanine pulled up in front of Melanie's house. "I'll be right back." Jeanine watched her go inside the house and waited a few minutes. Melanie had to have gone to the restroom. It was taking her too long. She caught a glimpse of something in her rear view mirror—a man was walking toward the car with a strong sense of purpose, one of his hands in his jacket pocket. She glanced back to the house and knew immediately she was in trouble. Melanie opened the front door and collapsed, blood staining the front of her blouse. Another man ran out of the house and towards the car.

Jeanine punched it, tires squealing, as gun fire sprayed the side and back of the vehicle.

CHAPTER FORTY-SIX

Kelly napped after the funeral. She was wiped out. When she woke, the first thing to hit her was the amazing smell of garlic bread and something else. She glanced at the clock on her nightstand. It was already past six o'clock. What in the world? Then it donned on her Tony must have taken over the patrol for the night, and was making dinner. She couldn't help but smile. Then felt silly for doing so. She rolled out of bed and looked at herself in the dresser mirror. The stress wasn't wearing well. When this was all over, she was going to load her horse into the trailer, make the long drive home, and spend two weeks in the Kentucky blue grass —get back to her roots. She had some vacation time coming. Then a horrid thought hit her, what if this was never over? What if Jake's killer was never brought to justice and young women kept coming into ER with complications and dying?

She shook off the thought and pulled her hair back into a pony-tail. Mascara pooled under her eyes from tears and fatigue. She wiped her face with a damp cloth. Stevie T stretched out on the bed and let out a soft meow—obviously annoyed his human-sized heating pad had dared leave the bed. She reached across the sheets, scratched Stevie under the chin, and called the NICU to check on her patients, especially Baby S. Everything was status quo according to the charge nurse.

Walking down the hallway, she spotted Tony in the kitchen. He had his back to her and was standing over the stove, stirring a pot full of something. "That smells wonderful," she said.

He turned around, spoon in hand, and smiled. "This is one of my mother's specialties—Puttanesca sauce."

"Yum. But why did you do this?"

"I figured you probably had a hell of a day and a nice meal would do you some good." He handed her a glass of red wine.

She raised her brows. "Is this part of the patrol job? Or maybe I'm getting the upgraded version?"

He laughed. "Technically it's my night off."

"Oh. What gives?" Her stomach sunk.

"I thought we might be able to talk some more."

"And...?"

"Well, I...I'm working this case and you are a part of my case, and...oh god damn, I was just trying to do something nice."

She looked down. "I'm sorry. I appreciate it. Can we start over?"

"Sure."

She held up her glass. "To starting over."

He clinked glasses with her and they each took a sip.

Kelly sat down at the kitchen counter and drank her wine. "I'm sorry if I seemed ungrateful. I guess I'm not used to anyone making me dinner, and considering the circumstances, I definitely didn't expect you to."

"I'm sure you didn't, but just because I'm a cop doesn't mean I don't have a heart. I wanted to do this." He took a spoon and skimmed the top of the sauce. Holding his hand underneath, he carefully reached it across the counter and offered her a taste.

Kelly took a bite, feeling awkward at the intimacy of the moment, but the earthy, tangy taste of the sauce instantly removed the tension. "Oh my goodness, that is delicious!"

He smiled and nodded. "I know."

His smile was pretty damn delicious, too.

As he continued to fix dinner and Stevie T found Kelly's lap, their conversation turned toward family. They were both trying to avoid discussing murder, sick babies, or why Tony was there in the first place.

"Tell me about your little boy," she said.

"Ah well, he's a great kid. He really is."

"I'm sure."

"It hasn't been easy though. Raising him. Not because he's a bad kid, obviously." He laughed.

"My parents are getting older and they really help me out a lot. Without having a mom around, it has been kind of hard. We lost her to cancer. The docs did everything possible but she lost the battle after two years. I think the hardest part for me to deal with is knowing he will never really understand how much his mother loved him. I mean, I can tell him, but he'll never know first-hand." He looked at her and she felt herself getting drawn in by his dark, magnetic eyes.

"Don't be so sure about that. Your little boy will know exactly how much his mom loved him."

He glanced at her quizzically. "What do you mean? What makes you so sure?"

"My mom died when I was a little girl. A car accident. Rainy night and, well…" she waved a hand, fighting tears. "Lost control of the car. I was seven. I'm not sure how old your son was when his mom died."

"Only two."

Kelly nodded. "He'll still know. I see babies every day. Very sick kids. And I see their parents. I see very devoted, loving parents, I see some who are disconnected, detached…and then there are those who never show up. The babies who thrive are the ones with family who come every day, who talk to them, and, if they can, hold them. My little strugglers are those babies who have no one outside the medical staff to care for them. Of course, we love them and do what we can to make them feel cared for and wanted, but there is something about having a parent there, and the maternal bond is very strong. I am certain your son was bonded to your wife, who was probably a wonderful person."

"She was. She really was."

"I also know first-hand what it's like being a kid who lost a parent at a young age. Like I said, I was seven. Not as young as Lucas, but still young enough, and when my mom died, I thought I would forget her. It scared me. But you know what?"

"What's that?" He poured her another glass of wine.

"Whenever I am feeling really down or things are not going well—kind of like lately—I feel a warm presence around me. It's hard to explain, but I know it's my mom. I know she's guiding me in some way. And I know she is letting me know things are going to be all right. I am sure Lucas can feel that sometimes." She laughed wryly. "I don't mean to sound hokey."

He sighed and smiled at her, shaking his head. "You know, you're not hokey at all, Doc. In fact, I think you're pretty cool. You surprise me at every turn."

She felt heat rise to her cheeks. Stevie T let out a meow, breaking the tension. She laughed. "Stevie T is rather opinionated."

"I guess so," Tony said.

"Feed him once and you will have a friend for life."

He grimaced. "Yeah, see me and cats...we don't really do well together."

"Oh, you're one of those cat haters?"

He pursed his lips and nodded. "I'm a dog guy. Lost my shepherd last year on a bust."

"Oh wow. I am sorry." The poor man had definitely had his share of troubles.

"Yeah. So, no cats."

"You never know, Stevie T is special. He might grow on you."

"Hmm. Not too sure about that, but I suppose stranger things have happened. So, you know a little bit about me and my family. What's your story?" he asked.

"I grew up in Kentucky. Lexington."

"Horse country."

She smiled. "Yep. Blue grass all the way."

"Horses?"

"Of course. My dad was an assistant trainer for years and then finally saved up enough and is now doing his own training. He might even have one or two horses in his barn this year who could win him some big money."

"Cool. I had a horse when I was a kid," he said.

"You did?"

"Trigger. Old quarter horse. My dad grew up on a ranch here out in Norco. His family moved over to the states when he was a baby. My grandparents always had horses back in Italy, so once they moved to California, they got more horses and Dad grew up around them."

"I think your dad and I have some things in common." She laughed.

"I think so. My mom was never much into them though. She came over for a vacation with her family, met my dad, and never went home. They got married, started a family, and then when I was about eight or so, he bought Trigger for me."

Kelly clutched her heart. "That is so sweet. How romantic. I mean your parents' story."

"It is, but after fifty years of marriage, the two of them fight like cats and dogs."

Kelly laughed. "So the horse. Tell me about Trigger."

"I thought we were talking about you."

"No. No." She waved a hand. "Your story is more interesting."

"Doubt it. But yeah, Trigger. We boarded him at the equestrian center because my folks didn't own any property to speak of. I rode for a couple years until my sister took him over. We had him until he colicked and died when he was twenty-eight."

"I feel fortunate to still have a horse. A mare. Her name is Sydney but I call her Syd. I board her over at the L.A. Equestrian Center."

"Maybe one day you could take me out there."

Once he said it, they both blushed and took a sip from their wine glasses. He immediately turned back to the stove. "Oh. Looks like it's ready."

She rubbed her hands together. "Let me get the plates." Kelly stood and walked around the counter. She grabbed a couple of plates from the cupboard. He took them from her and scooped up the pasta, handing her a piece of bread.

"Want to eat in front of the TV?" she asked, figuring maybe it would ease back whatever was going on between them. At that moment, sitting at her dining room table eating a meal he had prepared for her seemed a bit too date-like. Maybe TV would diffuse any chemistry between them.

"Sure. Oh, I brought backgammon with me. Maybe we could eat at the table and then play a game?"

"Oh. Yeah. I guess that would be a bit more, um…yes. Let's eat at the kitchen table."

Over dinner and without the television on, Kelly told Tony about her life as a kid breezing race horses. Why she had chosen to go to medical school and how she'd wound up in L.A. The talk was easy and the food amazing.

"I have to ask," he said while finishing up the dinner.

"What's that?"

"Your name? Kelly. It's, well, it's…"

"Not exactly Latina?" she said, reading his mind.

"No."

"My mother loved Grace Kelly. She named me Kelly Grace."

"That's very..."

"Silly."

"No. It's, it's, it's cool. Sweet. It makes sense. You don't look like Grace Kelly but you certainly are as beautiful. Oh wow. I'm sorry. Out of line."

"I'm not complaining, Detective." She smiled and the heat she had been feeling between them all evening intensified. "Want some dessert?"

"Love some," he replied.

As she cleaned dishes, he scooped them some ice cream. She turned to get some spoons and bumped directly into him. "Sorry." He held her gaze for several seconds. Neither of them moved.

He broke the silence. "What's going on here? Between us?"

"I don't know," she whispered.

He took the spoons from her hands. "I should leave. Maybe call in another officer."

She didn't answer.

"Forget it." He kissed her. Soft and slow at first. It quickly turned intense and passionate. Before either of them knew it, they didn't care what was going on between them. What they did know is it felt amazing. As they made their way to her bedroom, they forgot why he was there, and how they had met.

CHAPTER FORTY-SEVEN

They must have found her through the cell phone. But god dammit, who were they? Jeanine tried to keep the tears from coming again. Last night, she'd been stunned by what happened. It had been just after eight when they had driven back to Melanie's and her poor friend had been brutally murdered.

Jeanine knew they were all in serious trouble. She didn't know who to turn to or trust, and she definitely didn't trust herself at the moment.

She'd taken the kids back into Manhattan and ditched the car near Grand Central where she bought train tickets using cash she had found the purse her friend left on the front seat when she'd gone back into the house. They'd boarded a train to Port Jervis, a city bordering New Jersey and Pennsylvania, and it happened to be the last stop on the commuter line. She rented them a room for the night at a Days Inn and tried to plan her next move.

But all she could think about was Melanie? *Oh God.* They'd killed her. Jeanine was sure of that. Those men had killed her best friend. Jeanine had tried to shake the image from her mind —Melanie stumbling out the door, covered in blood.

The kids had all slept through the night and now they were awake and wanting to know what they were doing. "Mommy, why are we here?" Chloe tugged on her pant leg.

"Remember our train ride? Now we are going on another adventure."

"I don't want to," Taylor whined.

Jeanine got on her knees and forced a smile for the girls. Baby Oliver was on the floor lying on the blanket Jeanine had laid down for him. He had his feet and hands in the air and was watching them with curiosity. Thank God he was a mellow baby. "I know you're tired of the adventure, girls, but when we are done, Mommy is going to buy you something wonderful."

Chloe's jaw dropped. "Barbie Dream House?"

Taylor clapped her hands.

"Yes! Barbie Dream House it is. So, we are going to be really good today, right? And we are going to go get on a bus and go to Auntie Camille's cabin."

"We are?'"

"Yep."

"Is Oliver's mommy going?" Chloe asked.

"No sweetie." Jeanine fought back the tears. "She needs us to watch him for a few days and take good care of him."

"Okay. He is a good baby," Taylor added.

"He is." Jeanine laughed. "Now let's get ready to go."

"Hey, Mommy?" Chloe asked. "Will Daddy be at the cabin?"

Again, she had to fight tears. "I hope so, baby. I hope so."
She pulled both of her daughters in close and hugged them tightly,
tears sliding down her face.

CHAPTER FORTY-EIGHT

Stevie T stared at Kelly with disgust. He was lying on her chest when she opened her eyes. The cat meowed discontentedly as she inhaled the warm, pungent scent of fresh coffee. Last night came rushing back. What had she been thinking, sleeping with the detective! Stevie T was obviously wondering the same thing. Kelly did not sleep around. Ever. So what in the hell happened?!

As she stretched and sat up, she heard Tony's voice coming from the kitchen. She started down the hall and stopped as she heard him say, "She has no idea. I've got this covered. You have nothing to worry about, boss. I am telling you, she's clueless. I have it all taken care of." He paused. "Yes. Lunch time. I will meet you. It's all good. But we have to be quick."

Kelly thought the conversation was odd. What did he have to take care of and who was the *she* he kept referring to? Well, one night with him certainly didn't give her the right to start asking him questions about work. He'd obviously been speaking with his boss. But it still made her uneasy. Until she reminded herself Tony had a life outside of whatever was going on between them.

She rounded the corner into the kitchen. "Oh, hey," he said. "I made some coffee."

"Thank you."

As he was pouring her a cup, the doorbell rang. "Simmons."

"What time is it?"

"Almost seven. He's a few minutes early," he said. "Sorry. I was hoping we could spend some time together, but you were sleeping, and I know you must be tired."

"Yes, I am," she said.

The doorbell rang again. "I better get that," he said.

"And I need to get ready for work."

"Let's…um, well, I will call you, okay?" Tony said as he walked to the front door.

"Sure. Absolutely." She ran her hands through her hair. God this was awkward. Before she said something stupid, she turned and walked to the shower, hoping he really would call. She turned the shower water to cold and berated herself for sounding like a school girl and also acting like a woman who falls in bed with every Tom, Dick, and Harry. How stupid had she been? But she didn't think she could help it. Detective Tony Pazzini had gotten under her skin.

CHAPTER FORTY-NINE

Tony stared at the report on his screen. He was not happy. Apparently Gem Michaels' fingerprints were found on the sliding glass door at Chad Wentworth's place. On top of that, his crew had found wire and phone taps—all of it with Michaels' prints on them. Damn her. She'd denied having any direct contact with the man. He sighed. All he'd wanted to do was write this thing off for what it appeared to be—a straightforward suicide. But clearly there was more to Wentworth's death than that. Gem had not been careful. The funny thing was, her prints were in the database for perfectly legit reasons: she'd been fingerprinted in order to act as a driver/chaperone for her sons' private school.

Dammit. He really did not want to deal with this today. It seemed from the moment he walked into the station it had been one thing after another. He hadn't even had a chance to check on Luke—or call Kelly. Speaking of which, he had definitely thought about her. A lot. Last night had been pretty damn incredible and as much as he wanted a repeat, he knew he'd made a mistake. So much for his ethics. He needed to ground himself again. Maybe when this thing was over, he could pursue something with her. Damn! Where had his brain been? The moment had been primal and passionate and if he admitted it, the best sex of his life.

He picked up the phone to call someone else in to cover for him that evening. But then set it back down. What would one more night hurt? No. He could *not* go there. But before he made the call, he needed to deal with Gem Michaels.

He grabbed his keys and headed out to *The L.A. Times*.

Once at the newspaper's offices, he flashed his badge and asked for Gem. A nervous receptionist led him down the narrow hall of a large, cubicle-filled room. No one seemed to notice him... apparently police officers were a common sight around here. The receptionist stopped at the door of a tiny office at the end of the hall. Gem was typing furiously at her keyboard.

"Hey, Michaels. We need to talk."

Gem looked up from her computer and studied him for a second. He was pretty sure he caught a glimpse of "oh shit, caught red-handed," in her eyes. But she covered her emotions swiftly and smiled cordially up at him. "Detective? To what do I owe this pleasure?" She gestured to a chair across from her desk. "Please, have a seat."

He shut the door behind him with a soft push of his heel and sat down across from her. "Chad Wentworth. Your neighbor."

"Yes? I thought we covered everything this morning."

"Me, too. Here's the thing. My boss wants this case sewn up nice and neat. But I have a small problem."

She leaned back in her chair and eyed him. "What's that?"

"Let's start with the fact that you lied to me."

"Excuse me?"

"Earlier you said you'd never been to Chad Wentworth's place. That you'd never been inside his home, or had any conversations with him, other than to say an occasional hello in passing."

She nodded hesitantly.

"So can you explain why your fingerprints were found all over his sliding glass door and also on a bed rail in the loft upstairs? Oh and while you're at it, you might want to let me know why in the hell you were bugging the guy's place. I assume that was you as well. I've met your ex. Decent P.I. by the way. He taught you well."

Gem sighed. She paused a few seconds before responding. "Not well enough obviously. Okay, so yes, I was in the guy's place and I bugged his phone, but I don't think you're going to like my answer as to why I did it. It certainly won't help you close this thing up nice and neat like you hoped."

"I figured. But for your sake, I think you better lay it on me."

"Right. Just so you know, I only kept this from you because I think there's big story here, and I want to be the one to break it without any, you know, interference or complications."

"Obstruction of justice would be a pretty severe complication for you, I imagine."

"Are you threatening me, Detective?"

"Nah. I'm just stating a fact."

"I do have certain rights as a journalist in a free country."

He nodded. "You do. I can arrest you and then you'll have all the freedom in the world not to talk."

"Arrest me for what?" she asked incredulously.

Tony slammed his palms down on her desk. She jumped back, startled. "Look, Gem, don't fuck with me. You said you would tell me what was going on. If you have some kind of hot story here, I will do what I can to make sure you keep on rolling with it. But I think I may have a murder case on my hands now, and I need to know what you know about Chad Wentworth. And as far as coming up with a reason to arrest you, breaking and entering is a crime. One I can prove you committed. And there are a few other charges involving privacy laws and such."

She studied him for a few seconds, then started to tell him what she knew from the moment she received the e-mail from Chemmadderhorn to sneaking in and out of Wentworth's place and hearing his racist rant. She told him there was a chance the grisly Petersen murders had not been orchestrated by the Mexican cartel.

Tony sucked in a deep breath. "Do you still have the e-mail?"

"Yes. I was going through my inbox when you walked in. I'm behind."

"I would say, what with tailing a senator's nephew and all."

She didn't respond but pulled up the e-mail and printed it for him.

He took it. Read it a couple of times and although it didn't prove much, it did make him suspicious Wentworth had been murdered. "How would this guy, or whoever sent you this e-mail, even know who you are or where you live, or who the hell your neighbors are?"

She eyed him knowingly. "I guess it must be someone who knows me."

"Yeah. Or someone who knew Wentworth, and who also might have a connection to you."

"I wouldn't know anyone that guy was connected to. We run in very different circles, my being part-Jewish and all."

"Well, Gem, you are a journalist and Wentworth had powerful connections. He was attending law school, so I am sure he had political aspirations, maybe wanted to follow in his uncle's footsteps. Have you ever written a story about the Wentworth family?"

"God no. I do homicide stuff, Detective. You know that."

He nodded. "I need to find out where this e-mail came from. I'm going to have a tech guy pay you a visit."

"Not here." She sighed. "Please. I mean can't you trace IP addresses just by logging into my e-mail account?" She didn't want Stuart to get upset that the cops were sniffing around. If he'd known the extent she'd gone to in order to get the story, he wouldn't have approved.

"Yeah. We can. Want to give me the password info?"

"I suppose I'll have to."

"Good guess."

"You're not going to arrest me, then?" she asked.

He smiled. "Nah. You didn't kill anyone, and you told me what you know. I think we can keep this conversation between us. I'm a detective. I did some detecting and I learned some things. Now I have work to do. But I will be in touch. I'd also like to make a suggestion."

"Okay. What's that?"

"Lay low, Gem. I don't like the sound of any of this. You're an excellent reporter. You seem like a good lady." He winked. "I wouldn't want you to get hurt."

"Oh Detective, you care!"

He rolled his eyes. "Stay close, Ms. Michaels. I may need to talk with you some more. Don't change your password info until I give you the okay."

"You got it."

Tony left Gem's office with a pit in his stomach. He now had two very strange cases on his hands, and if Kelly was correct in her theory about Lupe Salazar, it was possible he had three.

CHAPTER FIFTY

Kelly had finished her morning rounds, but even her little patients couldn't stop her from thinking about last night. The heat rose to her face again. Things between her and Tony had certainly gotten out of hand. It never should have happened, but damn his touch was amazing and sent her nerves and emotions to a place she had not been in a very long time—if ever.

Tony said he would call some time during the day. So far, he hadn't, and it was already lunch time. He was busy. That was all.

She headed to the parent waiting room where she was sure she'd find Simmons. She felt like leaving the hospital and heading over to her favorite taco shop around the corner. But she needed an escort.

Kelly reached the waiting room and peeked in to see a mother reading a paperback, a father speaking softly on his cell phone, and another older woman, probably a grandmother. But no Simmons. "Excuse me," she said.

The mother and grandmother looked up. "Hi. Sorry to disturb you, but there was another gentleman here, and…uh, he had jeans on…and a plaid shirt."

"Goatee?" the young mom asked.

"Yes." Kelly nodded.

"He had to leave for a few minutes and said if a doctor came for him, to wait because he'd be back shortly."

"Oh. Okay." She frowned, hoping everything was all right.

Damn. She really wanted a carne asada burrito. The food at the hospital left a lot to be desired. She thanked the woman and decided the hell with it. It was broad daylight outside and the hospital was located in a busy area. She doubted she'd need to worry much about crazed lunatics lurking nearby.

Before heading out, though, she checked in with Eric to see if he wanted to go with her.

"No. I brought my lunch today and I have another hour before I take my break," he said.

"We can get some chipotle fries," she said trying to tempt him.

He rubbed his stomach. "You can't run a sleek machine like this on chipotle fries."

"Ah, you back on the workout program?"

"You know it." He winked at her. "Never know who I might need to impress."

Kelly took a quick look at Baby S. who was sleeping peacefully. The withdrawal symptoms she'd had seemed to be dissipating, and there were good indications her internal bleeding had stopped. "She is precious, isn't she?" Kelly said.

"Completely," Eric agreed. "And, I think she is getting stronger.

"She is."

"She's a special baby. Don't get me wrong…all our little guys are special, but I feel really bonded with this little sweetheart. I've been wondering…with her being placed in social services, there might be an opportunity to adopt her. When she's on the other side of all this, of course." He gestured towards the tubes and incubator where she slept.

Kelly peered at her friend. "Wow Eric! I think that would be wonderful! Let me know if there's anything I can do to help." She felt herself choking up, which was so not like her.

"If I get that far, I would just need someone to vouch for me. A referral or something like that. You know, some people might not think my lifestyle is conducive to raising a child. But they've done a few big studies over the last few decades that show kids raised in same-sex households do just as well, if not more so, than many of their heterosexual family peers."

Kelly nodded. "You don't have to prove anything to me, Eric. Especially considering we see ALL sorts of families here. " She looked down at Baby S. and smiled. "Fact is, any child would be lucky to have you for a dad. I only wish there were more people out there like you to provide loving homes to the thousands of children in need."

He leaned his head on her shoulder. "You're a good friend, Kelly."

"Goes both ways. Now, are you sure I can't entice you with a taco or maybe a carnita platter?"

"No. Now stop! If I am ever going to find someone to spend my life with, it will be a lot easier to manage without this damn muffin top hanging over my jeans." He gestured at the virtually non-existent bit of flesh on either side of his narrow hips. Kelly rolled her eyes and laughed.

"Whatever, Eric. I'll see you in an hour, okay?"

As she walked to Cotija's, Kelly couldn't help but look over her shoulder a couple of times. God, she had become so paranoid lately. She planned on calling Tamara when she had some time alone after lunch. The vet might be able to help her make some sense out of the lab findings. In any case, Kelly owed it to her to let her know why she'd asked her to run the labs in the first place.

The early May afternoon was warm, bright, and blue with only a few clouds dotting the sky. The typical Los Angeles smog seemed to have been cleared away by a nice easterly breeze. Perfection.

Kelly sighed in relief as she sat down at the small table after ordering lunch. She decided to call Tamara now. To her dismay, the call went immediately to voice mail. This almost always meant the vet was on some kind of emergency call. Kelly checked her texts and voicemail to see if Tony had tried to contact her. Nothing. She wondered if she should call him. But what if he hadn't called because he felt like last night was a mistake? Kelly didn't have the best luck with men. She always seemed to pick emotionally unavailable guys—or flakes—and had eventually decided she might be better off alone.

Her craving for carne asada satiated and lunch almost over, it was time to head back to work.

As she neared the hospital, she made a rash decision. She would call Tony. If he seemed uninterested, she'd act like she called to check on the evening's schedule. Damn. She felt like a school girl. Just as Kelly pulled her phone from her pocket, someone called her name.

"Dr. Morales? Dr. Morales!"

She turned and watched as a fair-haired man dressed in a polo and jeans jogged up to her. As he came closer, she was certain she'd met him before. "Yes?" She responded, "Do I know you?"

"No. Not yet anyway. I'm, um, well I am a soon-to-be parent."

She gave him an odd look and nodded. "Okay. How can I help you?"

"I'm sorry to bother you, but a friend of mine said you're the best neo-natal doctor on the West Coast. I think you know him, Tony Pazzini. Detective Pazzini?"

Kelly stared at him for a minute, still trying to place his familiar face. "I'm sorry, but how did you know who I was? I was just coming from lunch."

"Oh." He laughed. "Tony described you to me. I was right over there at Starbucks." He pointed across the street. "And I hadn't even planned to meet you today. I was simply hoping to schedule an appointment to discuss the birth of our twins. We, uh, we live up in Big Bear and my wife's doctor recommended she be seen in the city because he's worried about complications."

Kelly started walking again. His story didn't jibe. And Tony had never mentioned this guy. Then again, he hadn't called her all day. "You know, um, Mister…"

"Oh, call me Mark. Mark Pritchett."

"Sure. As I was saying, Mr. Pritchett, Detective Pazzini didn't mention you to me."

"I'm sure he didn't have time. I was lucky to get a hold of him. His son, Lucas, was born over at Cedar's, so I thought maybe he would know a great doctor. I actually spoke with him like an hour ago. He's on some case. It's just a coincidence that I needed to come into L.A. for personal business. I thought I'd call him, see if he thought his doctor would work for us. He said you might be a better bet, because of the pregnancy complications."

The man obviously knew Tony. But something still didn't feel right, plus she needed to get back to the unit.

"Right. Well, I hate to cut this short but I need to get back to the hospital. Your doctor should have placed a call to me. What did you say your doctor's name is?"

"I didn't."

Before Kelly had a chance to think, the man grabbed her by the arm and forcefully twirled her around so her backside pressed up against him. She felt something hard in her back. "Listen, Doc, be a good girl and no one will get hurt. If you scream or do anything stupid, I will shoot you."

She didn't respond and the man pushed her slightly. "See that grey sedan over there? That's where we're walking. Nice and easy. Your friend, Tony, is waiting for you there. He wants to talk to you."

"Oh my God!" she gasped. "Did you hurt him?"

The man laughed. "Of course not. He's working with me."

Kelly's stomach dropped. She didn't believe him. How could that be?

She walked slowly towards the car and watched as someone stepped out of the passenger seat and opened the back door. Before her mind could actually process what was happening, her protective instincts took over. Years ago, in college, Kelly had taken a self-defense class at her father's insistence. She'd never been more grateful for that class than at this very moment. She jabbed the man sharply in the ribs with her left elbow, catching him off guard. He dropped the gun and it skittered across the pavement. She forcefully hit his face with the palm of her hand, causing him to stumble back and bring his hand up protectively to his eyes. In her peripheral vision, she saw the other man in the car start after her. Kelly didn't hesitate. She took off running as fast as she could.

She ran into the street, darting in and out of traffic in an attempt to get away without being run over. Kelly heard the squeal of tires nearby and saw the grey sedan speed toward her. She turned sharply down another street and nearly collided with a car. There was a bang and the sound of crumpling metal behind her. She glanced back to see the sedan and another car smash together. For a moment, she thought she could stop to catch her breath. But then Kelly spotted two large men running after her.

It was then, with a sharp, sinking feeling, she realized one of her pursuers was Simmons. What the hell?! But she couldn't stop running now, because one of the guys was closing in on her. She needed to get away, fast.

Directly in front of her, beside one of the medical buildings, was a large parking structure. Kelly dashed inside, figuring it would be her best bet at this point.

She darted another look behind her, but didn't see any of the men. However she did spot a white Mercedes pulling out of a parking space. Without the slightest hesitation, Kelly pulled open one of the passenger doors and jumped in.

The fortiesh looking blonde woman behind the wheel stared at her incredulously.

"I'm a doctor," Kelly breathlessly panted as she flashed her I.D. badge. "Sorry about this but there's an emergency. My car won't start. Can you drive me to the—oh, God, where was it? The train station. A woman just delivered a baby there. I need to get to her as quickly as possible." Kelly knew her story sounded ridiculous but she was desperate.

The woman popped a piece of pink bubble-gum into her mouth and said, "Sure, hon, no problem. Want a piece of gum?"

"No thank you. Um, but I kind of need to hurry." Kelly hunched down in the seat as they eased out of the garage.

"Would you look at that?" the driver remarked, shaking her head.

Kelly peeked carefully over the passenger-side window at a crowd gathering around a body on the ground. Then she saw Simmons looking up and down the street. She dropped back down.

Not even the police had been able to protect her, and if what that man said was true, then the police were behind this—whatever *this* was. Maybe even Tony was behind this.

Could that be true?

Could Tony and Simmons somehow be involved? Could Tony have been in that car? Is that what he'd meant earlier today when she'd overheard him talking to his boss on the phone? Her mind was racing, along with her heart.

Simmons had disappeared and Tony had not been in contact all day. And that phone call he'd been on that morning. Oh God. Had he been talking about her? Kelly was beginning to wonder who she could trust.

"Hey, hon, I hate to be a busy body, but you sure you're heading out to take care of some woman who just had a baby? I wasn't born yesterday, and if truth be told, you look like someone on the run."

Ah, so she hadn't bought her story. She sighed heavily.

The woman glanced back at her. "Listen, I've had my own share of problems and I really don't want to pry. If you need to get out of town quickly, I wouldn't travel via Amtrak or even LAX. Trust me. I can drop you at the Burbank airport. Hardly anyone goes there these days."

Kelly didn't know whether to laugh or cry. "You know, I think that is a good idea. Thank you."

The woman laughed. "My horoscope said today would be full of surprises. " She blew another large, pink bubble and merged smoothly into traffic.

CHAPTER FIFTY-ONE

Redding felt a sharp stab of anger rise through his body when he heard the police were now considering Wentworth's case a murder. Redding had an informant at the LAPD, and the unofficial word was the suicide had been staged. Fuck. The reason he'd told Connor and Thomas to have Mark make it look like a suicide was murder cases were investigated by police he had no control over. And he'd wanted this whole thing to create sympathizers for Senator Wentworth. On top of it all, Ryan Horner was still missing. Peter did not like any of this. His stomach burned and his head pounded.

Things went from bad to worse when he received a call from his man handling the situation with Horner's wife and kids. She'd been located in New Jersey visiting a friend but had narrowly escaped with the children. However her friend had been killed by two of his henchmen. This was not good. He shook his head, downed another scotch, then switched over to speaker phone. "What the hell happened, Jeff?"

Jeff White had worked within The Brotherhood for more than a decade. He handled the dirty work on the east coast. He was good at it. But it seemed White had lost his touch. Or his team had. It only took one moron, one peon, to turn a strong organization into a house of cards. Peter wasn't going to let that happen.

"I'm sorry, sir. Things got out of hand."

"I don't understand." Redding was trying hard to stay cool. "Things got out of hand? What does that mean, Jeff?"

"We located the wife and kids sir."

"Yes, and you also murdered an innocent woman, Jeff!"

"She was a Jew, sir."

Peter slammed his empty scotch glass onto the table next to him. "I don't care if she was the Queen of the Jews! Killing her raises questions…questions bring cops. You prepared to take a fall for The Brotherhood if it comes to that?" There was silence on the other end of the line. "I asked you a question!"

"Yes, sir, for the higher good of humanity and what we stand for, I am prepared to make any sacrifice necessary."

"Good to hear, Jeff. Now tell me, do we know if Mrs. Horner is aware of anything her husband was involved in, or if he somehow leaked information to her?"

"She changed her hair color and cut it. She also cut the hair off the little girls."

"She knows. Any idea where she was going?"

"No. She's in her friend's car and we have the make on it. She's also got the other woman's infant with her. The police may find her first. She's wanted for her friend's murder and for kidnapping the baby."

"Interesting. I want her before the police get her. And I want her found alive. No more killings at all. Do I make myself clear?"

Redding hung up the phone and then placed one more call. "Hello, love."

"Peter?"

"Of course. I was thinking how nice it would be to see you tonight," he said.

"I don't know if that's a good idea. The police were here yesterday before the funeral and asking questions."

"Really? All the more reason for us to meet. See you at eight." She would come. Redding needed a distraction and Susan Hamilton would do just fine.

CHAPTER FIFTY-TWO

Gem knew Pazzini could have been a lot harder on her and she was grateful he'd let her off easy. Now she needed to learn as much as she could about Wentworth and Craig Johnson. Because the two deaths were far too coincidental. Two powerful men with money. One young. One old. Both strongly opinionated and not in a good way. Johnson she didn't know much about but she'd heard enough from Chad that night while hiding in his upstairs guest bedroom. Yes, she'd heard enough to convince her Wentworth was a very hateful young man. But what about Johnson? Who was he? Would the cops be able to connect the dots?

Pazzini was a smart guy. A good detective. If anyone could make the puzzle pieces fit, it would be him. But she'd see what she could do to help him out.

Gem googled Johnson's name and pulled up a variety of articles. Some were about his wealth and rise to fame. Others were about his unpopular views about immigration, race, and women. There were even a few about his philanthropic efforts. Gem couldn't help but laugh. "Who knew bigoted racists had philanthropies?"

After a couple hours spent reading through various materials, two articles caught Gem's attention. One had to do with Johnson's support of Senator Wentworth. The other covered a grant

Johnson's technology company had underwritten. Her jaw dropped when she saw who the grant had been written for; L.A. County Hospital's Pathology Department and Dr. Jake Hamilton.

CHAPTER FIFTY-THREE

Pazzini had promised Kelly he would see what he could find out about Lupe Salazar. He had tried giving Kelly a call a few times, but got her voicemail. She was likely in surgery. He'd changed his mind about calling another cop in to be with her for the evening. If anything, the two of them needed to talk about what had happened last night. He wondered how she felt about last night. He knew one thing for sure—there was a part of him that regretted it because he'd crossed every boundary possible, but there was another part of him that had no regrets at all. He hoped he had not screwed up with her because he was *very* interested.

Trying to maintain focus on his job, he headed into the Women's Shelter where he had learned Lupe Salazar had been living for the past few months. He was immediately led into an office where he met a lithe, petite woman of about fifty seated behind a desk. She stood and shook his hand. "Rosa Gonzales. How can I help you Detective?"

"I'm here about a young woman who I understand was staying here. Lupe Salazar?"

Rosa sat back. "Yes. Lupe. It was tragic what happened to her. I can't believe she's gone." She shook her head. "Do you know how her baby is doing?"

"The baby is holding her own. She's in the Neo-Natal-Intensive Care Unit at County."

"Poor thing. Such a shame. Lupe really wanted the baby and to do right by her."

"So, she did want the child? Tony asked.

"Oh yes. There was no doubt. She came here about four months ago. She asked me where she could go to get some care for her child and herself. I sent her over to the Women's Health Center just three blocks from here. I know she kept regular appointments and was eating well. That kind of thing."

"And did she have friends here? A boyfriend? Do you know anything about her family?"

"No. I don't know anything about a family. She says she was abused at home and ran away. She was nearly seventeen. We don't ask many questions of these girls. It's obvious they have some real issues. As far as friends, she really kept to herself. Did a lot of reading. Was attempting to finish up her G.E.D. and get a diploma. There was no boyfriend that I was aware of, but again, the girls are semi on their own. We have an overcrowding problem and there is only so much any of our counselors and myself can do. We are all volunteers." She ran a hand through her long, silvering hair.

"What about drugs or alcohol? Did you ever notice anything like that with? Where you may have suspected she was using or on something?" he asked.

"No way. The kid was a good girl. I can spot the users, Detective. Lupe Salazar came from a violent home, she wanted to do the right thing for herself and her baby, and so she got out and away from people who were bad to her. I don't believe she was wrapped up in drugs or alcohol."

Pazzini sighed. "Okay. One more thing. Did you know Naomi Williams or Desiree Jones? They were both teenage girls. African-American. Both pregnant."

Rosa nodded. "I do remember Naomi. She came here a few times for meals. I didn't know she was pregnant though, and I haven't seen her for some time. I've never heard of the other girl before."

"Do you know where Naomi was living?"

"I couldn't say. It's possible in the tenements seven blocks from here. Sometimes we get girls or women who come in from there just for a warm meal. Remember, Detective, I keep a discrete place. I know the hardships these women face so I try and watch my boundaries with them."

"Right. Well, thank you for your time, Ms. Gonzales."

She stood and they shook hands.

Pazzini headed out of the shelter more baffled than before. So, this Lupe Salazar was a decent kid according to Rosa Gonzales. Not a druggie at all, and Naomi Williams had been here a few times. Was this shelter the link to Dr. Hamilton's murder?

Maybe he would get some more answers if he visited the health center Lupe had been seen at. He started to head the two blocks up when his cell phone rang. It was Simmons. "Yeah? What's up?" he asked.

"Oh man, uh, I am so sorry but the doc…she's gone. She's missing, Pazzini."

CHAPTER FIFTY-FOUR

The plane screamed down the runway. Kelly glanced at the rows behind her. She wasn't sure what she was looking for, but all the other passengers seemed oblivious. No one took note of her. She leaned against the window and sighed.

What the hell was she doing? Running, of course. But from who? And why? She replayed her last conversation with Jake over and over as the plane headed north. "Leave this alone, Kelly. You could get hurt." And he'd been right. Those men had meant her harm. And was Tony involved? It didn't make sense. She fought back her tears. And that man, Mark Pritchett. Probably not his real name, either. Something about him looked so familiar.

What did she know? There was Lupe and the drugs in her system that transferred to Baby S. There had been at least two other cases similar to Lupe's. Then Jake was murdered after he'd warned her. She'd told Tony her theory about a new street drug. And she spent part of the afternoon running for her life. The more she thought about it, the more it seemed Tony was on the take. He was a dirty cop and so was Simmons. Their whole charade about wanting to protect her, shadow her, and all that was just to keep an eye on her and discover what she knew. It all made perfect sense.

Or did it? She remembered the night before, with Tony. The way he'd looked at her, touched her, kissed her, made love to her.

Had it all been a lie? She felt the sting of tears again. Kelly quickly downed the rest of her cocktail. She didn't know what to believe any more.

What did they think she knew? Where was she supposed to go and what was she supposed to do? Should she contact the FBI? And tell them what exactly? She leaned her head back on the seat and closed her eyes.

No matter what, she had to figure this out. And she had to figure it out quickly because there was no way in hell she was going to wind up dead. Kelly was going to get out of this thing alive, if that was at all possible.

CHAPTER FIFTY-FIVE

Only moments after he hung up with Susan, Redding decided to head out and purchase a nice gift for her—something to ensure her continued allegiance and silence.

Once he'd found the perfect diamond tennis bracelet, he had the driver stop by the liquor store and purchase a bottle of Dom. He was not going to allow all of his hard work to go up in smoke. He was going to celebrate all he had already accomplished and what was to come.

Champagne and gift in hand, Redding was on his way home to await his companion for the evening and release some of this pent up tension. His phone rang and he sighed heavily before answering. This couldn't be good. It seemed lately every time he answered a call, it was not good news. He was right.

"You lost the doctor?! One defenseless woman against three men and you completely screw it up?" What kind of fucking idiots did he have working for him?

"There was a cop following us. We could only do so much. And Thomas is dead. He was hit by a car."

"What?!" Redding screamed into the phone.

"Yeah. I'm sorry. I am." Redding heard the tremor in Mark's voice. He should be afraid. Redding had clearly jumped the gun by moving this moron up in the ranks. "Where's Connor?"

"I don't know. We scattered and went our separate ways, you know. The cops were everywhere."

Redding could feel the blood boiling inside of him. "Listen to me, Mark, and listen carefully. You have twenty-four hours to find Dr. Morales."

"How?"

"That's your problem, isn't it?"

"What if we can't, sir?"

"Well, Mark, as you know there are consequences for ineptitude. Bring in the doctor."

Peter hung up the phone and looked out the window. This was unbelievable. The organization was ready for the next step. Not a step backward. He had to do some damage control where Thomas was concerned. The good news was The Brotherhood had rules about keeping one's identity low key. If the man had followed those rules, the police would have a hard time discovering anything at all on him.

The other real problem at hand was this Dr. Morales. If he could track her down and work some of The Brotherhood *magic* on her, she could prove very useful. She ran a NICU unit in one of the biggest welfare hospitals in the state. Yes, she was Hispanic, but maybe that was exactly what he needed at the moment. Things were way out of hand. If he could bring in a minority, threaten her, threaten who and what she loved most, he'd have her in the palm of his hand. The key was finding the bitch, and fast. If she had any inkling what was going on, and took that information to the right person—he and everyone in The Brotherhood would be royally fucked. He could not let that happen. He had worked too hard for their ultimate goal. A white America. A white world!

It would all start with Senator Wentworth. Good old Lawrence. Peter hand-picked him long before Wentworth had any idea about The Brotherhood's existence. He'd been following the senator's career since their early days in college. Fraternity brothers. There were things Peter knew about Wentworth that would curl the hairs of his constituents. Wentworth was a lot like Peter in many ways. Not so much in others. The two of them firmly agreed on what the country should look like, what a new world should look like. And Wentworth had that All-American, apple-pie image going for him, which made people trust him.

Peter had it all worked out. The campaign money was rolling in from all sorts of private sources: White Power kingpins, pro-abortion liberals, feminists. Wentworth was preaching health care for everyone, but still allowing the wealthy to choose their own private physicians. Sure, presidents had tried to do it before. But Wentworth would be able to get it done and make everyone happy on all sides. Granted, the health care ruse would cost an arm and a leg, but through private funds, the deal would be signed, sealed, and delivered before anyone knew what was going on.

Health care facilities would be planted right in the middle of impoverished areas—places like Watts, Harlem, Detroit, all along the Mason-Dixon line—with their huge number of surplus people. Once the facilities were established, the plan would kick-off with free prenatal care, which would supply the women with free *vitamins* mass produced by Frauen Pharmacueticals, of course. In addition to being highly addictive, the vitamins, containing *Pure,* would also induce spontaneous abortions, causing most fetuses to die long before birth.

The beauty of it was the drug could be put into birth control pills. The same chemical reaction causing the abortions would also induce sterilization. The last piece of the puzzle Peter needed to figure out was how to get men to ingest the chemical. But this wasn't strictly necessary, because if the surplus hordes couldn't procreate, in eighty to a hundred years, the problem would be eliminated anyway.

The bigger problems they would encounter would likely be political. But Redding felt sure he had that figured out as well. The key would be initiating and keeping the right men involved in The Brotherhood.

A president could only be in term for eight years, but there were others The Brotherhood would line up. There would be supporters and the support would grow. Good, politically correct white Americans would begin to see the errors of their ways. Half of them hid their real feelings anyway about minorities. Redding was certain of it. The drug could be introduced as a street drug in the long run. Once out there on the streets, The Brotherhood's plans for a new type of humanity could really take hold. The trials within these health care facilities were nice and controlled. They made it easy to see if the drug worked. On the street it would be more difficult to tell. Once the drug was working within the controlled test facilities, then a release on the *undesirable* populations as a whole could go into effect.

He knew he wouldn't be alive to see his final solution realized. But he felt secure knowing the world would be a much better place without millions upon millions of wretched mongrels ruining things for the white race. Policies could be introduced forbidding non-European immigrants from entering the United States. Hell, if the peons of the world wanted to kill one another, why should the U.S. step in and try to make things better? Peter never understood this shortsighted policy. Once he and The Brotherhood were in charge of The White House, changes would take place, big changes. But first, Peter had to gain back the control slipping from him.

As the car parked in the drive and the driver opened the door, Peter stepped out and immediately felt something different in the air. Something was not quite right.

He had a visitor. Senator Wentworth was waiting for him in his den. His eyes were red rimmed and he looked very upset.

"Senator?" he said.

Wentworth stood up quickly from the chair he'd been seated in, "I know you killed my nephew, Redding!"

Peter walked over to the bar and poured himself a scotch and soda. With his back to Wentworth, he said, "I am sure you're upset about your nephew, Lawrence. It's such a shame, and I am terribly sorry. He was an asset to us."

"Fuck you!" Wentworth shouted.

Peter turned. "Now, senator, that doesn't sound very presidential of you. Go bury your nephew, put this bad business behind you, and move on with your campaign. You can probably use this suicide thing to your advantage considering it's one of those ugly tragedies no one ever talks about." He took a sip from his glass.

"Chad did not kill himself, Peter. He was murdered. By you."

Peter set his drink down on his desk and walked very close to Wentworth. His voice pitched low and threatening. "Listen to me and listen carefully. You are currently in a position to become the leader of the free world. The question you need to ask yourself is not how Chad died, but who is padding your pockets to ensure you become the next president of the United States." He gave Wentworth a shove and pushed him back down into his chair.

The senator winced.

"I think the most respectful thing you can do for your deceased nephew *and* your constituents is focus on the future. Now, I have business to attend to. Is there anything else you wanted to discuss, Lawrence?"

Wentworth stood and stared at Peter. He nodded his head once and walked out of the room. Peter sighed heavily and downed his drink. The last thing he needed on top of his problems was a loose cannon politician. If he had to, he'd cut the strings on his puppet and find another way to bring his plans to fruition.

CHAPTER FIFTY-SIX

Mark knew he was in deep shit. He'd made a serious error in judgment. As he threw what little clothes he had into a duffle bag, he realized he'd allowed his obsession with Dr. Morales to get in the way. Mark wasn't so stupid he couldn't see the writing on the wall. He was a dead man walking if he didn't come through for Peter Redding and The Brotherhood. But that was okay, he had a back-up plan: get the hell out of Dodge.

Yet, Mark knew going on the run meant he'd always be looking over his shoulder. Every time he turned the key in the lock to whatever hellhole he wound up in, he'd be wondering if Connor or some other henchman would be waiting for him. At least he didn't have to worry about Thomas hunting him down. That had been an ugly scene and all Mark could do was get the hell out.

Right now though, he had to get out of his place. Period. And he had to make an effort to find Kelly Morales.

Where could she have gone? She was scared shitless and with his made up line about the cop working for him, he was pretty sure he had her really freaked out. Looking back now, he realized what a brilliant ploy that had been. Sure, he hadn't expected her to get away but now that she had, the last thing she'd be doing was call the detective. But she would need someone. Wouldn't she?

Mark chugged down his second Budweiser before ditching his dirt-bag apartment. Friends…he belched and then started laughing. He had a good idea which friend she'd reached out to. And maybe that friend would know where the good doctor was hiding out.

Time to pay someone a visit.

CHAPTER FIFTY-SEVEN

Jeanine had just finished feeding the kids and sat them in front of the television where they were watching the Cartoon Network and keeping baby Oliver entertained. She could not believe they had actually made it to the cabin. They had taken the bus out of Port Jervis at noon, and seven hours later, finally wound up in a taxi in front of the bus depot in the Catskills. The driver had dropped them off at the cabin at nearly eight o' clock.

Time was running out to give Gem Michaels a phone call. After getting everyone settled, it was already after six in California. The number Ryan gave her had obviously been Ms. Michael's work phone. She hadn't bothered to leave a message because she wasn't sure what to tell her via voicemail. However, she realized as the minutes past, she might not have a chance

Jeanine was grateful Aunt Camille currently lived in a nursing home. Before they left for Germany, she'd handed Ryan and Jeanine the keys to her cabin, telling them it was her way of getting them to come back home soon. The cabin was pretty remote and conveniently isolated…not the ideal place for an elderly woman to live but perfect for a woman and three children on the run. She hoped.

Jeanine knew she was on borrowed time. Getting in touch with Gem Michaels was vital. She fished the card out of her purse with the journalist's phone number on it. She closed her eyes and prayed she would answer. Her eyes opened when someone picked up. "Gem Michaels, speaking." The woman's voice was deep, slightly raspy.

"Oh my God, finally! Thank goodness." Jeanine could not believe it.

"Yes. Who is this?"

"I'm sorry, I'm, I'm...my husband, he met you and he...we are in a lot of trouble. He told me to call you."

Oliver cried out from the room upstairs. Jeanine hoped he could hang in there until she was done talking.

"I'm sorry, who is this?"

Jeanine spoke up. "My husband is a chemist. He sent you an e-mail." The baby began wailing loudly. "Hang on please. Please don't hang up." Jeanine dashed down the hall into Oliver's room and carried him back into the kitchen. He instantly settled down and played with the coiled phone cord. "Ms. Michaels are you still there?"

"Yes."

"My husband's name is Dr. Ryan Horner."

"Okay."

"He sent you an e-mail, asking you to keep an eye on your neighbor. He signed it Chemmadderhorn."

"Uh-huh."

"You have to believe me. He works for some very bad people in Germany."

"You're in Germany?"

"No. Please listen. Ryan is and we are in serious trouble. These people, they killed my best friend. Her name is Melanie Schneider. You can verify that. It should be all over the news by now. Ryan is in hiding, I think, and I am on the run. I don't know who I can trust but he was certain we could trust you. His boss is a man named Peter Redding. Redding is the CEO of a private pharmaceutical company, Frauen Pharmaceuticals. I can't give you more details about what's going on but my husband said it's bad and we need help."

There was no response on the other end and for a moment Jeanine thought Gem had hung up on her. "Please, Ms. Michaels, are you there? I...we need your help."

"I'm here. I will help you. Can you tell me where you are?"

Jeanine hesitated, but Ryan insisted the woman could be trusted. "We're at my aunt's cabin. In the Catskills. Can you jot down the address? You should be able to find us on Google Maps."

Gem took the information from Jeanine, including her phone number. Her final words were, "Don't go anywhere. Help is coming."

Jeanine hung up the phone. There was nothing more she could do. Her family's fate was in the hands of Gem Michaels.

CHAPTER FIFTY-EIGHT

The sun was setting as Kelly leaned against a bench at the wharf. She'd been sitting there for at least an hour, unable to make any decisions. Not knowing exactly what to do after she had taken a cab from SFO into the city. Stevie T was going to need food. First things first.

She called Eric on his cell phone. His shift was over by now and she crossed her fingers he would pick up. He did.

"Eric. It's me. Kelly," she said, pitching her voice low in case of eavesdroppers.

"Jesus, Doc! Where the hell are you? The cops were at the hospital asking all sorts of questions. What is going on?"

"I don't know. I really don't."

"Okay. Listen, calm down and talk to me," he said.

"I can't. There is something really terrible happening. I probably shouldn't have called you, but I don't know who else to trust."

"You can trust me."

"I know," she said. "But I don't want you to get hurt."

"Kelly, you aren't making any sense."

"Where are you?" she asked.

"I'm home. Just got here."

"I need a favor."

"Sure. Anything," he replied.

"Can you go to my place and feed my cat? There is an extra key hidden in the back yard under a gardenia plant I have in a Mexican-style pot. It's blue and green and yellow." She knew she sounded off her rocker. "But be careful. I don't know if anyone is watching my house."

"Kelly, I would do anything for you, but I have to say you aren't making any sense. Tell me what's going on and maybe I can help."

She sighed. He was right. She did need help. "We both know Jake was in trouble. I think those same people are after me now." Her stomach sank as she said the words. She knew she should just hang up the phone and pray everything worked out. But she needed more than blind faith to survive.

"Oh hell. Where are you?"

She didn't say anything for a few seconds.

"Doc? Kelly? Are you there?"

"Yes. I'm sorry. I'm just worried about your safety."

Eric chuckled. "I can take care of myself. I have a black belt in Aikido. I'm not worried about anyone hurting me."

"Yeah, well, do you own a gun?"

"I actually do. I was attacked in college once, and trust me, Doc, that won't be happening again in my life time."

"Please take it with you when you go to my house."

"Okay, but will you tell me where you are and what's going on?"

She closed her eyes and blurted out the story. "I had some specialty labs done on Baby S. Turns out she has traces of Ketamine and a drug used to sterilize mares in her system. The only way the drugs got there is through her mother."

"Okay…Mares? As in horses?"

"Exactly. It sounds crazy, I know, but I think someone murdered Lupe Salazar and Jake knew who the killer was. I think Naomi Williams and Desiree Jones were also murdered. You said you saw Jake get into a limo last week. We both agree it was strange Dr. Pearson took off on vacation after the death of Desiree Jones and her infant. And then there was Naomi Williams. This is all connected. Mark my words."

"I don't know what to say," Eric said. "But, Doc, there was another case today. No one could find you and there were people asking. A lot of them are worried."

"Oh my God. Did the mother…did the baby?"

"They died, Kelly. I'm sorry. Things are not good. What happened to you?"

"I don't know if you'll believe this but I swear it's true. Today I was crossing the street and some man came up to me with a story about his twin babies needing a good doctor. Then he pulled out a gun and tried to drag me into a car. But I got away."

"Oh my God. What about the police? Why didn't you go to them?"

She sighed heavily. "Because...because...I'm not sure I can trust the police. I told the detective handling Jake's case about my theories, that maybe there was a new street drug out there. In less than forty-eight hours after telling him, I was nearly abducted."

Eric let out a low whistle. "You think he's a dirty cop?"

Tears stung her eyes. "I don't know. I really don't. And right now, I don't know where to go or what to do. I questioned Brightman and he was an ass about it. I think he knows more than he let on."

"Well, I doubt anyone is going to get much information out of him any time soon."

"What?! Why?"

"He turned in his resignation today. Rumor has it he bought himself a villa in the Cayman Islands and ran off with one of the ER nurses. Left his wife. His kids. He's gone."

"Holy shit!"

"I know, it's crazy, but that's the word on the street."

"Oh my God, Eric. I know we get paid well but how in the hell could Brightman afford a Caribbean villa?"

"My thoughts exactly."

"He knows something. I question him and then he takes off..."

"I can snoop around over here," he said. "See what I can find out."

"No. This is dangerous."

"I want to help. I'll feed Stevie T and see what I can learn about Brightman's sudden departure. Is there anything else?"

The lump in the back of Kelly's throat left her speechless for a moment. "Just please be careful."

"Always. But what about you? Where are you going? Where are you staying?"

"I don't know."

"I don't think you should use your credit cards. Do you have cash?"

"A little," she said. "About a hundred bucks."

"Not enough. Where are you?"

She hesitated. "I'm in S.F."

"Okay." He paused for a moment. "Listen, I have a friend there in the Castro district. Julio Velasquez."

"Oh no, Eric. I've already involved you enough."

"No. Trust me on this. I was in Iraq in the 90's with this guy and we well we were together for some time. Anyway, he was Special Ops. He has some connections. Julio can take care of

284 | P a g e

himself and protect you as well. I'll give you his address. Write it down and ditch your cell. Toss it into the bay if you have to."

"Wait…do you think this call is being traced? Oh no! What if they come after you?"

"I promise I'll be fine. I am worried about you, though, and better to be safe than sorry. Julio will get you a new phone." He proceeded to give her the address of his friend's place. "I will get a hold of him. Let him know the situation. Go there. Go now and I will do everything I can to help out over here. I'll bring Stevie T to my place."

"I don't know what to say."

"You don't need to say anything. Give Julio my love. He is good people. You can trust him."

"Thank you," she said.

"Be careful, Doc."

"You too," she whispered as she shut off the phone.

She watched as the sun dipped down over the bay, its golden rays hitting the water. Kelly stood up and tossed her phone into the bay as far as she could. It was literally out of her hands now. Eric would have to do the detective work, and she would go to a stranger's house and hope for the best.

She took the cable car to Powell and Market, then walked several blocks to the Castro. When she arrived at the colorful Victorian duplex, she walked up the front stairs to the entry way and hesitated before knocking. Images of the past week flashed through her mind. Abruptly deciding she couldn't continue to involve Eric and this total stranger in her troubles, she turned to leave. As she descended the stairs, the door opened behind her. On the landing stood a well-built, strong-looking man. He appeared to be in his mid-forties. He held a trash bag in one hand.

"Kelly?"

She thought for a second before identifying herself.

"Dr. Morales? Right?"

"Yes."

"Please come in. I'm Julio Velasquez. You're safe here."

Obediently, she walked up the steps. Although she knew it was foolish to trust someone this quickly, she also realized if she didn't, it would only be a matter of time before she wound up dead. "Thank you for taking me in. You've saved my life."

He set the trash bag down on the landing. She looked at it, and then down at the trashcans at the bottom of the stairs.

He waved a hand. "Don't worry about that. I'll take it down in the morning. Now please, come in," he held out a hand and guided her up to his second floor apartment.

Julio's place was immaculately clean, with modern Latin decor. The scent of garlic and other familiar spices filled the air. "I thought you might be hungry," he remarked.

Kelly suddenly realized how awful she must've appeared. She hadn't seen herself in a mirror for hours. Any makeup she'd applied that morning would have disappeared. But Julio didn't seem to mind her appearance at all, and he insisted she sit down so he could bring her a plate of food.

Julio gestured to a yellow futon, "Please, have a seat."

He sat down across from her. "Listen, Eric tells me something horrible happened to you. I think maybe if you talk about it, I can help. I'm not sure what Eric told you about me, but I have some connections in high places and maybe together we can solve this thing. Or at least get some answers." He got up and went into the kitchen, returning seconds later with a bowl of black bean soup and a thick slice of bread. Julio went back into the kitchen and came out with a glass of sangria. "My mother's recipes."

"Thank you. It smells and looks delicious." Kelly took a sip of the sangria. "This is great. I can't tell you how much I appreciate everything and really, your offer to help me is, well... it's overwhelming."

"No need to thank me. Anyone who is such a dear friend of Eric's is okay in my book."

"Thank you."

Julio sat down across from her. "I was in special ops for over twelve years and then I was injured by a street thug while home on leave. I'd had a few drinks and wasn't at the top of my game. Guy and a few of his buddies jumped me and stuck a knife in my back. I wound up getting the best of them, but they punctured a lung, and I was discharged honorably, but still…"

"That must have been difficult."

He shrugged. "I use my skills now in other ways. I spent some time working for the government. But now I work in the private sector."

"Doing what, if I may ask?"

He smiled wryly. "I'm a bouncer at a local club in town, but I also help out people in need from time to time. I, um, well let's say I do some security detail and protect those who need protecting."

Kelly smiled back. "I think I might qualify. And Eric, you've known him for a long time?"

"We used to date. Thankfully it ended on good terms. I think my line of work bothered him and then he moved to L.A., and, well, the long-distance thing didn't work out. But I would do anything for him. Now you. What's your story? Eric gave me some info…but I need details in order to help you out." He ran his hand through his short dark hair.

Kelly started with Lupe's death and went from there. Julio listened intently.

"A new designer drug," He rubbed his clean-shaven chin thoughtfully. "That has merit. Create a date rape drug with a euphoric effect but one that also causes women to abort or prevents pregnancy. Perverts would love that."

She frowned slightly. "Okay, but if that's the case, why does a women need to be addicted? Why not design it like a roofie? You know, for one-time use."

"Maybe that's all it was. You said Lupe Salazar claimed she didn't use. Maybe someone just gave it to her one time."

"The other girls, too? Remember the two other cases. And, when I spoke with Eric earlier, he said there was another case today. On top of that, one of the doctors who oversaw one of the cases is now on an extended vacation, and the other has apparently resigned and left the country. Eric says the rumor is that doctor—Brightman—purchased a villa in the Cayman Islands and ran off with one of the nurses. So, two docs involved with these cases are MIA. And then there's Jake's murder."

Julio didn't say anything for a few seconds. "Let's talk about the pathologist, your friend, Jake. Suppose he was ready to go public with what he knew. Publicity would slow cash flow for the bad guys."

"I don't think so. I think he was too afraid to go public. He was too afraid to even tell me what was going on. I am the reason he was killed."

He frowned thoughtfully. "His office was bugged."

Kelly's eyes widened. "Of course! I didn't even think about that but it makes sense."

"Obviously your friend was being watched carefully. There are definitely others tied into this who work at the hospital and it sounds like the police are involved as well."

She swallowed a lump in her throat and nodded. "When I questioned Dr. Brightman, he blew me off...like I was some sort of idiot. Now he's gone."

"So let's think. Who has the necessary cash flow to keep people quiet? The mafia, maybe. But they aren't as strong as they once were, at least not out here. There are offshoots of various gangs and the Mexican drug cartel, but they tend to use more heavy-handed tactics. In my opinion, this thing has cover-up written all over it. As in government cover up."

"What?!" Kelly was having a hard time following Julio's rational.

"I know. I sound paranoid and ridiculous. But trust me, our government is so huge...there are things going on, bad things, our government either has no clue about or wishes to sweep under the rug."

"Do you mean like a conspiracy?"

Julio nodded solemnly.

Kelly shifted uncomfortably. She wasn't sure where he was headed with this rhetoric, or how she felt about it. It definitely made her uneasy. "But why? What are they covering up? If it is the government, what are they trying to hide?"

"We answer that question and we solve the puzzle. I think we start by locating these two doctors who have gone AWOL."

"I'm still trying to figure out why anyone would do this," Kelly took another deep drink of the sangria. "Who benefits to gain from killing mothers and babies?"

He smiled sadly. "Infanticide is not as uncommon as you might think. The Chinese kill baby girls all the time. Same in India and parts of Central Asia. And consider the Middle East where baby girls die of exposure and "misbehaving" women are routinely executed. Ask yourself why. Now, ask yourself why the American government would want to kill off babies and mothers. How old were these women?"

"Between thirteen and twenty."

Julio nodded. "Street kids?"

"I believe so."

"Minorities?" he asked.

"Yes. One Hispanic. The other two were African-American. I don't know about the woman from today."

"Is this happening in other hospitals?"

"I don't know," she replied.

Julio stood and started pacing. "Tax payers are paying a lot of money into the system. They're not happy about it. Many average Americans view girls like these girls as charity cases at best, dead weight at worst. Our government is in a lot of debt. Maybe eliminating some of the "lesser thans," the uneducated, welfare folks, and some tax payers—probably the wealthy who support campaigns and such—are happier." He sighed heavily and didn't say anything for a few moments. Suddenly, he stopped pacing and turned to her. "I've got another idea."

"What?" she asked.

"I need to take you somewhere." He grabbed a coat from the front closet and handed it to her. "It's cold. I know it's going to be big on you, but it's better than nothing."

"Okay." The intensity in Julio's voice made her curious and a bit fearful, but she followed him to the door and outside.

CHAPTER FIFTY-NINE

Pazzini was at a loss. He could not believe what had happened. When Simmons called him and told him Kelly had gone missing and that he'd last seen her when she was being chased by some thugs, he'd pretty much lost it.

One of the suspects wound up dead after a car hit him— some loser named Thomas Martin. Not much info about the guy yet. All Simmons turned up was that he lived in Studio City, drove a silver Mercedes sedan—which the police had confiscated—and he kept to himself according to the neighbors. No prior record. No job they could track him to. It was all very strange and spoke of a man who worked for someone with a lot of money and knew how to keep a low profile. Common criminals didn't drive around hundred thousand dollar cars, live in a decent house, and not have any connections, any job known to anyone. No way. Whoever this Thomas Martin was, he had been after Kelly along with a couple of other men. Hired guns. But why?

Simmons handed him a fresh cup of coffee. He shook his head. After Tony chewed his ass out royally, Simmons was obviously walking on egg shells. "Hey man, I am sorry. I'm really, really sorry. I don't know what happened. One minute I'm in the waiting room with a group of parents, you know, knowing I gotta grab some lunch soon with the doc. The next minute I'm getting a call from someone saying he's a doctor in Long Beach and my sister's been in an accident with her new husband. I couldn't hear the guy real well, so I stepped out for a minute."

"Apparently that's all they needed." He took the coffee from Simmons. He was trying to ease off the guy. His anger had tempered some over the past few hours since Kelly had gone missing. "I know you didn't do any of this on purpose, but it's obvious the doc is in some real danger. The fact that she hasn't called me makes me wonder…"

Simmons nodded. "We will find her."

"Yeah. I don't know who or why anyone is after her." Pazzini thought about Kelly's theories. Maybe she had really been on to something. After speaking with Rosa Gonzales, Pazzini was pretty much convinced somehow Lupe's death and possibly the deaths of the other girls were linked to Jake Hamilton's murder.

Damn. Where was Kelly? The last place she'd been seen was dashing into a parking garage next to the hospital. But the police had combed through the area with no luck.

Simmons phone rang. A minute later he hung up and said, "We got the video surveillance from the garage. Want to take a look?"

"Absolutely."

They went into the viewing room and sat through about thirty minutes of tape, narrowing it down to the approximate time

Kelly had been in the area. Pazzini stood and leaned in close to the screen when he spotted her jumping inside a white Mercedes. "Bingo!" He rolled back the tape and enhanced it so he could read the license plate number.

"I'll run the plates," Simmons said.

Moments later, he came back with the information on the car—a Mrs. Carla Hopkins of Bel Air. Forty-five minutes later, they were seated inside Mrs. Hopkins garishly decorated mansion showing her a photo of Kelly. Carla Hopkins wore what appeared to be a kimono-style silk robe and a pair of red, heeled slippers. She held a martini glass in one hand.

"I certainly didn't take her for a criminal," Carla Hopkins remarked in a long, slow drawl. She offered them a drink, which they refused.

"She isn't," Pazzini replied. "But she is in trouble and we want to protect her."

Mrs. Hopkins looked at them suspiciously. "Really?"

"Yes, really, ma'am," Simmons chimed in.

Carla told them she'd dropped Kelly off at Burbank airport.

Once back at the police station, they had finally been able to get a hold of the various flight manifestos. They eventually found the one Kelly had been on...to SFO.

Pazzini shook his head. "She could be anywhere up there. Have we gotten any hits off of her cell phone or her ATM and credit cards?"

"I'm still working on it," Simmons said. "Let me give Patty a call and see if she's come up with anything."

Simmons called Patty O' Brien, their records and surveillance specialist, to see if she had learned anything. After a brief conversation, he hung up and turned to Tony.

"Looks like she made one phone call after landing in S.F."

"To who?"

"Eric Sorensen. He's an RN at County and he works in the NICU. O'Brien already checked and he lives off of La Cienega."

"Let's pay Mr. Sorensen a visit."

CHAPTER SIXTY

Ryan was done with this sitting duck bullshit. He couldn't wait any longer. He had to take the chance and get to his family. Jeanine had now had enough time to contact Georgia Michaels and hopefully the savvy reporter had done her due diligence and by the end of today, he would hopefully wind up in the arms of his wife.

He left the motel and headed to the train station. Ryan berated himself again, realizing how selfish it had been to send Jeanine by herself with the kids. In reality, he should have told her he wanted a divorce, let her go live a life with their daughters without ever knowing the truth. It would have possibly been the only way to keep them safe.

He continued to keep his head low and glanced occasionally over his shoulder, making sure he hadn't attracted any interest. So far, so good as he traveled the three blocks to the train station. He purchased a ticket to London. Heathrow was a major hub and a huge airport. The vast expanse might allow him extra time to get out of Europe.

Once aboard the train, he sat down and looked around. Again, no one seemed interested in him in the least. Maybe he would get away with this after all. Maybe he would get to the states and expose these bastards. Maybe the day would simply be one of safe travels.

CHAPTER SIXTY-ONE

Mark found Eric's apartment without a problem. The jerk was listed! He shook his head. Who still listed themselves publically anymore? Whatever. Made his job easier.

The nurse lived off of La Cienega near the Beverly Center. Nice digs. Outside was all Euro-style or whatever the hell rich folks called it. Who knew nurses made such decent cash? Because of the location and the fact that the nurse lived in such a quaint place, Mark knew he would have to be smart, careful. He checked his watch. A little after eleven. Perfect. Everyone should be tucked in bed and those who weren't were either watching late night TV or getting a piece of ass.

Now wouldn't that be interesting if Nurse Eric had a bed buddy? That would so not be good. Especially considering he suspected Nurse Eric of having a thing for guys. The last thing Mark needed was a confrontation with two dudes…especially if they were in the buff. He grimaced distastefully.

The gate at the front entrance was locked, but that wasn't a problem for him. Mark took a quick look around, keeping his head down. There were likely surveillance cameras, so he had to make sure he could get the locked picked quickly so it appeared as if he were a resident simply having a hard time opening the gate. It was easier than he'd imagined…open in under one minute. "That was easy," he muttered.

Mark passed by the pool and hot tub. There were a couple of late nighters fooling around in the Jacuzzi. He wanted to yell, "Get a room!" but decided against it.

He quickly found the stairwell and climbed the stairs two at a time until he reached the second floor. Not even remotely winded. His workouts had been paying off. He smiled.

Two minutes later he was at the nurse's front door. To knock or not? NOT!

Two minutes more and he was inside the nurse's darkened apartment. Ah good boy. He was in bed.

There was a night light on in the hall. The place was pretty good sized for an apartment in L.A. But not so big that it was hard to find the bedroom.

"Hello?"

The nurse had heard him. Mark stayed perfectly still next to a bookcase. Then he heard, "Must be the kitty. Here Stevie! Here kitty, kitty. Shit. Maybe I should have left you at Kelly's."

A-ha! So he had the doc's stupid cat. He purposely took a coin from his jeans pocket and tossed it onto the tile flooring. He needed to rouse his victim.

"Dammit, Stevie. Come on. Where are you!?"

The light went on in the nurse's bedroom.

And then he got up.

Nurse Eric walked into the family room and Mark grabbed him around the neck from behind, shoving a knife underneath his throat. "Hey Nurse Eric."

Eric grunted.

"Surprise! It's not Stevie T. But since you have the doc's cat, I think you know where Dr. Morales is hiding. Tell me or I will slice your throat."

"Fuck you," the nurse said.

"Not nice. Play nice and tell me where she is, and I'll let you live."

Without further comment, the nurse brought his hands up to Mark's arm and pulled down hard. Mark lost his grip on Nurse Eric. Who knew the fucker was so strong?!

Mark stumbled back into the bookcase. The only light was the dim one coming from the bedroom.

Mark lunged at the nurse with the knife and he knew he'd hit something good because the man yelled out and lurched to the side. He wobbled a bit and Mark went in for the kill, but the nurse stood straight and threw all of his weight against Mark who fell back hard and down onto a glass coffee table, shattering it on impact.

Mark felt a sharp, horrible pain slice through his chest. He grabbed a piece of glass and swung it at the nurse. His aim was off but he hit pay dirt when he felt the glass connect with skin somewhere on the man's body. The nurse went down. Mark was sure with all the commotion someone had already called the cops. He didn't think leaving through the front door was a good idea. And he was really hurt…he could feel the blood dripping from his side.

Mark spotted a sliding glass door across the room and headed for it, limping as quickly as he could. The nurse was on the ground, moaning. Mark unlocked the door and went out onto the balcony. He didn't know if he could make the jump. Two stories? It was worth a try. He wasn't going down without a fight.

He could hear someone pounding at Eric's front door, and that's when Mark took a chance and leapt off of the balcony.

CHAPTER SIXTY-TWO

Julio was silent as they walked down Castro and up to Market. Kelly, usually assertive and questioning, remained silent too. They their destination ten minutes after leaving Julio's place. A group of people milled around holding up signs, many of them yelling. Kelly realized it was a protest against gay rights. "You think they'd pick a more receptive venue." Julio smiled sadly. "But every day you can find these bigots here in front of this church."

Kelly glanced at the church door with a large, rainbow flag hanging in front of it. She took note of the small cluster of people carrying signs with things like, "Burn in hell, Fag" and "Homosexuality is a lie. You have forsaken the Lord. Romans 1:18-31" or "Faggots are the Devil's spawn" written on them. She was astounded by the hatred from so-called Christians. She'd never been a huge church-goer but even she knew Christ spent a lot of time preaching about loving others without judgement. So where did these people get off?

She looked over at Julio. Why had he brought her here? What did this have to do with Jake or dead girls?

Julio took her hand and squeezed. "Can you feel the negative energy? The hatred?"

"Yes."

"It's negative to us but to many, it's intoxicating. Addictive. It has a malicious charm in and of itself."

"They remind me of the Nazi collaborators in old newsreels, burning books and smashing the windows of Jewish shopkeepers."

"Yes," Julio said with cold contempt, "many Nazis considered themselves *good* Christians, too. At one time, Hitler was even a Catholic seminarian. He was always careful never to displease the Vatican, which signed a peace agreement with him, and even helped prominent Nazis like Klaus Barbie escape Europe after the war."

She looked at the group of people again. "Their signs certainly quote the Bible a lot."

"Of course. Quoting scripture allows them to justify their hatred," Julio answered. "But it's no different than what white America did during the civil war. People just like these carried signs quoting chapter and verse to prove the Bible sanctioned slavery, and that Africans—being the descendants of Ham—were an inferior race. The bottom line, millions of people are prepared to kill one another to defend their own prejudices—their God given right to hate. Frankly, it doesn't matter what country you live in, what religion you follow, what socio-economic background you belong to. Hatred within the human race runs rampant and is an evil I don't think will ever be contained."

Kelly didn't respond. Her mind was racing. The girls who had come into the hospital were minorities. The idea of actually murdering minorities simply because they were a minority seemed far-fetched, but seeing the blatant racism standing in front of her, it was also oddly plausible. "Okay. I get it," she said. "Maybe this whole thing is race motivated. But what do we do now?"

"Go have a drink and figure it out."

They walked up to Powell and Market and caught a cable car to Fisherman's Wharf. "Might as well do the tourist thing while you're here," Julio quipped with a smile. They jumped off at the end of the line and walked half a block to the Buena Vista Café.

The old-fashioned bar had a cozy, warm vibe that instantly cheered Kelly. She removed the wool pea coat Julio lent her. He took off his coat and placed them both on a nearby coat rack. They tried to find a place to sit at the crowded bar.

"Is it always like this?" Kelly yelled above the din.

"Always," he replied.

They squeezed through a mass of people and by sheer luck, found a young couple standing up to leave. Julio sat down and placed his hand on the stool next to him. Kelly sat on the leather seat and swung herself around to take in the ambience. She liked it. There were groups of people sitting at various round tables, chatting. The walls were lined with walnut and painted in green trim. Everyone appeared to be drinking Irish coffees. The bartenders were expertly mixing the drinks and sending them hurtling down the bar at patrons. Julio ordered two. He winked at Kelly. "It's what they're famous for.""I sort of got that."

The coffees came and after a few sips, she felt noticeably more relaxed. Kelly decided to dive into the deep end. "You think there is some kind of conspiracy to wipe out pregnant minorities?"

"I think when you want to destroy a group of people, the easiest, most vulnerable targets are young women and children. And by starting with pregnant women…" he shrugged. "Well, yes, I think it is plausible."

"But a government thing? It just sounds so…well…crazy."

"We are headed into an election year, my friend, and many have not been happy with the current administration. On top of that, lots of people feel the country has gotten too liberal, bordering on socialist."

"Okay, but there's a big jump from not liking liberals to killing off entire groups of people simply because they're minorities."

He nodded. "Maybe. Maybe not. What you think looks like basic civil liberties, may look like communism to an extremist. And as we've seen here…people with extreme viewpoints don't seem to have a problem sharing it publicly. The anger is palpable. It doesn't take much to imagine someone taking the obvious next step."

"You think we have people in Congress or the senate who are that extreme?"

He smiled sadly at her. "I have a difficult time imagining *any* politician fundamentally believes in any one philosophy. They seem to go whichever way the wind blows. However, if more and more of your constituents seem to be spewing anti-immigration rhetoric and expressing a desire to return to the "good, old days", you'll give them what they want, especially during an election year like this one." He took a long sip from his coffee.

"So what do we do now?" she said. "I mean, we're still talking about "what if" but we don't have any proof, any leads... just a growing body count and some creep chasing me around the streets of L.A."

"We start with the missing doctors. You said one of them was in the Caymans?"

"Yes, Dr. Brightman."

"Okay. You feel like taking a quick trip to the Caribbean?"

Kelly laughed out loud, "What? Are you serious?"

"As a heart attack."

"Wow. Okay then." She cocked her head to the side. "Why are you doing this?"

"Because Eric said you needed help and I'll do anything for a close friend. Also, I don't like the sound of this business. If I can remove some more assholes from this planet and help restore the balance, I'll do what it takes."

"You're a good guy, Julio. A hero."

"Nah, just a guy who wants to get the bad guys. You game?"

"When do we leave?"

CHAPTER SIXTY-THREE

Since hanging up from her chat with Jeanine Horner, Gem had been busy gathering information. She had immediately Googled Melanie Schneider plus murder. A handful of stories popped up.

The New Jersey Centennial read:

Local Mother Murdered in Cold Blood, Baby Abducted

Melanie Schneider (38) was found shot to death outside her home in Bergen County this evening. Her nine-month old son Oliver Schneider is missing and believed to be with her long-time friend, Jeanine Horner, of Balkinese, Germany according to Mrs. Schneider's husband, Robert. The two women were spotted having dinner at The Franciscan Country Club earlier and left together. Police believe Horner was involved in a plot to murder Mrs. Schneider and abduct the child. A search is underway for Horner who is also traveling with her twin daughters. Her husband, Dr. Ryan Horner, has not been reached. Police are also looking into the possibility of another assailant who helped Horner.

Gem had sat back in her chair as if sucker punched, shaking her head. Holy God, what a mess. What in the hell is going on?

Think. Think. Think. She leaned back over the desk and Googled Frauen Pharmaceuticals, then Peter Redding, and finally now—after two hours—she once more opened her file on the Petersen case, and started to connect the dots.

When Gem finally looked up from her computer screen and saw the darkened hall, she felt momentarily uncomfortable. No wonder, considering all she'd been involved with lately. Thankfully she wasn't completely alone…she could still hear the janitorial service cleaning the office next door.

Gem leaned back in her chair and stared up at the ceiling, trying to make sense of the facts swimming around in her head. Dr. Hamilton had been murdered in cold blood. He'd also had a grant funded by Craig Johnson. Craig Johnson hung himself on his yacht two days prior. Her neighbor, Chad Wentworth—nephew to Senator Wentworth—shot himself the same night as Johnson's suicide. Johnson and Chad Wentworth shared the same radical views. Wentworth and his high-brow, white cronies apparently hung out at an estate out in the boonies doing who knows what.

A week ago she'd received an e-mail from Chemmadderhorn telling her to keep an eye on her neighbor. Now, Chemmadderhorn's wife, Jeanine Horner, tells her his real name is Dr. Ryan Horner. The woman claims she is on the run and her friend Melanie Schneider has been murdered. Okay, confirmed. The original e-mail also mentioned the horrific Petersen murders.

Damn. Dr. Ryan Horner…her brain was searching memory bank because she knew she'd heard the name before.

Details.

Gem took a swig of her cold coffee and rubbed her tired eyes.

And now, the kicker. Peter Redding and Frauen Pharmaceuticals. The one thing she could find on Redding was he owned the private pharma company that mainly produced products for women…pre-natal vitamins, meds for menopause, an anti-anxiety med, a med for depression. Frauen Pharma's returns were good. They'd shown high profits for the past five years.

The one tie-in she'd found to bring this whole thing together was Redding was a major supporter and contributor to Senator Wentworth's campaign.

There were two things Gem needed to do. One was fill Pazzini in on what she'd learned, and then find Jeanine Horner. Because Gem had the distinct feeling Mrs. Horner was in serious danger.

As for Dr. Ryan Horner who called himself Chemmadderhorn there was not much on him at all. He's a chemist, as his wife had said, and works for Frauen. Then it hit her. That detail part of her brain. She remembered exactly who *the chemist* was and where she had met him—in that town car, three years ago just after The Petersens' murders, in front of her townhouse. In front of Chad Wentworth's townhouse. Jesus! What was going on here?

CHAPTER SIXTY-FOUR

Redding reached across the bed and twirled Susan's long blonde hair between his fingers. She was glorious. And she had been pivotal in moving the Covert Reich Project forward. Funny how things have a way of working out. Who would have ever thought meeting Susan Hamilton at a bar after an argument with her then-husband would have worked to his benefit?

Susan rolled over onto her side and faced him. The fireplace in his room still crackled with the last embers. Susan had certainly done the job of alleviating his tension for the past few hours. She propped herself up on the pillow. "You know it's been a lovely evening, Peter, but we need to talk."

"I say we talk over breakfast." He reached his hand out and caressed her breasts.

She gently pushed his hands away. "No, this is important. That cop. That detective. Pazzini. He was at my house asking me and my daughter all sorts of questions. I'm afraid, Peter. I'm afraid he could tie us together and somehow discover I am an accomplice to Jake's murder."

"That won't happen, Love. I'll take care of him." He kissed her lips hoping to quiet her.

"How do I know that?"

He sat up now. "Because you trust me. We have a relationship based on trust."

"Yes well, I want more. I'm no longer content with being your convenient fuck buddy. Jake is dead. The cops are on me and I want them off because I plan to move into this house with you."

"Excuse me?" Redding said.

"You heard me. I'm done being ignored until you need something from me, especially sex. You're not going to get the milk for free any longer."

A wicked smile spread across his face and he started laughing.

"What's so funny?" She asked, pulling the sheets up around her bare chest.

"You, dear. You're hysterical."

Her eyes narrowed into slits. "I'm glad you think I'm keeping you entertained…but let me remind you, I'm the one who made this all possible. Without me, your little project would never have made it off the ground. If I don't get what I want, there will be hell to pay."

"You're not only hysterical, Susan, but you're delusional as well. I would think twice before you make threats toward me. I'd watch your step.

"Out of control?! I am not out of control and I won't allow you to continue to treat me like this. I demand respect from you, Peter."

"Oh Susan. You're nothing but a whore who I used to help me get something accomplished. I appreciate your help. You've been compensated quite well, I might add. You're lucky I remained interested in you after I got the information I needed about your ex. If I wanted you out of the picture, all it would take is a snap of my fingers and you'd be history. So let me give you a word of advice. Threats don't work with me. If you don't want to wind up in a plot next to your ex, you'd better be a good little whore and keep your mouth shut."

Her eyes were wide with disbelief. "Sounds as if you're threatening me now."

"Simply stating a fact."

"And what if your facts don't impress me?"

"Then you're being a fool." Redding stood up and headed to the bathroom. On his way there he called back to her, "You know the way out, Susan."

A few minutes later, Redding came out to find Susan still in his bed. "I told you to get out," he said.

Tears were in her eyes. He sighed.

"I'm sorry, Peter. I am. I just panicked. I don't know what I was thinking. I'll do whatever you need me to do. I'm sorry."

He shook his head. How he hated groveling. Disgusting. And for a minute there, he'd been mildly impressed at the spine Susan appeared to have developed. He walked over to her and leaned down as if he was going to kiss her. She looked up at him with her big, tearful blue eyes. "I really am sorry, too." He placed a hand on either side of her neck and then snapped it. Her eyes were wide with shock as she died within seconds.

God, he was tired of problems. At least Susan Hamilton wouldn't pose one any longer. She should have left when he'd told her to.

CHAPTER SIXTY-FIVE

Ryan couldn't believe it. He'd made it to Heathrow and so far no one seemed to be taking any notice of him. Now he needed to find a flight back to the States. He still had the hunting knife he'd bought at the pawn shop. He would have to get rid of it before going through security but until then, he thought it prudent to keep on hand.

He checked the flight schedules and saw one was leaving in two hours for Newark. It would take a miracle to get on that flight. He had to try though. It would get him to New Jersey by 3:00pm and if he made it through customs and rented a car, he could be with Jeanine and the kids by nightfall.

Of course those two hours would give Redding's men two additional hours to find him in Europe. Once his name went onto a flight manifesto, it would raise certain flags. Ryan was not so naïve as to think Redding's boys couldn't find him anywhere at any time. They had means, methods, and more members than anyone imagined. But he had to take that risk.

The first thing Ryan did was head to the money exchange counter at the airport where he exchanged his spare Euros for Pounds to pay in cash for his ticket. Thank God he'd had the foresight to set a little cash aside every week for the last several months. But now he didn't have much money left after the purchase, and he knew once he was in the States, he'd have to use his credit card. But at least he would be one step ahead of the game.

He walked toward the security line and then remembered the knife. Backing away, he headed in the other direction toward one of the airport pubs. Ryan walked into the men's restroom towards a stall. He didn't have much time since the security lines were long. He had to act fast.

There were a couple of men at the urinals. Ryan closed the stall door behind him. He opened up his backpack and reached in for the knife.

Suddenly, the hairs on the back of his neck stood up. He hadn't heard anything out of the ordinary but something didn't feel right. Maybe he was being paranoid but better safe than sorry. Ryan grabbed the knife and put both feet on the toilet, raising himself just high enough to discretely peer over the stall door.

A guy was at the sink washing his hands. Otherwise the bathroom appeared empty. He could hear the flight announcements over the loudspeaker in the pub beyond. Ryan dropped silently down to the floor and shook his head. He was way too wound up. Right now, he needed to get rid of the damn knife and get through security. Once there, it would be a lot harder for anyone to come after him.

He turned to set the knife down behind the toilet, when the stall door was kicked in. The loud, metallic bang echoed off the walls. Hands immediately went around his neck and his legs were kicked out from under him. Ryan fell towards the open toilet but managed to grab the rim before hitting ground. Remembering the large knife he held in his hand, he jabbed backwards, hard. A scream sounded behind him and the hands around his neck dropped. He turned to face his attacker. Ryan recognized him immediately. Frederick Färber. He was the one who had taken him in San Diego and forced him to watch the DVD of the Petersen murders, and he had told Ryan he had been the one to murder Selena.

A rage stirred inside Ryan. Färber was bleeding from a slash mark on his right side. Ryan kicked the man in the stomach, sending him flying straight back through the open door and knocking him against a sink. Färber's head thunked hard against it. He staggered and regained his balance, desperately swinging a right hook into Ryan's face. Ryan stumbled back a few steps. His attacker lunged towards him, giving Ryan only seconds to swing the knife downwards into the man's chest. Färber took two steps back, his large hands covering the open wound above his heart, his eyes wild. There was blood everywhere. Ryan grabbed Färber before he collapsed and shoved him into a stall, onto the toilet seat.

Ryan arranged the unconscious man so he wouldn't fall off the toilet.

He quickly searched Färber's pockets for a cell phone and his wallet for money. If the guy woke up, he would have difficulty contacting anyone without a phone or cash. Then Ryan wiped down the handle of the knife and placed it inside Färber's jacket. He closed the stall door behind him, cleaned himself as best he could, and exited the restroom. He did his best to appear calm and ordinary as he rapidly walked away from the pub towards security, boarding pass in hand.

Ryan knew there was no turning back. One of Redding's other henchmen could locate and kill him, or he could be arrested for the attack he'd just committed. Amazingly, he made it through security, found his gate, and took a seat in the waiting area, trying hard not to look conspicuous even though he was terrified. Passengers were beginning to line up at the gate—the plane was boarding.

Ryan took Färber's cell phone from the man's his pocket and searched through the contact list. It didn't take him long to find Redding's information. Ryan knew exactly what he needed to do next.

CHAPTER SIXTY-SIX

It was already three in the morning, and neither Julio nor Kelly had gotten any sleep. After returning from the Buena Vista, they'd stayed up to see what they could find out about Brightman, Pearson, and Jake. They were looking for a connection...the missing puzzle piece.

It took some time, but they eventually uncovered a link between Pearson and Brightman. Thanks to Julio's "side jobs," he had an unusual amount of access to normally secure government databases. He'd spent part of the night on the telephone talking to different people and asking for favors. But the link between Pearson and Brightman wasn't found in a government or covert database. Instead, she discovered it four web pages in via Google.

Kelly let out a low whistle. "Hey, Julio, think we hit the jackpot. At least a little."

Julio was in the kitchen getting her another cup of coffee. He came over, setting a mug down on the table, and bent over the laptop. "What is it?"

"Read that." She pointed to the screen.

Julio leaned in closer and clucked his tongue.

The article was from an East L.A. community paper, dated 2009.

New Women's Health Center Opens in East Los Angeles:

A new women's health center opened on Monday morning in East Los Angeles. Located in one of the poorer areas of the city, the much-needed center is a welcome addition to the community. With a women's homeless shelter only two blocks away, many young women will receive the care they need. The center is non-profit and staffed by volunteer doctors. A top obstetrician and neo-natal pediatrician from County Hospital, Dr. Pierce Brightman and Dr. Joe Pearson, also serve on the board and volunteer one day a week at the center. Brightman says his main goal is to educate the women who come to the center. "We will provide free pre-natal vitamins to ensure pregnant women in the community are receiving proper nutrition and care."

"I had no idea either Pearson or Brightman were such good Samaritans," Kelly said.

"I doubt they were," Julio replied. "If I had to guess, I would say the three girls who died at the hospital visited this clinic. And they either lived close by or at the shelter."

"Lupe Salazar lived at the shelter for sure."

"Right. In any case, there's a good chance Brightman and Pearson are murderers."

"What? Like serial killers?" Kelly was skeptical.

"No, not exactly." Julio grabbed a few papers off the printer. "There were drugs in those young women and their babies.

At least we know for sure they were in Lupe and Baby S. And they weren't your typical street drugs, right?"

"Right."

"Okay. Look here." He pointed to the top paper in his hand. "This article came out in 1991. There was even a special on 60 Minutes about Farrakhan's rhetoric."

"Louis Farrakhan?"

"Yup. He had all sorts of crack-pot theories about how the U.S. government was out to get African Americans. For example, he accused the government of targeting forty-ounce beer specifically at black people, to disempower them. He also claimed the same about crack-cocaine, and even went so far as to say AIDS was a bio-weapon the government used to keep the population of various races down."

"Really?"

"Really. Now it sounds crazy and I personally think Farrakhan was off his rocker. But, like I mentioned to you last night, governments around the world have done things exactly like what Farrakhan claimed. In fact, in the 1970's, there was a college text book titled "Ecoscience: Population, Resources, Environment." It was co-authored by Obama science czar John Holdren. This guy and the co-authors stated that compulsory, government-mandated "green abortions" would be a constitutionally acceptable way to control population growth and prevent ecological disasters, including global warming, because a fetus was most likely not a "person" under the terms of the 14th Amendment.

"Where are you going with this?" Kelly asked.

"Hear me out," Julio said and took a sip of his coffee. "The authors of this text also suggested government-mandated population control measures might be inflicted in the United States against welfare recipients. They argued involuntary birth-control measures, including forced sterilization, may be necessary and morally acceptable under extreme conditions, such as widespread famine brought about by "climate change."

"You think the government is covertly aborting fetuses or sterilizing welfare recipients to try and control the population?" Kelly asked.

"I think it's possible, and I think Brightman and Pearson were on someone's payroll. I don't know how they are giving the drugs to the women, but I'm convinced it's happening."

Kelly sat back for a moment and thought about the various tests women have to undergo during pregnancy. Then she looked Julio in the eye. "It's the pre-natal vitamins. It has to be. It's something a pregnant woman takes regularly. Most of the other tests involve blood withdrawals but few require injections or medication."

Julio nodded thoughtfully. "I think you're onto something, Kelly." He stood, yawning. "And now, my dear, I say we try to get a couple hours sleep. I should have everything arranged for our island adventure by seven and then we're off to chat with Dr. Brightman."

CHAPTER SIXTY-SEVEN

Peter woke with a very bad feeling. Somewhere along the way he'd lost control. Killing Susan probably had not been a great idea, but she'd pushed him and he'd snapped. Literally.

But once he'd done it, he regretted it. After all, she was good in bed and had helped the project. He'd wrapped her up and carried her down to the basement. Thank God his place had one. He wanted her body as far away from him as possible. Now he needed to call in somebody to get rid of her. Good thing he had someone on the payroll who could handle it. He made the call, knowing by the time he was out of his morning shower, she'd be gone.

Susan's body was the least of his worries considering it was only nine o' clock and he'd started receiving calls three hours ago from a handful of colleagues on the board. They'd gotten word there was trouble and Wentworth was unhappy. Wentworth! Maybe he was another mistake too. Did these incompetents not understand their mission? The reason behind everything they did and everything they stood for? It was frustrating to say the least.

Now there were two women on the run: Doctor Kelly Morales and Jeanine Horner. And then there was Ryan Horner. He was probably the largest threat of the three. Kelly Morales likely didn't know anything, and whatever she thought she knew would sound like insane rambling to the authorities. Not to mention, Peter had quite a few authorities on his pay roll. As for Jeanine Horner, she may have information but unfortunately for her, she was now a suspect in the murder of her dear friend and the kidnapping of the woman's infant. But Dr. Ryan Horner knew too much. He had too many details. If he got the attention of the right person, or in this case, the wrong one, everything could come crashing down. Finding him was key.

Peter made phone calls to men who could help him get the answers he needed, and he'd learned a few things. Kelly Morales was somewhere in San Francisco and had spoken with a nurse from the hospital.

He paced the length of his swimming pool—his head pounding after last night. Although it was a crisp morning, he was perspiring. Fuck!

Peter threw himself into one of the lounge chairs and finished off his second cup of coffee. His cell phone rang. He wasn't prepared to have another conversation but the call was from Connor. Thank God for Conner. He'd contacted Peter after Mark had about the incident yesterday with Dr. Morales. As Peter assumed, Pritchett was the one to blame. Then again, when you looked at it more carefully, he was the one to blame. He should have never put Mark in the position he had. Now Connor was doing double duty because one of his other best men was lying in the morgue. Poor Thomas.

"Sir, I've located Dr. Morales," Connor said.

"Where?"

"She just boarded a plane to the Caymans. She's traveling with someone named Julio Velazquez. Ran a report on the dude. He's trained and smart. He's also a homosexual."

"I don't give a shit if he's from Mars. I want to find out how she knows him."

"I'll see what I can do."

"Good. This Velasquez, you say he's trained?"

"Special Ops. Marines. His file is closed. At least I have not been able to obtain access to it."

"Okay, well, it's likely he's not armed if he's boarding a commercial flight. He may have access to weapons once he gets there, but that will likely take him some time, and I expect you will have them handled by then. Kill them both. But do it so no one finds them. I can't risk more dead bodies popping up."

"Sir, they are on a private jet. The guy must have some serious connections."

Peter didn't say anything for a moment.

"The Caymans?"

"Yes, sir. What do you want me to do?"

"Meet me down there. You'll have some back-up as well."

"Where?"

"Are you listening, Connor? In the Caymans! I will fly in and we'll take care of Dr. Morales and her friend. I will let you know my ETA. I'm sending a plane for you."

Now why in the hell would Dr. Morales and some mercenary be traveling to The Caymans? Somehow he doubted it was for a tropical vacation.

CHAPTER SIXTY-EIGHT

Tony and Simmons pulled up in front of Eric Sorensen's apartment building. Tony was eager to hear what Kelly's friend and co-worker knew. It was late. Just past eleven-thirty. They took the elevator to the second floor.

The doors slid open and they walked down the hall toward Eric's apartment. When they got to his door, they were alarmed to see it was partially opened. Pazzini called out, "Police! Open up!"

There was no response.

He took his gun from his holster and nodded at Simmons who followed suit. They slowly opened the door and stepped inside. They hadn't gone more than a few feet when they spotted a man lying on the floor near the kitchen. He'd been badly cut. Blood was coming from his chest. Tony glanced up and saw the curtains from the balcony billowing through the open sliding glass door. He bent down over the man who stared at him, frightened. "Simmons call the EMTs. We need back up and search." He bent down over the man on the floor. "You're Eric, right?"

Eric tried to nod and winced. His voice was raspy and cracked slightly as he replied, "Yes. I stabbed the guy."

"Good for you, man. We'll get the bastard. Just stay still." Tony looked around and could see large drops of blood leading out through the balcony. The guy who came to take Eric down may have met his match, because from the amount of blood on the floor and walls, he'd been seriously injured before escaping. Tony wanted to question Eric about Kelly, but he was barely conscious. He managed to get one question in before the emergency crew arrived. "Do you know where Dr. Morales is? The man who tried to kill you just now is probably with a group who is after her. Please tell me if you know where she is."

Eric opened his eyes and mouthed the word, "Yes." Then he passed out.

Tony stayed with Eric, waiting for the EMT's. Simmons began casing the area looking for any signs of the perp. As the medics arrived and began working on Eric, Simmons called up to him from outside, "Pazzini, I got the perp. He won't be saying much though. He is d.e.a.d."

Tony stood and slammed his fist against the wall. Would he ever see Kelly again?

CHAPTER SIXTY-NINE

Gem called Pazzini who answered after the third ring. It was six o' clock in the morning but she figured he kept odd hours.

"Pazzini" his voice was sharp and curt. He sounded agitated.

"Hey, Detective. It's Gem Michaels."

"Oh, hey."

"I know it's early and I'm sorry, but I think I've got something."

"Spit it out. I'm in the middle of a situation here and don't have a lot of time."

"Listen, if you want in on this, meet me at US Airways. I've booked a flight to Newark out of LAX. Flight 7682. We leave in an hour and a half, so you better get moving. If I'm right I am going to lead you to Jake Hamilton's killer. I hope I spelled your name right for the ticket. Hope to see you on board." Gem hung up.

Yes, there was a strong possibility Pazzini would blow her off. She'd called him out of common courtesy because he'd allowed her to pursue her story without interfering, and had even given her a few decent leads. She'd also called him because she was scared. Gem did not know what she would find when she got to Jeanine Horner's cabin. Hell, she didn't even know if the woman had been telling her the truth. For all she knew, she was headed out on a wild goose chase…one that could potentially result in someone getting hurt, or worse. But she felt it was a risk worth taking. And she felt if she had given Pazzini all the info over the phone, he would have cut her out of the entire thing. She was too deep in this to allow that to happen. Gem crossed her fingers and hoped the detective would take the bait.

CHAPTER SEVENTY

Redding was mid-flight when he was finally able to log-in to his e-mail account. Based on the number of calls he'd received, he was certain someone had sent him an e-mail or two. Only a few people had his e-mail address and when he saw one from Frederick, his head guy in Germany who'd been tracking Horner, he immediately opened it.

Mr. Redding,

We have located Dr. Horner and family. They are in the Catskill Mountains in a cabin at 2893 Back Hills Lane. I am in pursuit and am boarding a plane from Heathrow to New York at 2:00pm this afternoon, my time. I will not let you down.

Färber

Sent from my iphone

"Yes!" Redding smiled.

He left a message for Connor to take care of Morales and her new special agent friend. Redding had a bigger fish to fry and damned if he wasn't looking forward to it. It had been far too long since he'd been in the field removing "problems" himself. He ordered the plane to redirect.

CHAPTER SEVENTY-ONE

Ryan could not help but feel smug. His hands shook for a good five minutes after sending the e-mail. He ordered a cocktail from the flight attendant, hoping to calm his nerves. He wondered if anyone had found that prick, Frederick Färber, yet. He hoped he was dead. Ryan did not feel guilty for killing that son-of-a-bitch and locking him in a toilet. Not in the least. He palmed the man's phone and thought about the day Färber approached him in the café parking lot in San Diego. How he'd taken him, tortured him with the horrible images of what was done to The Petersens.

He was going to get these bastards. All of them. He had a feeling Redding would show up at the cabin. And when he did, Ryan would take him out. He would certainly beat him there. Redding would need to get to the airport and then it would take six hours to fly east from there. Then he'd need a car, and that would take another three hours to make the drive. He'd likely take his time, assuming Färber was going after them, but Ryan was sure Redding would show. Ryan knew Redding wanted him dead and he was sure he would want to be involved. But Ryan had a head start…he was already 37,000 feet in the air and had been for three hours. He would beat Redding to the cabin, get the girls out, and lay in wait. By tomorrow morning, there would be no more Peter Redding and all of his plans would be destroyed.

Three hours later the plane landed, Ryan rented a car and then went to a gun shop in a seedy area of town where he illegally purchased a nine-millimeter glock.

He now had to get to his family and hide them, and then Redding would come to him like a horse to water. And with any luck, Redding would soon meet his maker. If it was the last thing Ryan Horner did, he would send Redding to Hell.

CHAPTER SEVENTY-TWO

Kelly and Julio were only a half hour from landing in The Caymans. Kelly slept a good portion of the flight. She woke feeling…well, not exactly refreshed but better than she had in days. Julio glanced over at her and smiled.

"Hey, sleepy head. Wait until you hear what I've found out."

Kelly rubbed her eyes and took a sip from her bottled water. "Do tell."

"The pre-natal vitamins being stocked at the women's center in East L.A. are supplied by Frauen Pharma. They're based in Germany and have a satellite office in Los Angeles. Apparently, they're supplying meds to half a dozen clinics around the country —just like the one in L.A. They're all located in poor areas, neighborhoods with a lot of welfare recipients, that kind of thing. I'm still trying to find out if there have been any pregnancy related deaths in the hospitals or centers near these clinics. Anyway, my guess is these six clinics were field test centers. They're distributing the drug to see how it works on real people. Once they get it right, they'll probably go national."

"Oh my God."

Yeah, and check this out. The CEO of Frauen Pharma is this guy, Peter Redding. Apparently his adoptive father was a pretty high up in the Ku Klux Klan."

"What?" Kelly sucked back a deep breath of air. She took a moment to digest everything and looked back at Julio. "In this day and age, to think people like this can actually put a horrible plan into action…it's, it's, I don't know…"

"Disgusting," Julio said.

"At the very least." She looked out the window, her thoughts scrambled and full of emotion. After a few moments she spoke again. "But…"

"But what?"

"The detective. The one I told you about. He's Italian. I mean he doesn't exactly fit the racist profile." She frowned. "I really thought he was one of the good guys."

"You like him, don't you?"

"I don't know. I mean…yes. I thought I did anyway."

"It could be a simple misunderstanding."

"Maybe." She wrapped her sweater around her shoulders. "Back to the issue at hand…I keep wondering about Brightman. I mean, why move to The Caymans?"

"Off-shore accounts. I already traced it. I got an address on the dude and in about an hour, I'll be paying him a little visit."

The plane touched down and Kelly shot him a look. "Wait a minute. You? What about us?"

He shook his head. "Kelly, this thing is bigger than I initially thought. I don't think it's a good idea for you to come with me. I wouldn't want you to get hurt...or worse."

She folder her arms against her chest. "I don't care. I'm going. I want to look that bastard in the eyes and get an honest answer."

Julio sighed. "You know how to shoot a gun?"

"Of course."

He opened up his duffel bag and took out a Beretta, handing it to her. "Think you can shoot this?"

"Hell yes I can."

He smiled. "I thought you might say that. That's why I brought an extra. I figured you weren't the type to stay behind."

"You figured right."

CHAPTER SEVENTY-THREE

Jeanine knew she had to make a move. The girls were hungry. They'd eaten the last of the Top Ramen stocked in the pantry. Oliver was almost out of formula and the diapers were gone. She'd been using towels and a pair of safety pins she found in her aunt's bedroom. The little guy was miserable and between the whining, the crying, and the hopeless feelings, Jeanine was close to losing it.

She'd parked the kids yet again in front of the TV and began flipping through channels, searching for a cartoon. She'd caught a glimpse of CNN earlier and was shocked to see she was wanted for questioning in Melanie's murder and suspected of kidnapping Baby Oliver. How was she was supposed to get out of this mess?

The sun was setting, and she knew she'd run out of options. Jeanine had to go to the police. She had to take the risk.

"Hey girls, Mommy is going to go upstairs and pack."

"Are we leaving?" Chloe asked.

"Yes."

"Good. I'm bored," Taylor said. "And he stinks." She pointed at Oliver.

Chloe giggled. The simplicity of youth. If they only knew the kind of trouble they were in. If they only knew it was likely they'd be placed with social services if caught until Jeanine could prove her innocence to the cops. And that was a *good* outcome, comparatively speaking. She looked at her blue-eyed girls and didn't know if she could do it. She did not know if she should take the risk and leave the cabin.

What choice did she have? They couldn't stay here and starve to death. She made her way up the stairs. Jeanine had just finished putting the girls' things into the pack when she noticed how quiet it had become down stairs. When it came to kids, silence was rarely a good thing.

She hurriedly slung the pack over her left shoulder and Oliver's diaper bag over her right. She grabbed a couple more towels for Oliver and then quickly made her way back down. Suddenly, one of the girls cried out, "Mommy, help! There's a bad man!"

Jeanine dropped the bags with a thud and leapt over the last four steps to the landing below. A man stood in the middle of the living room. He was dressed in a suit and tie. He had graying sideburns and could have been a businessman, if it wasn't for the large gun pointed at Chloe's head. Taylor was on the ground next to her sister with her head bowed between her legs. She was sobbing. Fortunately, the baby had drifted off to sleep.

"Mrs. Horner. Hello. So nice to meet you. I'm Peter Redding." He had a bag over his shoulder and with his free hand, pulled out a roll of duct tape and tossed it to her. "Your husband is a stupid man. Tried to trick me. But he is not a good criminal. I have people everywhere and the man he tried to kill, well, it didn't quite work out as planned." He glanced at the kids. "I don't like children much. Tape their mouths for me, or I'll kill them."

She fumbled for the tape and it fell to the ground.

"Pick it up."

Jeanine bent down, hands shaking, and grabbed the thick, silver role. How had he found them? "W-what do you want?" What did he mean Ryan had tried to kill someone and had messed up?

"Shhh. No time for questions now. We have to work quickly. If I'm right, your husband should be here soon to join the party." He chuckled warmly, sending chills down her spine. "Too bad for you and the little ones here that his little ruse didn't fool me. Now get to taping, Jeanine."

She bent down in front of Taylor first. "It's going to be okay, honey. I promise. We're just playing a game." She knew the guy was sick enough to pull the trigger at any moment. She figured the best chance they had was to follow his orders and pray Ryan saved them, if he truly was on the way.

"Get the fucking tape on the kid, Jeanine. Now."

Tears welled in Taylor's eyes as Jeanine put tape over her mouth. Jeanine tried not to cry. She needed to be strong for the children. She had to figure out what to do.

"Okay. Now tape her hands and feet together."

"No!"

Redding sighed dramatically. "Jeanine, I don't have much patience. You're a smart lady and you have cute kids. You might just live if you follow the rules."

She taped Chloe's mouth and gently bound her hands and feet. Jeanine looked up at Redding. "Can you put the gun down now?"

"I don't think so. Do the infant."

"He's asleep. He could suffocate!"

"Do you think I care?"

"Please don't make me do that," Jeanine begged.

"I could pull this trigger real easily, Jeanine." He waved the gun menacingly towards the sleeping child on the sofa.

With trembling hands, she placed the tape as gingerly as possible over Oliver's mouth. To her surprise, he didn't stir. She prayed he would stay asleep.

"Okay, kids! Everyone take a seat on the couch. We're going to wait for your daddy to come home."

Redding took the tape from Jeanine, tore off a strip, and placed it across her mouth. But before he could get her hands, she took one of the safety pins in her pocket, pressed it open, and stabbed it towards his face as hard as she could. It caught him on the check, just below his eye. He cried out in pain and jumped back, out of reach. Jeanine quickly raised her leg and with a sharp upward jerk, kicked him square in the balls. Redding grunted and grabbed himself. She tried to kick him again but he'd moved out of range.

"You fucking bitch!" He screamed, swinging out with his right hand and punching her hard across the jaw. Jeanine fell back onto the floor and Redding began kicking her in the ribs as she lay on the ground. He placed a foot on her and held the gun to her head.

"I don't like aggressive women, Jeanine," he grunted. He turned her around, tearing off another piece of tape while keeping his knee in her chest. She could hear the muffled cries of the children next to her. Redding deftly taped her hands together and then bent down to do the same to her feet. Jeanine closed her eyes and prayed for a miracle. Suddenly, Redding lifted off of her, and there was a loud commotion.

Jeanine rolled to her side and spotted another man on the ground with Redding. Then she heard the sharp retort of a gun. Her eyes focused and she realized the other man was Ryan. And he was bleeding. He'd been shot by Redding who was now standing up and coming back towards her.

CHAPTER SEVENTY-FOUR

Julio and Kelly rented a Jeep and drove it up the coast to Brightman's new home. The turquoise water and sandy white beaches seemed totally inappropriate considering the task at hand. But she couldn't help but gaze admiringly at the gorgeous setting. She'd always wanted to visit the Caymans but this wasn't quite they way she'd imagined it happening. The sun was slowly sinking down over the ocean. It was almost eight o'clock and dusk was fast approaching.

"Just follow my instructions. We want to have a nice conversation with this guy, okay? I don't know what kind of security he has, but I'm not terribly worried." Julio said.

"Why's that?"

"I've got a plan." He glanced over at her, grinned, and then focused back on the road.

Twenty minutes later, Kelly was standing in front of two large double doors. She rang the bell. Christine Wood, the former ER nurse, opened the door, a glass of champagne in her hand. She took a step back, a surprised look on her face. Kelly smiled broadly, "Hey, Christine!"

"Dr. Morales?"

Kelly pushed her way in. "Crazy, huh? I heard you two love birds moved down here and since so many doctors seem to be going on vacation, I thought I deserved one, too. So you on the payroll?" She winked at her.

Christine shook her head. "I don't know what you mean."

"Oh, okay. Is that how you want to play it?" Kelly glanced around at the lavishly furnished foyer. "My, my, my. They paid you, or should I say Pierce, better than me. I am jealous."

"Um. Uh…"

"Speaking of, where is Pierce? Looks like the two of you are celebrating. I want in on it."

Christine backed up and called out behind her, "Um, Pierce. We have company."

Kelly took in the brightly decorated room and waited patiently for Brightman to show. She heard the slap-slapping of flip-flops behind her and quickly turned to see the man himself enter the room. Pierce's shocked expression mimicked that of his girlfriend.

"Morales? What the hell!?"

Kelly frowned petulantly, gesturing at the surroundings. "You know, I knew those asses from Frauen ripped me off. You end up in a fancy villa in the Caribbean. Pearson gets sent on a Mediterranean vacation—and, by the way, he hasn't been seen or heard from since. Think he pissed them off like Hamilton did? Poor Joe could be fish food for all we know."

Brightman darted a glance at Christine and then back at Kelly. "Jesus, Morales. You're nuts! I don't know what you're talking about."

"Don't you?" Kelly asked, looking at him skeptically.

"Yes, don't you?" Julio slipped silently into the main foyer through a rear entrance, his gun pointed at Brightman. Kelly quickly slipped hers from her purse and turned to Christine. "I'm a federal agent, Dr. Brightman. We know you were receiving kickback from Frauen Pharmaceuticals and were involved in a plan to push harmful drugs at unsuspecting young women via women's clinics across the U.S."

"I don't know what you're talking about. I don't!" He was shaking his head vehemently.

"Right. Look, we have a line on your bank account here in the Caymans, and the reason no one has heard from Pearson recently is because we've got him in federal custody and he's singing like a bird. Frauen and its clinics have been under investigation for months. Your place is surrounded by federal agents. It's time to man up and do the right thing, Brightman."

Brightman glared from Julio to Kelly and back again. "I want my attorney."

"Of course you do," Julio replied.

Julio reached into his back pocket with his free hand and walked over to cuff Brightman. Suddenly, the sound of crashing glass echoed throughout the house. "Take cover!" Julio yelled.

Kelly dove behind a couch as she realized they were being shot at.

CHAPTER SEVENTY-FIVE

Ryan was trying hard to breath. Out of the corner of his eye, he could see Jeanine struggling to get closer to him. But Redding got to her first. Ryan tried to open his mouth. Speak her name. But he couldn't.

He glanced towards Chloe whose terror-filled eyes were full of tears. Taylor was next to her sister, lying prone on the floor and shaking silently. There was also a baby, red-faced and trying to scream…to breathe, with tape over its mouth.

It was over. Ryan was certain. He closed his eyes, praying the end would come quickly for them all. Then he heard a shot. And a loud thud.

Across from where he lay, he opened his eyes. Gem Michaels standing next to a dark-haired man he did not recognize. The man held a gun in his hand. On the floor next to him lay Peter Redding. Dead, in a growing pool of his own blood.

CHAPTER SEVENTY-SIX

Glass was everywhere. Kelly didn't know where the shots were coming from. Julio was with her, behind the couch. "They got Brightman," he whispered. "I think he's dead."

Christine, screaming, had run upstairs.

"Oh my God." Kelly's hands shook.

"Listen, stay low. The shooter is out by the pool. I think there could be two of them. Get ready, Doc. Shoot to kill, cuz they are. You go to the right in the kitchen and try to get a lock on anything that moves out there. But stay the fuck down."

"What about you?"

"I'm going out there." With that, he stood and started running towards the shattered glass, his gun firing.

Kelly darted into the kitchen and dove down behind a large butcher block, near the sliding glass doors. When she poked her head up, she could see a body on the ground outside. She heard a splash and saw two people fall into the pool. One was Julio. What to do now?

She sprinted through the open doorway towards a man on the ground, struggling to get up. His gun was close by. Kelly grabbed it, and kicked him hard in the ribs, trying to keep him down.

As she neared the pool, she could see the other guy had Julio under water. Kelly screamed and aimed her gun at him. The guy glanced up but didn't seem phased that she was pointing a loaded weapon his way. "Stop, or I'll shoot!" She yelled. But the man ignored her, and she could have swore he had a smirk on his face. "Fuck you, you stupid…!"

Something inside of Kelly snapped. She aimed, pulled the trigger, and fired. The guy flinched off of Julio and slowly slipped under the water, a dark trail of blood spiraling up behind him. Julio was gasping and coughing by the side of the pool. When he caught his breath, he came over and wrapped his arms around her. "You did good, Doc."

Kelly stood there shivering as distant sirens approached the estate.

CHAPTER SEVENTY-SEVEN

Tony turned his phone on as soon as the plane landed in Los Angeles. He was praying Kelly had called. She hadn't. He'd taken a huge risk flying to New York with Gem, not knowing what had happened to Kelly, but he also knew Gem was going to go on her own, and his gut told him she could be in danger. He also couldn't sit still waiting to find more news on the doc. Eric had been in surgery for half of the evening the night before and too groggy to answer any questions that morning, so Tony had left it to Simmons and had prayed the entire flight home Kelly had been found.

There was a voicemail from Simmons. "Hey, man, Linden wants to you to get your ass here as soon as you land. He wants a detailed report because the shit is starting to hit the fan. The feds are here and climbing up his ass. They all want to talk to you. I also have news about Dr. Morales. Oh, and Eric Sorensen is awake and doing well."

Tony turned to Gem as they walked slowly towards the plane exit. "The feds are at the station and they want a report. I think you better come with me."

"You got it."

He nodded and tried to stay calm. But once they were in his car, he placed an emergency light on top of the sedan and sped past traffic. Out of the corner of his eye, he saw Gem hanging on for dear life. She was a sport though, and didn't say a word.

They arrived at the station and were greeted by Simmons, Linden, and two federal agents—Karen Ross and James Denae. Denae was tall, blonde, blue-eyed. His partner, Ross, was petite with short brunette hair and engaging hazel eyes. She shook Tony's hand.

Linden looked pointedly at Gem.

Tony responded before Linden even had a chance to ask the question. "She's been involved from the get-go. Listen, the rogue chemist from Frauen, the guy was there because they'd threatened his family, contacted her via e-mail and provided her with some key information to look into. She has a lot to contribute to the story. Everything you thought you knew about the Petersen murders in San Diego three years ago is wrong. All of this is tied together and this lady here knows more than I do."

The agents looked at each other and nodded. The small group headed towards a large conference room at the back of the station. One they were seated with the door firmly closed, Gem started talking, beginning with Ryan Horner.

She paused briefly, "Speaking of Dr. Horner, have you guys been in touch? That poor family has been through hell."

"Yes," Ross replied. "We just received word that Dr. Horner is out of surgery and in stable condition. His wife is with him and we have field agents standing by to take their statements. That's why we're here with you…to provide the loose ends so we can piece it all together. We've already initiated a federal investigation. The Horners will be taken into protective custody until we can be assured of their safety."

Gem nodded feeling relieved the family was finally safe and continued with her story. When she finished, the agents turned to Tony for his statement. When he got to Kelly and her involvement, he stopped. "Listen, what do you know about Dr. Morales? Is she okay? Has she been found?"

Denae looked at Linden. "He doesn't know?"

Linden shook his head, "No."

"Know what?" Pazzini looked from the agents to his boss.

"She was located in the Cayman Islands. Dr. Morales took out a doctor named Brightman. And a couple of Redding's henchmen."

"What? What do you mean she "took them out?" In the Caymans? What the hell!?" Tony tried to keep from shouting as Gem reached out and touched his shoulder.

Linden quickly filled in the blanks. "She was with a former agent, Pazzini. It's how the feds got involved. Apparently Julio Velasquez worked for the government in special ops for over a decade." He looked over at Ross who nodded slowly.

"Yes. Former agent Velasquez was injured and decided to go into the private sector doing some security work. He was also a friend of the injured nurse, Eric Sorensen. Eric was the one who facilitated the contact between Dr. Morales and Velasquez."

"Go on," Tony said.

"Velasquez still has some contacts and he used them to trace Brightman to the Caymans. Dr. Morales and Velasquez confronted Brightman at his home. Seems he's been on The Brotherhood's payroll. Anyway, things got heated, then some fellows from The Brotherhood showed up on the scene. Velasquez and Dr. Morales managed to kill off the attackers. Brightman was killed in the melee," Ross said. "We're still looking for the other doctor, Pearson, for questioning. He was last seen on the French Riviera. We'll find him, dead or alive."

"She and Velasquez are on a chartered plane and headed back here. They are due to arrive in about two hours." Ross glanced at her watch. "Around six-thirty."

Gem squeezed Tony's arm. "I told you. I told you she would be okay."

Tony sighed and nodded. He finished giving his statement and shook the agents' hands. They stood and Denae turned to Linden and Tony.

"We would like a debriefing with Dr. Morales, Velasquez, and a couple of other folks tomorrow morning. May we use the facilities here?" he asked.

"Of course," Tony replied, and then walked out of the station and into the parking lot. He drove her to her car. Gem glanced at her watch. "Six o' clock, Pazzini. You've got just enough time to make it to LAX."

He smiled. "I'm on it!"

CHAPTER SEVENTY-EIGHT

The sun was beginning to set as Kelly and Julio's flight taxied and the stairs were lowered down from the private jet. She had to squint in the bright light to make out the figure at the bottom of the steps as she looked out the window. She gasped when she realized who it was. *Tony.*

Julio over at looked her. "You okay?"

She nodded. "It's the detective. Tony." Julio was grinning broadly. "Did you know about this?"

"I made some calls. After we talked and all that went down back there, I needed to see if this guy was dirty like you thought. I could tell you were into him. And I hated thinking he was a bad guy, that he'd used you. But he's not a bad guy. He's clean, Doc. Squeaky clean."

She stood up and headed to the stairs. Walking down the stairs, her stomach churned nervously. "Hi," she said, reaching him.

"Hi? Hi?!" Tony grabbed her and hugged her tightly. "Oh my God. I was so scared. I didn't know what to think."

Kelly laughed nervously, "You? I thought, well...I thought you were in on it. I thought you were part of all of this."

"Me?" He looked at her, stunned. "Why would you think that?"

She told him about the phone call she'd overheard back at her place, the morning before she'd been chased and fled to San Francisco.

He laughed outright. "That? Oh Kelly, do you know what that was?"

"Uh, no. Obviously." She was starting to feel irritated.

"I was talking with my dad. Boss is his nickname from way back. We were planning my mom's surprise party! She turns 65 this year."

Kelly felt the heat rise to her cheeks. "Are you serious?"

"As a heart attack." He put an arm around her.

"I feel so stupid. I assumed…"

"She assumed the worst," Julio said. He'd come up behind Kelly, reaching around her to shake Tony's hand and introduce himself.

"Thanks, man. Thanks for helping bring these guys down and for taking care of Kelly."

Julio smiled. "No thanks needed. Oh, and the doc can take care of herself."

"Yeah. I bet she can." Tony was smiling so hard his cheeks began to hurt. "Hey, why don't we go grab some drinks and have a little dinner? We can fill each other in on everything. We have a debriefing in the morning with the feds, but it might be good to wind down some, share notes."

Julio shook his head. "You know, I think that's a great idea…for you two. I actually want to go and see Eric." On the flight back, they had received word that Eric was in the hospital, recovering from an attack at his apartment.

"Oh, we need to go there, too," Kelly said.

"Tell you what, why don't you let me visit him tonight and you can swing by in the morning? Get some dinner." He winked at Kelly.

She smiled at Julio, getting the message. "Please give Eric my best…and find out how Baby S. is doing," She gave him a kiss on the cheek. "Thank you for everything."

Julio said goodbye and headed inside the airport.

She turned back to Tony and took his hand. "You know what?"

"What?" he asked.

"I would love to have dinner with you. But I don't want to talk about any of this."

He took her face in his hands and kissed her. After a minute, he pulled away. "Deal. Drinks, dinner, and maybe a little dessert. Doesn't get any better than that."

They headed into the terminal, holding hands.

EPILOGUE

One Year Later

"Champagne?" the waiter asked.

"Yes, please," Gem replied, taking the flute from a tray. She caught Pazzini's eye and raised her glass in his direction. He had one arm around Kelly's waist. A large diamond ring flashed brightly on the doc's left hand. She was so happy for them.

Across the room, Gem spotted Julio and Eric talking animatedly together. Somehow, they'd been able to patch up their relationship and, best of all, were now the proud parents of a little girl. Samantha (formerly known as Baby S).

As for Gem herself, well, things had gone from good to great. They were all there celebrating her bestselling book. *The Covert Reich Project*. It was the story of Peter Redding, The Brotherhood, and their demise. In it, Gem detailed first-hand many of the events that brought The Brotherhood to its knees. She'd worked with the whole gang: Pazzini, Kelly, Dr. Horner and his wife, Eric Sorensen, and Julio…all of them to weave a complex and riveting tale of greed and bigotry and heroism. Not only was her book a New York Times Bestseller, a movie was also in the works. Gem sighed happily and took another swig of the champagne.

"Cheers!" she called out loudly. Then, "More champagne please!"

Author Note

I hope that you enjoyed COVERT REICH. It is a book of fiction and meant for pure entertainment. To learn more about how the book came about and the reasons why I wrote it, I hope you will take time to visit my blog and at http://www.adventuresnwriting.blogspot.com and my website at http://www.michelescott.com.

I also would like to acknowledge those wonderful people who helped see this book through to completion; Jennifer Meegan who is an amazing editor, Jessica Park who is an awesome friend, Lori Gondelman who reads and honestly reviews my work, Cassie Hagey who makes sure the marketing runs smoothly, Aaron Keith who keeps me on schedule, and Mitch Edwards who helps me understand what it is really all about.

39253334R00202

Made in the USA
San Bernardino, CA
18 June 2019